I0710411

Copyright © 2024 by Sterling & Stone
This edition published by Johnny B. Truant and Nyfie Brothers Publishing.
All rights reserved.

No part of this book may be reproduced in any form or by any electronic or mechanical means, including information storage and retrieval systems, without written permission from the author, except for the use of brief quotations in a book review.

Thank you for supporting my work.

For the artists.

GORE POINT

I

THE RIFT

The trees grew strange as they approached the Gore Point, and Adrian Porter finally decided to tell Ray what was on his mind.

"Father James says Dad is going to Hell," he said to his brother.

But Ray wasn't moved. He was four years older and officially a teenager now. So of course he knew everything. "Father James likes to diddle kids."

Adrian didn't answer.

Ray's words didn't really mean anything. That was just the sort of thing he'd been saying lately, now that he no longer believed in the church.

In Adrian's experience, Father James was anything but a pedophile. He wasn't even creepy, and Adrian sometimes found the other priests creepy. And really, that right there was the problem. If Father James *was* creepy, then Adrian would be able to dismiss him same as Ray.

But Father James struck Adrian as reasonable and rational.

Father James didn't condemn kids to Hell for smoking or drinking or having sex or listening to heavy metal music. When new rifts opened and outbreaks spilled into the world, Father James hid like everyone else instead of throwing Holy Water and hoping that God might save him. He was actually a lot like Dad, except he wore a collar instead of swinging a Rollard.

So when Father James said Eldon Porter was going to Hell, Adrian had taken the idea seriously — even if he wasn't sure whether or not to accept it literally. Father James hadn't said "going to Hell" like a priest. He'd said it like a scientist reaching a foregone conclusion. It'd come out like a fact about their father, like how he lived on Chance Street and was six feet tall.

"I'm serious, Ray."

"I know you're serious. That's what's so sad about it."

At first Ray said nothing else. They walked on, dead leaves and twigs snapping underfoot. It was almost noon and the air was dark gray, like gaseous ash. Ray's flashlight helped less than it should. About thirty feet out its beam was swallowed by the gloom, as if it'd been eaten.

Ray climbed over the strange, low-hanging arm of a Teardrop tree, then leapt over what seemed to be a long-dead body. It'd been picked down to the skeleton — a grizzly discovery that Adrian took pains to walk around. The bones were surely a suicide.

Even this far from the Flats, Freaks still came here to die.

Ray didn't even slow. Even though he wasn't yet out of middle school, the darker side of life behind the Rampart didn't bother him. He thought like Dad: Life began; life ended; life was random, so why bother worrying?

Adrian favored his mother: There was more to the world than eyes alone could see, and everything had meaning. The best time to worry was when you didn't know what that meaning was.

Ray stopped short of another Teardrop tree, then turned to face Adrian. Reluctantly, he donned his *you-suck-but-you're-still-my-little-brother* expression: the one that diluted his regular *know-it-all* with a parody of compassion.

"Listen. Hell's just a word. Dad's an exterminator, nothing more and nothing less. He's not going to Hell. He's never *been* to Hell, because Hell doesn't exist."

But Father James's declaration wasn't the only thing Adrian had been keeping to himself. He might as well get the rest off of his chest.

"Matt says Dad crossed a rift."

"Legions don't cross rifts. That'd be stupid. You can't breathe over there without a rig. Besides, it'd be like walking into a wasp's nest to get rid of the wasps. You kill wasps from the *outside*, dipshit."

"Well, Matt says he crossed one."

"Matt's a choad."

Adrian looked down and shrugged, wishing he hadn't. The ground this far in was teeming with scuttling beetles. Harmless, but unsettling. Half of the crunching under his feet had been leaves, bugs were the other half.

"How the hell would *Matt* know what's going on out here?" Ray continued. "He just sits at home all day playing D&D and pulling his dick."

"His dad's in the Brigade, too."

"Yeah. And Dad says he's a tool. Don't listen to Matt. I'm your brother. You should listen to me."

Adrian was considering this twisted bit of sibling logic when a massive cracking sound bent the air around them. It was like the sundering of the forest's biggest tree.

Adrian flinched. Ray lit up. All this unknown was a splinter under Adrian's skin, but his brother thrived on it.

Adrian often envied him. Ray's impulsiveness was always getting him in trouble, but Adrian didn't know anyone who lived more in the present, disregarding both past and future, lessons and danger. It made him a jerk sometimes, but also fearless.

"Hurry," Ray said. "That sounded like a big one."

Ray ran toward the sound without waiting for an answer.

Adrian found himself in an impossible frying-pan-or-fire situation.

Did he want to stay alone among the bugs and bones under the impenetrable canopy, or run toward something even scarier with Ray?

Adrian chose the latter. He was nine years old now and reluctant to let his brother know how much he needed him, but that was still better than walking the forest alone.

They reached the edge of the dead zone less than two minutes later, to a night and day demarcation. As strange and surreal as the undergrowth was in the forest behind them, it was at least life. Beyond the demarcation, there *was* no life. Supposedly even the soil itself had been barren (no worms, not even any bacteria) since the '50s, when the dead area first appeared.

By the time the Zen mines started closing, the area finally stopped expanding, but by then it had grown from the size of a baseball diamond to over ten thousand acres. Adrian had studied it.

Ray was wrong if he thought Adrian was afraid of the Gore Point. It was actually fascinating, so long as it stayed an academic subject read.

Without canopy overhead, the dead zone was ablaze with

noonday sun. The contrast from the dark was shocking, and Adrian had to shield his maladjusted eyes.

Ray didn't even pause. He wasn't academic like Adrian; he preferred the visceral nature of hands-on learning. His shoes churned dead soil as he ran — drawn to the ridge atop the rise ahead as much as Adrian felt repelled by it.

Adrian didn't move at first. He'd been wary of drifting toward the sound of an opening rift, but he was even more wary now that he knew the source of that sound was just ahead. But then he seemed to hear something whispering in the dark behind him (maybe nothing ... or maybe an escaped fiend) and sprinted to catch his brother.

"Ray! Wait!"

It was like Ray didn't hear him.

Adrian ran faster. "RAY!"

He finally stopped to let his little brother catch up, waving Adrian forward. He was all smiles — no fear at all.

"Hurry up, slug!" he chided. "The fiends'll be coming out any time now!"

Adrian's voice grew smaller. "I ... I want to go home."

Ray stared at his brother for half of a second. Then a look of utter scorn crossed his face and he turned to run again, upward toward the lip of the rise, sparing no speed lest he miss a moment of the excitement to come.

Adrian followed at a crawl. He had to force himself to move upward, but the effort would be worth it once he got there. Ray would probably choose to descend the other side once he reached the top.

Then Adrian would lose sight of him. He'd be entirely alone for a while, and right now Adrian would do anything for some company out here.

Ray reached the top, then continued down as predicted.

Adrian ran hard to catch him — *so* hard that he almost tripped, turning to look when Ray hissed his name.

"Ade!"

Adrian stopped, but he didn't see his brother.

Where had that voice come from? He felt his eyes go wide: classic deer in the headlights.

"Get down, numbnuts!" came Ray's whisper-hardened voice. *"You wanna get us busted?"*

Adrian's eyes darted, soon enough spotting his brother crouched behind a rock formation, waving feverishly and demanding that Adrian join him.

"Check it out, Ade," Ray said as Adrian came over. "Isn't this the coolest thing you've ever seen?"

Adrian didn't look right away. He couldn't share his brother's enthusiasm. His heart hadn't yet slowed from his uphill sprint, nor from the childlike certainty he'd felt that Ray, once his brother disappeared over the ridge, would be gone forever.

His stomach had clenched with permanence, unwilling to relax. He had to pee, certain on some level that he was just inches from pissing his pants.

Steeling himself, Adrian peered over the rock. The vista — which he'd seen many times in photos — was both awesome and obscene.

The black lake loomed ahead: a tiny thing perhaps five hundred feet across at its widest, located close to the center of the original quarantine area. It looked filled with ink, a perfect blot of ochre in all this nothingness.

Ray and Adrian's father had told them the first rift opened near the lake, and that scholars now theorized there were smaller rifts at its bottom. Creatures were always emerging from what passed for its water, covered in bile.

They percolate up from the bottom, Dad had once quipped, *like smoke from a bong.*

But looking at the lake now, Adrian didn't find himself thinking of the original rift. His eyes gave him a terrible sense of *déjà vu*. Their grandfather had shown them photos of himself as a child, fishing in this exact spot back when it had still been Cecret Lake. The difference between those photos and today's reality was startling.

Back then, the pool of water had been liquid paradise in the middle of a wild, green national park. Now, it was a wasteland.

"Holy crap," Ray said, staring toward the area Adrian's eyes had been avoiding, which was about sixty degrees to the lake's left side. "Dad was right. He's always right."

Ray respected very few adults (he claimed himself an independent, but in truth was more of a scoundrel), but Dad was his unabashed hero — maybe the only person in this world Ray truly wanted to be.

He probably *would* be, too. People said that Ray was Eldon in miniature — something Ray took as high flattery. They both had the same broad, square, effortlessly handsome face. The same thick chests and wide shoulders, though in Ray those things were still mostly a promise. They had the same moxie. The same bravery — though Mom had a different word for it that she'd shared privately with Adrian: foolhardiness.

They'll be the end of themselves, Mom once said to a friend. He wasn't supposed to have heard that, but he had ... and in recent days Mom's words and those of Father James had entwined in Adrian's fears like a braid.

End of themselves. Going to Hell.

It felt like a case of first one, then the other.

"It's right where he said it'd open up," Ray continued. "Holy shit, Ade. What do you think that is? A four? Maybe even a five?"

Adrian understood the question, but was too freaked-out

to weigh in. Their father had explained: Rifts were graded using the Minghai system, modeled after the Richter earthquake scale. The smallest rifts were ones, with the largest rifts in the range of six. But academic Adrian understood two important things that Ray probably didn't.

Just like the Richter scale, the Minghai scale was logarithmic. A 2.0 rift wasn't *twice* the magnitude of a 1.0, but instead *ten* times as big.

The second similarity was that neither had an upper limit. How big could an earthquake be? How big could a *rift* be? It bothered Adrian that the makers of the scales had allowed for the theoretical answer to be "infinite."

He forced himself to look at the fiery gash in the valley ahead. It made an enormous flaming eye that seemed to float ten feet above the ground. It was one of the bigger rifts Adrian had seen, though all the others were from behind the safety of a computer screen. This rift wasn't a four point anything. It was a five at least: a thousand times the size of the much more common 2.0s, and ten thousand times bigger than the tiny but troublesome 1.0s — the micro-rifts Brigades hated because they were like gnats: almost too small to find, fight, and close.

"Look!" Ray said. "There's Dad!"

Now Adrian wanted to tell Ray to keep it down, because his exclamations might get them caught out here where children absolutely should not be.

But there was no real danger of loud voices giving them away; rifts above 3.5 roared with the sound of a blast furnace.

Simple thermodynamics, Dad had told him once. *Hot air is excited. It wants to move, so it moves toward us.*

Adrian, thinking he was smart, had added, *But only when the air inside the rift is hotter than the air outside, right?*

Eldon had gone serious at that. *Son, ain't no place on Earth where our air doesn't feel sub-zero to them.*

Adrian had always been strong in the sciences. But seeing those same simple thermodynamics in practice didn't feel scientific at all. The air inside even the most timid rifts was hotter than his grandmother's oven on Broil. In person, watching the other plane's environment trying to equalize with autumn in Utah felt nothing like science.

The Legions, who stood closest to the opened rift with their face shields down and Rollards at the ready, all leaned forward against the onslaught of the great eye's exhale. Even the Stitchers, who would stay at least fifty feet back until Legions cleared the first wave, wore thermal coats like firemen, the bottoms of each flapping like flags in a hurricane.

Ray was squinting at the far-off action as if it might turn his eyes into telescopes. "This is bullshit. Let's go closer!"

"Ray! No! We're already—!"

But Ray didn't answer because he was already gone, sprinting toward a group of rocks much closer to the action. A single member of the Brigade turning their heads would prematurely end this adventure, but Adrian would be secretly relieved.

The ground was nude; not even grass to hide him. Only the bones of the most stubborn trees had survived the last seventy years, and even then half of those had fallen over decades ago, hardy roots dissolved as if by salted earth.

Ray found shelter, unnoticed. He waved again for Adrian to follow. Ray was much closer to the Brigade now, but even from where he was Adrian could see his mouth making silent words: *Come on!*

He'd be safe to follow. The Brigade wouldn't see him right now if he grabbed a dozen people and started a can-can line. All eyes were on the rift, waiting for the fiends to come.

More reluctantly than ever in his life, Adrian came.

"Look at Dad," Ray said with pride. "He's right up front. Tip of the spear."

It wasn't a surprise. Eldon Porter had been the world's first Legion, and today he was easily the best known. He was also a showboat like Ray, and saw every job as a photo op. There was no press here now, but still Eldon was in the middle of the forward defense line. Combined with the rearward line behind it, the formation made a pair of jutting V's like migrating birds.

Adrian kept comparing his hobby to this startling real-world reality. The popular version of riftfare was a highlights reel; Adrian understood that now. Despite his interest in the family business, he'd never seen (nor sought) footage of a repellance from end to end. He'd never had the stomach for it.

"Where are their Paulson rifles? Shouldn't they have their goms out?" Adrian asked.

"They have to see what comes out first. Different fiends need different weapons."

"But ... they can't just fight them hand to hand, can they?" Adrian knew the answer to that one deep-down, but he negated it now.

"They have to. Fire a gom at a Classical and you just make it mad. Paulsons are even worse. Paulsons fire Zen rounds. You *do* know where Zen Element comes from, right?"

Adrian punched Ray in the arm. He wasn't an idiot.

"The first wave is always a scrap," Ray said. "The forward line holds them back with Rollards while the rearward line figures out what they're up against so they can pull the best weapons for whatever class they're facing. Then the lines switch places. The rearwards fight with their new weapons while the forward line equips themselves the same way. Then the Stitchers—"

Apparently Adrian was going to have to say it. "Shut up, Ray. I'm not stupid. I know how it works."

"Then stop being a butthole, will you? You're going to make me miss the exodus. You know what *that* is, right?"

"I said shut up," Adrian told him.

Then they waited. And watched. And waited. All the while, the red eye roared with breath hot enough for the boys to feel from their hiding place. A trick of planar light made the thing seem to have an aura of blue and purple flame. The eggheads at GEN supposedly called it "the aurora" because the inter-planar burn charged particles Adrian was far from understanding, and made them shine in miniature undulating curtains — like the aurora borealis.

"Any minute now …"

A Legion in the forward line flinched as the formation waited, gripping their Rollards. Then another flinched beside him. Dad said the time between a rift's opening and the exodus was longer when the rifts were bigger; nobody but maybe the aforementioned GEN eggheads knew why.

It made the Legions edgy. They kept wanting to false-start the way overeager defenders false-started in a football game.

But then the fiends came — and as they swelled the temperature increased: the sheer breadth of their movement shoving even more superheated air through the rift.

Adrian found himself too terrified to even catalogue those that exited, though a defensive part of his brain recited random (and not even accurate) fiend names to keep his eyes open and his attention present.

Headbeater. Winker. Rolldog. He knew them all — as well as the classes — but in the moment Father James's word was the most appropriate of all: *Hell.*

Demons. That's what the world beyond the Rampart called the fiends.

It was like seeing every horror movie Adrian had ever watched playing out live in front of him. First came a line of fiends that seemed to walk in backbends: bipedal creatures that scampered mostly bent over as if their spines were broken. Blended into the mix with them he saw upright brown-and-red halfskulls: creatures that looked like humans burned and gnarled by fire, with their heads half chopped off just above the grinning mouth.

He made himself focus, trying to figure out which class of fiends this was.

Which class had halfskulls? And what of the fat, hoglike things now buzzing through on tiny wings?

There was only ever one class of fiends in any expulsion, Dad had told them: something to do with the geography of their plane and the conditions on their side of the rift.

That was a good thing — arguably the only thing that made the Brigade's job possible. All classes contained both small and large species … but every fiend within a given class was subject to the same weapons and style of attack.

That was how the classes had been defined: sorted into groups based on how they died.

Fiends are mindless like locusts, Dad had told them. *But they also* multiply *like locusts. If you fight humans, there can only be so many of them. When they see friends up front dying, they get scared, and that makes them easier to fight … and more likely to run away before you have to face them. But have you ever tried to fight a swarm of ants? Step on all the ants you want and they keep on coming.*

The thing Dad said next had given Adrian nightmares.

Now think about this, boys. Let's say you're fighting ants … but now every one of 'em has to be killed in a different way. Some of the ants you can step on, but others you've gotta stab with a toothpick, or burn in the sun. You can spray some with ant spray … but be care-ful, because spraying the wrong ones will just make them stronger.

That's what things would be like, if we had to face more than one class per rift: ten thousand fiends coming at once, but we'd have to fight them one on one. It would be impossible to stop them, boys. If they came at us that way, I'd die thankful for the Rampart. The nuclear solution for an outpouring of that size would be nuking everything behind the wall. But what then? Who's to say a nuke wouldn't just open the mother of all rifts?

Mom had overheard Dad telling Ray and Adrian that particular bedtime story. Two years ago, when Adrian was seven and Ray had still been young enough to admit he was scared. Mom had kicked Dad out of the house that night. He'd been drunk, and drinking always brought out the bastard in him.

Quietly terrified ever since, Adrian had done research that made him feel even worse. The only thing that eventually killed *every* kind of fiend turned out to be brute force, which usually happened at the business end of a Rollard ... assuming the fiend was small enough for that particular weapon to do more damage than a pinprick.

Adrian watched the forward line doing that now, shivering inside at thoughts of what would happen if the Brigade had to fight hand to hand for more than the thirty seconds it took for the rearward line to find its bearings. A drawn-out hand-to-hand battle (the kind that would result if rifts expelled multiple classes, rendering projectile and energy weapons useless) would be like fighting Dad's theoretical one-by-one swarm of ants.

It would mean the end of the Brigade. The end of Fortune. Maybe, if the Rampart didn't hold, the end of the planet itself.

Ray had none of Adrian's existential horror. He held his fist in the air as he watched, practically cheering. Forty yards away, Eldon Porter was making mincemeat, swinging the axe end of his Rollard one way, then striking on the backswing with the fork. The speared holding end of the weapon even got a few licks in: every few swings Eldon would parry and shove the sharp part backward, then pull it from his enemy with the help of his boot.

The rearward line acted fast. Soon enough they had fitted their weapons and were now each holding what looked like Thor's hammer.

"Rattlers," Ray said, naming the hammers. *"Cool."*

The lines swapped places and rearward moved up.

Once the frontward line equipped with rattlers of their own, the two lines became one: a horseshoe formation that haloed the rift.

Fiend bodies started to fall much faster now that the Legions had equipped. The use of rattlers meant this was a Dorn-class rift full of Dorn-class fiends, and that was excellent news. When Adrian had seen the rift's magnitude, he'd worried his father's Brigade might be overcome with volume, but rattlers were an efficient weapon, able to handle vast swarms all at once. Using a rattler was like shattering glass with sound: the Zen Element in their heavy metal heads resonated with the chorus of a million crickets.

Apparently Dorn fiends couldn't take whatever waves they sent out; their bodies ruptured and they collapsed. It was an efficient way to clear a first wave — and, by Legion standards, a relatively safe way as well.

The pulse of fiends slowed to a trickle, then to nothing. The Legions called *Clear*, then yelled for the Stitchers to come forward and close the rift.

But apparently that wasn't all the rift had in store.

The ground shook. Even Ray's eyes grew alarmed. At first Adrian had no idea what was happening, but then he realized what it was. The king daddy of the Dorn class must be approaching the rift from the other side: a twelve-foot macerator, rumored to be so dense in structure that it weighed almost thirty tons.

"*Oh, shit,* Ade. I heard about these things from Matt." Ray grinned hard at his brother, his disparagement of Matt apparently forgiven. "When they're rattled-at, *their heads explode.*"

The Stitchers held their positions at a gesture from the Legions. The Legions, in turn, held their rattlers at the ready. They'd hit the macerator the second it emerged ... and then if Ray was right, everyone in the valley would be slathered in its gore.

But what came out of the rift wasn't a macerator, with massive gnashing teeth and absent eyes. Instead it was a thing that looked like the Devil himself: a towering twenty-five foot hellbringer with horns so enormous, the creature had to duck through the rift.

Ray was still grinning. He didn't realize the terrible, impossible thing had just happened. Ray was still waiting for his grand finale, wherein the Brigade would simply dispatch a different boss than the one they'd expected.

Adrian knew otherwise. He, like the baffled and backing-away Brigade ahead, understood that the hellbringer wasn't a Dorn-class fiend, which it should be. Instead, it was a Classical.

Rattle at a Classical-class fiend and it'd draw strength. Rattle at *that* big son of a bitch, and it'd be the last thing the Brigade ever did.

"Ray. *Ray!* We need to get out of here!"

But Ray didn't seem to hear Adrian's panic. His pride had subdued his common sense; he seemed only to notice Eldon taking point all by himself and all the other Legions retreating.

To Ray, this was a glory moment in the making, but Adrian knew better. Equipping for the first time took a well-oiled Brigade thirty seconds, but *de*-equipping and *re*-equipping to fight an entirely different class might not even be possible as far as Adrian knew. Swapping gear mid-repellance was never done. Until now there had never (ever) been the need.

"Ray."

Ray's face shifted, maybe seeing the writing on the wall.

"RAY!"

But all Ray said as reality dawned was: *"Dad?"*

The hellbringer looked down on Eldon and roared. The sound was claws down a human spine. Adrian *did* lose his urine then, far past caring. Still he found the wherewithal to grab Ray and tug, craving the primal protection of curling up with their faces in the dirt.

But Ray was too strong; Ray held the rock and stayed put with eyes wide and mouth open. And because *Ray* was strong, *Adrian* stayed upright too, failing to unseat his brother.

They were both there, in full view of everything when the demon raked a massive red hand through the space where Eldon had been — and then Eldon, as an intact human body, existed no more.

Blood gushed. Body parts flew. Someone screamed.

At first Adrian thought it was only Ray, but then he realized that his own yelling was louder.

Over the hellbringer's cry and the roar of the rift, two among the Brigade looked and saw them.

They rushed for the boys as the others fell back. Adrian was running hard toward his father's body when a Stitcher named Halstrom tackled him, pinning the boy to the dead earth with his body.

There were sounds after that — sounds Adrian later understood to be the Brigade's split-second solution to the problem.

He learned the next day that someone had gotten behind the wheel of the squad's truck and rammed the heavy vehicle into the the hellbringer's leg hard enough to hobble the beast.

The remaining Legions surrounded it after that, beating and slicing at the fiend with Rollards until a backup Brigade arrived and re-equipped, with Classical armaments, to deal with the creature correctly.

All of those things, Adrian learned later.

In the moment, covered by Halstrom's protecting body, he knew only the suffocating heat of fear and blood and loss and sin.

2

CHAOS

Twenty Years Later

Someone took Laurel by the upper arm as she pushed her way toward the kitchen. She looked back in confusion, at first thinking she would see Russell Adler; the hand was big enough to encircle her arm almost entirely, and she'd noticed him in this traffic jam before attempting to pass it.

But Laurel turned and saw Ray instead. He was on the couch with Matt Baker and one of the other Legions, watching the soccer game. As usual, Matt was doodling. He had a little lizard thing he drew all over the place, as if it was his mascot.

"Hey. You gonna give me a kiss?" Ray asked her.

She shook her head. "Not today, Ray."

"But it's my birthday." The word came out like *burstay*. His breath was the inside of a never-washed-out garbage can: the sour-reeking sludge at the bottom, where nature performs its chemistry experiments.

"You're drunk."

"Of course I am. It's my *burstay*."

If they were alone, she'd shake him off. If he was sober, she might slap him. Laurel wasn't normally a reactionary person, but Ray wasn't being innocent. He only *pretended* to be innocent around her.

Knowing Ray, he was also overemphasizing his inebriation, using it as an excuse to touch Laurel the way he did all the time, always with a different reason as to why she was over-sensitive to care about something that didn't even matter.

Instead, because it really was Ray's birthday and because he was among friends, she gave a not-entirely-believable smile and pulled gently away.

When Ray's hand finally dropped onto the back of the couch, he groaned in a way that suggested Laurel was no fun; she was a party-pooper and spoilsport. Same as always.

"Come sit with us," he said.

"Where's Adrian?"

"It's not Adrian's birthday."

"Where *is* he, Ray?"

Ray sighed as if to say, *I give up, but only because this girl is no fun.* "Where do you *think* he is?"

Laurel walked away. The Brigade House was packed. Not only did almost every Legion and Stitcher seem to be present (six shifts, all here at the same time), but many of them had brought dates. She saw many unfamiliar faces, along with plenty she knew: GEN liaisons, mostly, including Denny's protege Erika Dale.

She waved at Erika and Erika waved back.

Erika was strange, but she was at least a coworker — an oasis in all this testosterone. And not because she was a woman; in truth just under half of the Legions were women along with just over half of the Stitchers. But riftfare was a testosterone kind of work, with all the chest-bumping and guttural shouting and *boo-yah* it implied. Everyone here knew how to snap a towel, all of them adrenaline junkies to some degree. The Brigade House even had a leveled-up dartboard. It used massive 1980s-era lawn darts instead of the little kind.

The kitchen was mobbed, filled with kegs, and at least one full-grown adult doing keg stands. The rest was wall-to-wall plate-fillers, heaping high with chips and chicken wings.

Laurel skirted it all, squeezing into the locker area and then the garage. Inside was an echo, as if the repellance trucks missed their people.

There was a spiral staircase in the corner. Laurel ascended it, crossed the on-call bunk room above the party, then descended the staircase on the other side. The back hallway, being mostly offices, was quiet.

The door to Captain Kaur's office was ajar, of course. Even though he was almost thirty, Adrian still left a light on at night and every door at least a little bit open. He said he hadn't liked tight spots or dark spots ever since his father died, even though Eldon had perished under a blazing sun, in the middle of a wide-open valley. Laurel didn't try to psychoanalyze, nor did she mind. Leave everything on and open as far as she was concerned. She slept like the dead.

He looked up. Kaur's desk was spread with Adrian's detritus. "Hey."

"You're missing the party."

"Oh, I'm not *missing* it," Adrian told her.

"Ray's annoyed. He thinks you're being a douche."

"He *said* I'm a douche?"

She shook her head. "I can just tell."

Adrian's eyes returned to his work.

Laurel came over and put her arms on his shoulders. He was five inches taller than she was, so the embrace felt like preparing to climb a ladder.

She looked at the desk: photos of live rifts and the aftermath of closed ones, where enormous piles of dead fiends lay waiting for the Zen recycler to come. He'd spread out research reports — many from GEN's own R&D team, all annotated by way of many Post-Its bearing Adrian's angular scrawl. There was a map showing rift incursions within the Gore Point, as well as a larger map of Fortune and an even larger map showing lands inside the Rampart.

They were all marked up: all of them Adrian's private copies, not the captain's or the Brigade's.

She picked up the largest-scale map, about the size of an unfolded newspaper. Small red notes had been made all over its surface, none inside the forest or dead zone.

"What's this?" she asked.

"Possible incursions outside the Gore Point."

"*Outside* the Gore Point?"

"I know."

"No, you really *don't* know, Ade. Zen Element is bio-consumptive. If rifts were opening outside the Point, we'd know about it because they'd create zones of inhibition."

"What's a 'zone of inhibition'?"

Laurel came toward him, softened her automatically-abrasive tone into something more understanding, and pinched the photo from his hand. It was one of the first forensics pictures taken by the division now led by Denny Brennan, showing a scene twenty years, two months, and three days in the past. She knew the timeline because her man obsessed over it.

The day his father died had reset something inside Adrian, as if he was a stopwatch forced to start over. He had been born twice: the first time literally, the second time in spirit. At nine years old, Adrian Porter had become an adult whether he'd wanted to or not. Seeing your father ripped to shreds — and under such unexplainable circumstances — could do that to a person.

"It's a kill radius," she said, putting the photo gently away. "Wherever a rift opens, Zen expulsion basically salts the earth around it. People would be reporting report dead circles on their lawns."

"I've never seen that," Adrian said.

She turned him to face her. "That's because rifts always open inside the *original* zone of inhibition, which is massive. The dead zone is one big sector of inhibition, out there at the Gore Point. Open new rifts under lab conditions and the effect is obvious."

"You open rifts in the lab?"

She shook her head. "Brennan does. It's one of Erika Dale's specialties. It's why he brought her on. They're not real rifts, baby, and they're about the size of a grain of sand. Don't worry. I'm there to make sure they don't make your job harder."

He looked back at the map.

"Come have a drink with me."

"I'm not thirsty."

"That's not why people have drinks. Come on." She had a few of his fingers in hers, but when she pulled, his hand slipped away.

"Ade."

He was already staring at the desk full of documents again. "There's a pattern. I know there's a pattern."

"To the places rifts open? Or to your obsession?"

"Laurel," he said, narrowing his eyes at her.

"*Ade,*" she repeated.

They were looking at each other, at friendly impasse, when a heavy form slouched against the hallway doorframe. Laurel and Adrian glanced up to see Ray, two beers in two hands.

"I'll tell you the pattern," Ray said.

"That's okay," Adrian replied.

Ray leaned off of the doorframe, came forward in a careful drunk-walk, and slapped one of his glasses onto the desk hard enough to slosh beer over the edges. "The pattern, is that you're a dick."

"Good one."

"Have a drink," Ray said, eyeing the partially spilled beer. "It's your big brother's birthday."

"I don't drink, Ray."

"You drink." Ray half-squinted, as if this was checkmate.

"Technically, I guess I drink. But I don't 'drink' in the same way *you* 'drink.'"

"Oh yeah? And what way's that?"

"Like—"

Ray saw it coming almost too late. "Don't say 'like Dad.'"

"Yeah. Like Dad."

"Oh. I see. So you don't want to be like your father. Is that why, twenty fucking years after he bit the shit, you're still trying to make sense of something that's obviously senseless? Does Kaur even know you're in here?"

"He said I could use his office."

"And *that's* why you're in here every second he's gone. Tell me, Baby Brother. Are you still a Stitcher? Or are you a desk jockey now?"

Ray moved closer. Laurel could still smell him; his breath reeked like Oktoberfest.

"You wanna know something?" Ray peered at him.

"No. Not from you."

"This—" He waved his arms to indicate the desk full of paper and photographs. "—is like your own personal rift. But instead of closing it, you're keeping it open. Dad's case was shut twenty years ago, Adrian. *Twenty years*. Maybe you've convinced yourself that this is just being thorough, and that's why you're still doing this. *Thorough*, not obsessive or anything. It's not like you're on some Quixotic quest for—"

"You know the word 'Quixotic'?"

Ray leaned even closer, their faces now six inches apart, their tones soft and full of ill promises. "I know shit, Ade. Just like I know there's no goddamn *pattern*. You wanna hear another big word? I looked it up just for you."

"Not even a little bit."

"'Apophenia.' It's when people see meaning in things that *have* no meaning. Like when they see shapes in clouds, or—" He tapped one finger hard onto the desk blotter, shifting papers enough to spill the beer further. "—when they think that if they just keep looking, they'll find a *reason* their father died instead of accepting that sometimes, shit happens. Why can't you just be a man? Why can't you just *let it go* like the rest of the world?"

"A *Classical* fiend," Adrian argued. "In a *Dorn* rift. That's never been seen before."

"Exactly. *Never been seen before. Never been seen since.* It happened *once*, and you're still trying to find patterns."

"Aren't you curious?"

That was the wrong thing to say. Ray's warning tone was replaced by a more overtly angry one, his lips spitting as he spoke.

"No I'm not *curious!* There's nothing to be curious *about!* Dad died protecting this city, and that's all there is to it! You think you've got me all figured out? Maybe *you're* the predictable one. *Twenty years,* Ade. I thought we were past this, but then the anniversary of Dad's death hit and the magazines started doing interviews again to mark it and *that's* when you started bringing all of this bullshit up again. Was it a coincidence? Or was it just you being nostalgic? Wanting to try one more time to find meaning in it all?"

"I—"

"Did you have an actual *reason* to bring all this old horse-shit into our lives again? Some new and brilliant idea, to make this relevant all over again — to give you a reason to drag it all back out, not just for you but for everyone? You think this doesn't affect me, Ade? You think *I* want to think about this anymore?"

"The incidence of new rifts has increased by thirty percent in each of the last two years," Adrian said. "You don't think that's worth looking into?"

"*Shit happens!* More people get into accidents for no reason; more people burn their houses down for no reason; and yeah, more fiends decide they want to claw their way through to the other side for no motherfucking reason. Sometimes things just *happen*, Adrian! Why does there always have to be a reason?"

"Boys," said Laurel.

Ray turned on her. "Why are you with him? Huh? Is it because the planets lined up? Is it because you met on a sunny day following three days of clouds? Was that the *pattern?* The *meaning* in it all? Or is it because my name has an odd number of letters, so you needed to leave me for someone even? What happened the day you moved in together, Laurel? Did five new Starbucks open that day, too, and that's why it happened? *It must all be connected!*"

Laurel got behind Ray and tried to push him toward the hallway. "Who cares. Let it go. You've got friends out there waiting to share your birthday."

"*Yeah.* Everyone but my brother. What's *that* pattern? Tell me, Adrian. What was the pattern in our house after Dad was gone? What's the pattern in—" Ray began ripping papers off of the desk, throwing them around in a tantrum. "*—all! This! BULLSHIT!*"

Now Adrian snapped. "I'm not just going to give it up!"

"No! You aren't! It's just everything *else* you're willing to give up on! Mom! The Brigade!"

"I never *once*—"

"Dad's legacy! You still remember Eldon Porter, don't you? Most celebrated Legion there ever was? First of the breed? But do you even *try* to do him proud? Or do you run whenever the press wants us together, making some obscene assumption that we're a team worth rooting for? *The famous Porter Brothers.*" Ray snickered. "'At least one of them remembers what their father stood for.'"

Adrian started to come around the desk to tackle Ray — bigger, stronger, and better-trained but still not above taking a beating from his younger brother — but Laurel got between them.

"Stop it!" she snapped at them both. "Why don't you guys just grab a ruler and get it over with?"

"Don't need to," Ray said. "You can just tell us who's bigger."

Now she did slap him, and hard. "Go back to your party. Kaur listens to GEN. I can still get you fired."

Ray seemed to consider challenging her, but instead he sniffed and glared in his brother's direction.

"Not everything has meaning," he sneered. "You know why you never fit in behind the Rampart? Because in this place, *things just happen.* There's no divine guidance. No higher order. It's not Hell we fight. 'Hell' is a luxury that the people out there," he pointed at the wall, meaning the world outside of Fortune city limits, "are able to have because they don't live here. It's just another pathetic attempt to find 'meaning' in a cosmic accident."

He stepped closer again.

"Do you know what the Brigade's real job is? We're not here to understand the Gore Point. We're not even here to stop it. Over fifty goddamn years that thing's been open, and what advances have we seen in that time? *Better weapons. More efficient closure. Faster detection.* The fine folks at GEN haven't given us ways to end it — just to put up with it better. The Brigade's job is to protect people from something that *can't* be ended."

"For now," Adrian said.

"You know what the Gore Point really is, if not the doorway to Hell? If it's not even a 'junction between planes of existence,' or however Brennan puts it? The Gore Point is *chaos.* You won't find meaning or patterns because there are none. It can't be understood because *there's nothing to understand.* So if you're smart, you'll stop trying to put out a fire that can't be extinguished. Your job is containment, not elimination. Maybe it's time you grow up and realize that."

They glared at each other.

Until Adrian looked down at the glass. "You spilled your beer on the captain's desk."

"That's *your* beer, little brother. Happy fucking birthday to me."

Ray stumbled out, mumbling to someone in the hallway as he nearly crashed into them.

Then the someone replaced Ray at the threshold: Captain Darren Kaur, who'd sent his regrets to the party for reasons unknown but had now arrived after all, and at the most awkward of times.

He eyed his office, then looked up at Adrian and Laurel. "Porter. A word?"

"I'm sorry, Captain. Ray—"

"It's not about Ray." He turned to Laurel, then back to Adrian before closing the door. "I guess you can stay for this, Ms. Gantry. I assume he'll tell you anyway."

3

SPREAD AND CONTAINMENT

After the door was closed, Kaur made a silent request with his eyes for Adrian to clean up his mess.

He began gathering and stacking files. Adrian had been exaggerating slightly with Ray; the captain hadn't allowed Adrian to "use his office whenever he wanted" so much as he'd given permission for Adrian to grab Brigade files whenever Lieutenant Brennan's office needed them.

Adrian had defaulted himself into the role of interdepartmental liaison simply because he always had his nose in the investigations anyway. Brennan was constantly asking for repellance case reports and Adrian was always *just asking*, so pairing them up had seemed a logical fit — and a way to keep Adrian's questions from irritating the captain to annoy Brennan instead. But the liaison position was nothing official, and certainly no reason to befoul the office while the boss was away.

"I looked into your request, Porter." Kaur sat at his desk.

Adrian stopped shuffling. He turned his head toward Laurel to see her looking at him with mild surprise. A "request" between Adrian and Kaur could be many things, but Laurel right now was thinking of what it had actually been: an ask to transfer out of the Brigade — ideally outside of Fortune.

Laurel looked surprised that Adrian had finally opened his mouth. For two years now, he had been promising they'd pack up and move outside the Rampart "next month."

"It's denied. I'm sorry. I need you here."

"Captain."

"Just nod and say 'Yes, sir.' I sounded willing last week because things were different last week. This is now. I know you have problems with your brother—"

"It's not just that, sir. It's—"

"—but now I *need* you, Porter. We're understaffed and underfunded. I guess you didn't ask to be Ray's brother. Or, let's be honest. His sidekick."

Adrian laughed. That's how the world saw them, all right.

Ray Porter did amazing things in cool and impressive ways, somehow always scoring his most crowd-pleasing kills while the TV cameras were rolling. Adrian, on the other hand, had never done anything impressive-looking on TV. Big Showy Ray mowed down fiends, then puffed his chest and called for Obedient Adrian to stitch his freshly cleared rift.

Ray was a sponsors' wet dream, with an uncanny ability to impress the investors. When Gillette was sponsoring the Brigade, Ray managed to shave fiends' scalps right off their heads. When Energizer stepped up, the repellance that day had turned out to be a Max Juke rift requiring weapons that spit electricity. Someday, Adrian hoped Kraft would sponsor one of their missions — but the joke would probably be on Adrian, with Ray somehow finding a way to battle through it, using only cheese.

"It's just a preference," Adrian said. "I've been studying the halo effect. I think that if I'm transferred out of the epicenter, I can be of more use to the effort somewhere outside the Rampart wall, where the energetic halo caused by the Gore Point is—"

"The Gore Point isn't the whole story, Porter. So do me a favor."

Adrian waited.

"Just nod and say 'Yes, sir.'"

Adrian looked at Laurel. She looked away as if this was his fault. As if she'd been asking to move away from Fortune forever and he'd only brought it up to Kaur recently, which was true. He was trying to play like *Don't blame me, Baby*, but Laurel's IQ nearly doubled his. Adrian's games were only insulting himself. She should be used to it by now. Eldon had been dead for two decades, and still Adrian took his side every time these issues arose.

"Yes, sir," he said.

Laurel rolled her eyes, shook her head, and walked out.

Kaur waited for the door to close, then eyed Adrian once to see where his loyalties were. There was a beat after that in which Kaur didn't comment on the doghouse Adrian had just booked himself into and Adrian stood tall to look like he was still inside by the fire.

Then Kaur waved him forward.

"Sit down, Adrian."

Adrian sat, but did so with his antennae raised. The captain only used his people's first names when guards were down: when facing delicate or intimate issues, where more than departmental rules applied.

"Do you know why I wasn't here earlier tonight?"

"Ray said you had a personal thing."

"Officially, that's exactly why I wasn't here. I'm thinking 'illness in the family' is as good an excuse as any. Unofficially, though, I couldn't attend your brother's birthday because of a meeting. With S&C."

Adrian frowned. "Why would Spread and Containment want to talk to the Brigades? Wait. Do they think something's getting past the GEN detectors?"

"No. Nothing's getting past. They're sure because they sent a team around to check every single one of them. GEN's work is flawless like always. Any unshielded Zen Element crosses the perimeter, we'll know about it. From what I'm told, the threshold is set so low, they'd know if a fiend the size of a gnat got through."

"What, then?"

Kaur drew a deep breath, looked at his open wall of windows, then seemed to decide they were alone enough, that he was going to take a leap and involve one of his grunts in something he probably shouldn't.

"I saw the maps. Where you marked them up?"

"Those are actually my personal maps, sir. I'd never—"

"Relax. I know they're your maps. I was interested in the conclusions you seem to be drawing." He paused. "And so was S&C."

"You took my maps to S&C?"

"I didn't have to. They had maps just like them. Tell me, Porter, so I don't have to be the one to say it: What do the marks on them mean? What are they maps *of?*"

They faced each other in silence. Adrian understood why Kaur wanted him to say it. His was a ridiculous conclusion to draw, and even Laurel hadn't believed him.

"Well, sir ..." Still he hesitated. "I know it's hardly proof, but ..."

"Just say it."

"I think rifts might be opening outside of the Gore Point."

Kaur waited for a few seconds of heavy suspense, then nodded. "Yes. That's exactly what S&C thinks."

"L—" He stopped himself from saying Laurel's name. This felt top-secret, so probably best to keep her out of it. Adrian rephrased, then said what he meant in a new way. "I thought that when rifts opened, it created a Zone of Something Or Other. An area around the rift dies off. That's the one thing that doesn't jibe."

"'Inhibition,'" Kaur completed, nodding again. "It actually does jibe. S&C says they're seeing Zen spread outside the perimeter, and there's no other source of Zen Element other than rifts and fiends. One way or another, it has to be brought over from their side. It's not passing the GEN detectors and it can't be shielded, so we know the Element they're finding is new, not something stockpiled. The only way it could be happening is through new rifts. But S&C's been modeling it for a while, and their detection's a little better than yours."

Kaur tipped his head toward Adrian's stack of maps, which weren't based on "detection" at all — just records, given locations after the fact. "They think the rifts outside of the Point are temporary. They're only open for a little while."

"Rifts don't close on their own."

"No. They don't. You're my best stitcher, Adrian. How long did you train before you could close your first rift?"

"A month. Maybe two?"

"Two months. Using confidential, departmental protocols. You've seen the folk remedies out there: freaks walking out into the woods and praying to the Lord of the Flies or whatever, trading tips on what to do when you're camped in the dead zone and a rift opens nearby. My favorite DIY stitching method is to rub peanut butter on the rift. How would that even work?"

"Captain. What are you saying?"

"I'm not saying anything other than that the public estimates are low. According to S&C, new rift incursions aren't up thirty or so percent this year. They're up almost *two hundred* percent."

"Two *hundred* ...?"

"Most of them outside the established Gore Point. Short-lived, in-and-out rifts. Some that stay open, too; Brennan's team has quietly closed sixteen small, outside-the-circle rifts in the past two months. And who knows how many are being missed. His people found a rift with no notable fiend activity that was slowly leaking Element. Discovered it by mistake after closing a rift the size of a sewing needle. It was leaking at a rate of one-tenth of a picogram of Zen Element per week. The detection threshold is around a picogram. That rift would have leaked for three months before it would have even been detectable. Who knows how many others are out there? Two hundred percent might turn out to be conservative."

Adrian looked at his hands, sitting with all he'd been told.

"I need you to keep this quiet for now, Porter. Don't even tell Ray. Try not to tell Laurel — should be easy, now that she's pissed at you."

Adrian's eyes went to the door. He had fences to mend.

"S&C wants a stitching expert on the inside to help with this investigation. They need to find out what's causing so much new spread and why it's so unusual. Fifty years we've been dealing with this shit, and this twist is brand new. Really fucking unusual."

Adrian nodded. It *was* unusual. As unusual as two different fiend classes coming from the same rift the day Eldon died — an obsession of Adrian's that Kaur knew perfectly well.

"I'm already working with Denny Brennan, sir. He works with GEN and S&C both."

"I'm talking about working with S&C directly. They're sending an agent."

"You mean a scientist."

Kaur shook his head. "I mean an agent, and I need you to be his man inside the Brigade."

An agent. From S&C.

"Jesus, Darren," said Adrian, forgetting himself enough to use the captain's first name. "What do you think's going on?"

"I told you. I'm not thinking anything just yet."

4

TRUST YOU

He caught up with Laurel in the most logical place: talking to Erika Dale. They worked in the same non-Brigade office, and although Adrian barely knew Erika (Laurel herself didn't know Erika well), it made sense that the two GEN workers in the middle of all these Legions and Stitchers would cordon off for protection.

He watched from a distance, trying to gauge Laurel's mood. A no-bullshit kind of girl, she didn't pine, sulk, or play games. At least Adrian never needed to wonder if she was secretly mad at him.

When Laurel finally walked away, Adrian followed her through the party crowd at a distance. She disappeared into the back halls.

He paused, no longer camouflaged, loitering beside an ice-banked keg and a stack of red Solo cups. Had he gone through a time warp and found himself at a frat party?

"Bathroom," said a female voice.

Adrian turned his head. It was Erika Dale. She looked less like a forensic investigator's research assistant and more like a goth dropout. She was supposed to be brilliant, but Adrian had only ever seen her in Brennan's shadow. She was probably around thirty but still looked like his niece, there for the day because she'd gotten kicked out of girls' school and her mother couldn't pick her up yet.

"Oh. Okay, thanks," Adrian said.

"You're one of the Porter brothers, aren't you? I've seen you on TV."

"Yeah."

"The Stitcher."

"That's right. Adrian."

"Not the one everyone likes."

Adrian waited to see if she'd realize her gaffe, but instead she kept waiting.

He extended his hand and introduced himself. "Adrian."

She took it like a foreign object, then shook with no introduction.

"You're Erika?"

"Erika Dale. I'm allergic to peanuts."

Adrian wasn't sure what to do with that information, offered for no reason whatsoever. There weren't even peanuts nearby.

"*Deathly* allergic," she elaborated.

"So ... you're Denny's girl?"

"I'm very much not 'Denny's girl.' I'm my mother's girl."

Drunk, Adrian decided. "She must be very proud."

"She's dead."

"I'm sorry."

"Me too. But it was a long time ago."

Adrian turned to face her, figuring he should address this weirdness head-on. "I work with Denny, too."

"I know. He talks about you."

"And apparently my brother. The one everyone likes."

"Mr. Brennan doesn't talk about your brother. He might be the only one." Erika laughed and it was like some artifice snapped. A normal, human smile crossed her face. "I'm sorry. I'm being weird."

"You're not being weird." But she was.

And where was Laurel? He'd come out here to talk to Laurel, not to occupy her conversation partners while Laurel was gone.

"Yes, I am. It's a lab rat thing." She shook her head and blinked, as if trying to fend off any residual weirdness. "I work long hours and rarely get out to where normal people live. Not Mr. Brennan's fault. I'm sort of obsessed. I've heard the same about you."

It was usually easier to roll with these things instead of denying them. Besides, it was a party. "Oh yeah? What am I obsessed with?"

"Your father's death. He was your father, right? Eldon Porter?"

"Yeah, that's right."

"I'm obsessed with my mother's."

"Was she in riftfare?"

"She was a teacher. She died of breast cancer."

"I'm sorry to hear that," Adrian said, still craning to see where Laurel had gone.

"But it's all connected. Everything's connected. Don't you ever get the feeling that there's some sort of a grand plan?"

Adrian turned to face her. "What?"

"I work with your girlfriend at GEN."

"Right ..."

"You know what we do at GEN."

"All I know is that our best weapons and detectors come from you guys, and that Denny acts as a go-between with GEN and the Brigade. He helps you understand what we need. Right?"

"Right. So. You're a Stitcher."

Adrian couldn't keep his bearings. There was something about Erika's mode of conversation that wouldn't let him settle in or get comfortable. Must be the lab rat thing she mentioned: geeks kept in laboratories at all hours, unable to learn simple human social behavior.

"Yeah. I'm a Stitcher."

"What goes in your welder?"

"Filler rods."

"Right. And you know what's in filler rods?"

"Will there be a quiz later?" Adrian asked.

"Zen Element. It's fascinating stuff. In the ways that matter, we don't understand the Zen Element any more today than we did back in 1954. My work is on the biological implications of Zen thermodynamics. When my mother died, when she was fighting through the last of her cancer, I couldn't shake a feeling that—"

"You've met," said Laurel, arriving after Adrian looked away.

"Oh, yes," Adrian replied. "We've seen each other around, but ..."

"I should get back anyway." The *anyway* struck Adrian as incongruous. Had someone told Erika to leave while he wasn't watching?

"Thanks for coming," Laurel said. "See you tomorrow."

When Erika was gone, Adrian said, "She's weird."

"She's a scientist."

"*You're* a scientist. You're not weird."

"She's one of the actual smart ones. I just do press and try to look pretty."

"Well," he moved closer, "you're certainly good at your j—"

"So is that it? Are you staying?"

Adrian felt whiplash. He'd been about to wrap an arm around Laurel's waist and lean in lecherously, thinking he'd dodged a bullet, but she was shooting straight as ever.

"You're angry."

"No, Adrian. I'm not *angry*. 'Anger' is a well-behaved form of what I'm feeling. What I am, is *pissed*. Pissed at you."

"I asked for a transfer."

"How sad are you that Kaur denied it?"

"I—"

"How strongly worded was your request? What arguments did you make?"

"I said that we'd both put in our time and wanted a quiet life."

"So you made it all about you."

"I ... Well, yeah. What the hell was I *supposed* to make it about?"

"What's your IQ?"

"How the fuck should I know?"

"You know because you broke into your school files so you could measure dicks with Ray. He was the strong one. The handsome one. The one everyone loves, whenever he swings his Rollard for the cameras."

"This is a great pep talk, Laurel. Thanks. If you know so goddamn much, why don't *you* tell me my IQ?"

"It's 131. Which you know because it's the single ace you keep up your sleeve. The one way you can beat Ray, whose IQ is 122."

"You act like I say it all the time," Adrian told her.

"It's practically bedroom talk. Maybe you don't remember the way you slipped it in when we first started dating, so I'd know that I was upgrading on intelligence grounds. So now answer me this. As a man with a good IQ — not an amazing one, but a good one—"

"Again, thanks."

"—are you seriously trying to tell me you thought you'd be making a solid case to your captain, for a transfer outside the city wall, by telling him how happy you'd be if he granted it?"

"I—"

"Because if that's what you did, Ade, then I'm guessing there must have been some mistake with your IQ test. If *the very best you could do* was *not* to tell Kaur why a transfer would benefit the entire department and instead just tell him, 'I'll be so *happy* if you grant the transfer my girlfriend wants but that I secretly don't want—'"

"I do want to transfer!" Adrian blurted.

"Yes! That's what you told me and what I believed! *Stupidly*. There was a mistake on my test, too, because I actually thought you'd try, do your best knowing how fucking sick and tired I am of living in this city, behind this goddamn wall, surrounded every day by—"

"What the fuck do you want, L? They need me! For Christ's sake; he told me there are ..."

He stopped. She waited. Kaur's words were still in Adrian's ear, asking him not to share news of temporary and shifting rifts opening outside the Gore Point with anyone — not Ray, not even Laurel.

He certainly couldn't tell her about the S&C agent the captain had told him he'd soon be paired with, as S&C's "man inside the Brigade."

"There are *what*, Ade?"

"It's like I said earlier. There are more and more rifts opening every year. Someone has to liaise with Brennan while he liaises with you at GEN. We need to figure this out. What if another Gore Point opened somewhere else in the world? Right now, everything's nice and neat behind the Rampart in Utah. This is when I can help to figure things out and make a difference. This is *where* I can help. Here. Inside the Rampart."

Adrian thought Laurel might yell at him, but instead she looked toward the corner and shook her head. She looked ready to surrender, or like she might cry from frustration and fury.

"You promised we could leave Fortune. You told me we'd sail around the world. What do you want, Ade? For me to leave without you?"

"No!" He saw his moment, moved in and took her hands. Her anger was over; his job now was the same as at work: Contain the damage and stop the spread. "We kept talking after you left. It's a temporary task force, I think. They ..."

He could say this much, right?

"They want me to work with someone at Spread and Containment. They're ... cataloguing. Studying the rifts and their clauses from a different angle. I won't let him keep me long. They just need help from someone inside the Brigade. I'll talk to the S&C guy. Get him all set up. I'm just some random Stitcher, L. They don't need *me*."

"*Public Relations* needs you. That's what's always bothered me. You and your brother ..."

"I know. 'The Famous Porter boys.' Root for Ray. Or for Adrian if you're crazy. Come for the fiend battles, but stay for the sibling rivalry."

He squeezed Laurel's hands. "I'm not on this planet to be a side show. Right now, I'm best known for fighting with my brother. We're the best thing since the guys from Oasis. Do you really think that's a legacy I want?"

"The Brigade wants it."

"To attract funding. To attract a TV audience. But money's not the issue anymore. We've got stockpiles of filler rods for the welders, plus plenty of weapons, armor, and gear. They've already got us wearing sponsor patches on our jackets, but for what? Not for departmental funding; more for padding salaries. Keep up this freak show any longer and riftfare will become like the NFL. It's not a game. I want to make a difference. Right now, I can make one here. But once this new thing is set up, my best contribution will come from outside the Rampart. Doing research and archival study. With you, far from here."

Laurel looked like she believed him. It really *would* be a setup job. He'd insist on it. He didn't want to be in Fortune any more than she did these days … and if he didn't get some distance from Ray soon, one of them was bound to snap and kill the other. They had done their stint as a drama-filled reality show. *Brigade* could go into its fifth season as a simple documentary series. He was done with talking in front of confessional cameras, having his brotherly tensions poked and prodded into maximal, crowd-pleasing drama.

"Very far," Laurel said. "On a boat. Sailing around the world."

"Research can be done from anywhere," he replied with a nod. "All I need is a satellite internet connection."

"You can't even sail."

"I'll learn."

"Tell me we'll get an RV. It's much more believable."

Now he drew her closer. "I don't want an RV. I want to sail."

"We'll die at sea."

"Better than dying here."

They separated. They looked into each other's eyes.

"*Promise me,* Adrian Porter. Promise me that you mean it. This is the last thing. The last time you get sucked back in. Just an office job. You and Denny and some guy from S&C."

"I just need to brief them. Set up some policies and procedures. It won't last a week on-site. After that, I can work remote. On a boat. Wherever we want."

"You can't know it'll just be a week."

"I can," he said. "I'll insist. But give me two. Two weeks, no more."

"No more?"

Adrian shook his head.

"What if he denies your transfer after two weeks?"

"Then I'll quit. But I won't have to quit. Trust me, L."

She looked into his eyes. "I'll trust you. One more time."

5

INSIDE THE EIGHTH

Adrian tossed and turned through the night.

When he did manage to sleep, he dreamed of his father beckoning Young Adrian and Young Ray toward the rift on the day of his death, urging them forward with a long curling finger.

In the dream there'd been a mistake; in the dream the hellbringer had come and gone and Eldon was just fine. So when the boys came close, Eldon backed toward the rift and stepped one foot inside. Ray yelled out, but Eldon never stopped looking into Adrian's eyes, calm as anything.

The beauty of it, Eldon said. *It takes my breath away.*

Adrian startled awake as his phone began to blare like a foghorn. He'd only ever heard that alert twice, and both times had been in training, as an example. At first he didn't even know what it was.

"S'that? What's goin on?"

Adrian patted the pillow Laurel had pulled over her face before grabbing the phone. She was mumbling like an idiot. Laurel lost eighty percent of her brain every night and didn't retrieve it until after her second cup of coffee. If he silenced the phone's alert quickly enough, she probably wouldn't even remember waking up. Or what you got when you added two and two.

He snatched the phone, then trotted bare-assed into the bathroom. His brain wasn't working yet either, so it took him several extra seconds to figure he shouldn't just silence the sound, but instead had to answer the call.

"What?" he demanded.

There was a click on the other end of the line, then a droll recorded message that gave him a place (North Suicide Flats, near the Number 12 Brigade) and a time (ASAP). Seemed he was on duty despite his day off.

Laurel was sitting entirely upright when he emerged from the bathroom. She looked the way Adrian felt. He'd risen too quickly. His head was still in the dream — still watching his father disappear backward one step at a time, talking about the beauty of the other side.

Laurel's usually-tidy dreadlocks looked like Medusa on a bad hair day. Despite sitting up, her eyes were mostly closed — perhaps trying to catch an extra few winks upright. Her small gold nose ring winked in the early morning sun.

"The fuck's with your phone?" she asked.

"Emergency reverie. They want all hands out in Victorsville."

"Suicide Flats?"

Adrian nodded.

"That's way the hell across town. Is that even your jurisdiction? And ..." Her eyes opened, then closed again. "Is this Monday?"

"Sunday."

She fell back to the bed, then spoke to the ceiling. "You're not even on call."

He leaned in and kissed her. "I'll be back before the first strip of bacon."

Adrian gave his odds of keeping that promise as 50-50. If Laurel fell back asleep, she probably wouldn't wake again for another hour and a half, giving him at least that long to make it back home. That felt like an eternity of time, now that Adrian was experiencing it as a civilian trying to catch up.

While on duty, Adrian slept in the bunkhouse with everyone else. He was ready and on-site with the speed of a fireman whenever new rift incursions were detected. He'd never been called in on an emergency — from home, from off-duty — like this, though he'd understood the possibility. Now that he had been, what struck him most was the process's torpid pace.

Instead of jumping into his gear like he did when a call came to the station, Adrian instead had to run around the house, gathering necessities and getting dressed. Then he had to drive to the station for his gear, which had not been tidily put out the night before because he wasn't supposed to be on call. It felt like hours before he was finally back in his car and headed to the site. Surely whatever emergency had summoned him here had been dealt with by now.

But it hadn't even begun.

Adrian was waved to park in a grassy area by a parking lot commando who looked like he'd been called to active duty from middle school. Then, in full gear, he had to cross the street amid a crowd of gawkers as if he was just another lookie-loo in a cosplay outfit.

Another parking lot commando pulled back a barricade to let him pass, nodding and calling him "Mr. Porter" in a way that suggested VIP status. A series of police waved him through a broad no-man's land that curved down a hill and out of sight.

Whenever possible, officials tried to keep civilians from seeing the rifts. Their hysteria made things so much harder.

Adrian moved between two familiar people: Lee Barnes, still stitching into his fifties, and Kyle Watson, who looked like his son.

"Now it's a party!" Lee smiled at the sight of him. "Good. All these Twelvies were giving me the creeps."

"About that. What's up with Twelve? We've never called them to help out."

"Have you seen the site?" Kyle asked.

It was clearly ahead, judging by all the lights, sound, and laid-out gear, but there were too many people ahead to see.

"No. Why?"

"Go look at the site."

"Why?" Adrian insisted.

"It's not just us and Twelve here," Lee told him.

Adrian left the safety of his fellow stitchers and moved ahead, already starting to understand what Lee and Kyle were implying. The sightlines on-scene were blocked, even though sightlines were never blocked on an active rift site. There were too many people here, and there were too many people because it was like Lee said; it wasn't just their own and the Twelfth Brigade. Once Adrian started scoping shoulder patches, he noticed members of at least three other Brigades here as well.

And they'd called in everyone who had the day off? Must be one hell of a party.

"Jesus." Adrian craned his neck to see over the front line of standbys.

"Or not," said a voice.

Adrian looked. It was Dee Scott, a Legion who worked with Ray.

"Don't do the thing where you ask if you're seeing correctly," Dee said.

"Four rifts?"

"Seven, actually. There are two on the other side."

Adrian looked. If "the other side" meant what he thought it meant, there'd be rifts all around the valley. Now he felt surrounded.

"Is this even inside the Gore Point?" Adrian barely knew this part of town. The dead zone was amoeba-esque, not perfectly round like those bacterial zones of inhibition Laurel sometimes referenced.

Dee just looked at Adrian. That answered two questions, at least. Yes, this was still inside the Gore Point, and yes, everyone else still thought it was crazy too.

"How many rifts have shown up simultaneously before?" Adrian asked.

"One," Dee replied.

Adrian spied a waving hand, then followed it. Captain Kaur. Not far off was Denny Brennan, the forensics inspector, standing next to a tall, stern-looking man with a bald head. They seemed to be picking through rubble.

Between forensics and Adrian was a massive, inter-Brigade line of stitchers, standing and waiting with Rollards at the ready. The day was overcast and the halo light of four visible rifts danced on their face shields like reflected illumination from a moonlit pool.

"Captain, I—" Adrian stopped when Kaur touched an earpiece with one hand and held up the other.

"Down," Kaur said.

"What?"

"DOWN!"

Adrian ducked. Ahead, one of the rifts exhaled and its aurora glowed, and the Legions at that part of the defense line leaned in.

A wave of fiends — Dolor class, Adrian thought — emerged and hand-to-hand battle began immediately.

The forward and rearward lines swapped, duly equipped, and soon enough the wave was over, bodies were everywhere, and a corps of Stitchers was moving in with their rigs. The clatter of spent filler rods was ominous in the waiting quiet that followed — the *tink-tink-tink* of stitching in progress, dead rods falling to the rock underfoot for scrappers to collect later.

Adrian watched for a while, trying to see if any of the Stitchers now entering the rift to patch it from the other side were from his own Brigade. He spied only strangers.

Kaur straightened.

"What's going on, sir?"

"Dealer's choice," Kaur said, nodding toward the rifts. They were in a rough line, extending around a bend — probably to where the other three rifts Dee had mentioned were. "That's the second one to incur. The first was Max Juke class. It's like someone over there is testing us. Seeing if we can play whack-a-mole with a different class per rift."

"But only one class per rift, right?"

Kaur gave him the same glance that Dee had given him earlier. The fact of hellbringer appearing from a Dorn rift had been erased by the intervening decades as if it'd never happened. It was an inconvenient bit of outlying data: a single exception that, if heeded, would unravel their method of fighting fiends.

"Why aren't they all incurring at once?" Adrian asked.

"Above my pay grade." He touched his earpiece. "Here comes another. Brigade Two this time."

Adrian watched another battle unfolding. This was how they'd chosen to address the multiplicity issue: Many types of fiends required multiple Brigades, each equipping for only one type. It felt like a test, to see how much the entire riftfare department could handle at once.

To Adrian, who couldn't stop thinking how quickly this could all go south if the rifts incurred in unison (or if only one Brigade had shown up in time), it felt like a test they were failing.

When it was over, Adrian watched Two's Stitchers move in while Twelve's Stitchers finished closing the Dolor rift from earlier. Things went in orderly fashion — no real problem at all — like just another training exercise. He only flinched when the Anchor Stitcher stepped out of the rift for the others to finalize and close, fearing somehow (as always) that the Anchor would be eaten and unable to return.

Adrian was Anchor Stitcher as seldom as he could be. Although it had never happened (and there were safeguards in place to prevent it), he couldn't bear the thought of a rift closing with him trapped in the other plane.

Someone was yelling for him.

"Go ahead," Kaur said, seeing that it was Ray calling out — with, of course, an entourage of TV cameras behind him. "We're covering the southmost rift. But come back when you're done." He nodded toward Brennan and the tall, bald man by his side. "Want to talk a little more about what we discussed last night."

Ray was in full Big Brother mode when Adrian reached him. Belittling and micromanaging. "The fuck you been? You know they want us working together."

Ray clamped Adrian to his side and smiled for the closest camera.

Meanwhile all Adrian could think about was how they'd

left things at the birthday party. Ray's drunken words: *The famous Porter Brothers. At least one of them remembers what their father stood for.*

When the photos were taken, Adrian shoved his brother away.

"Testy?" Ray asked.

"Hung over?"

"I'm ready any time." Ray straightened his uniform with its many sponsor patches. "Unlike some people I know."

Adrian looked down at himself. "What are you talking about?"

"Where's your rig?"

"On my back!"

Ray gave him a *you're-so-stupid* chuckle. "Your breathing rig."

"*Also* on my back."

"That's oxygen," said Ray, stating the obvious.

"Well, what do *you* breathe?" Adrian countered.

"I meant your rebreather. You can't take oxygen across a rift. What if the tanks blow from the heat?"

"Across a—" Adrian scowled, understanding. "No."

"I was talking to one of the show producers. They're light on Adrian heroics. *Ray* heroics ..." He touched his broad chest. "Well, they've got plenty of footage there. But the second half of the Dynamic Duo is just shooting Ghostbusters beams at what look like flaming vaginas."

"I've got seniority. I'm done being the Anchor."

"Hey, what can I say? I signed you up." He shrugged. "You know. So you can make Dad proud."

Adrian flinched toward Ray, but a shout came from the front lines: the spotters, noticing the first signs of their rift's incursion.

Ray turned to go, then raised his eyebrows at Adrian. "Better be quick. Little brother."

Adrian swore. He'd have to haul ass to get the rebreather from Equipment and return in time for the opening volley. Stitchers weren't needed for a while after a rift opened (Legions needed to kill off all the incurring fiends first), but with the cameras already waiting, showing up after the battle began would make him look sloppy ... just what Ray intended.

He trotted around to where an inter-Brigade line of Equipment clerks had set up camp, under a tent away from the blast area, like concessions at a sporting event. But before reaching the tent, Adrian spotted a single Legion off by himself, poking around by a rising rock face.

Curious, he broke off and approached. All the Legions should be lined up to fight now, and yet this one looked like he was after rocks for his collection.

Once past the rear of the Equipment tent, Adrian was all alone with the Legion. He was about to speak when he saw what'd so fascinated the other man. He was actually looking into a cave that was just around a corner in the rock face, brilliant light warbling from it.

"Hey," Adrian said.

The Legion didn't answer. He was ahead of Adrian and moving farther away from him, closer to what seemed to be yet another rift — an eighth, and maybe not yet known to the wider party outside.

"Hey, do people know this is here?" Adrian called.

The Legion walked forward, closer and closer to the rift.

Adrian thought to call out, but he did so too late.

The man entered the glowing slit in reality, crossing the threshold and gone.

Adrian found himself blinking, unable to believe it.

He rushed forward, knowing he was being stupid, knowing he needed to report the new rift immediately, knowing that at any moment, a wave of fiends could emerge unexpectedly. In recent years, rifts never opened without a team of Legions waiting to kill whatever came out, but things weren't always that way.

Before proper Brigades, before Stitchers, rifts often emptied themselves into Fortune without forewarning. The days after made for a hellish game of hide-and-seek as the Legion tried to snuff out everything foreign.

Adrian was at the rift's lip before he knew it. He hadn't gotten his rebreather yet and Ray was right. Even if Adrian felt like entering, taking explosive oxygen into a furnace was a terrible idea.

Get out of here. If some dipshit Legion wanted to kill himself, that's on him. You need to run to one of the captains. Tell them there's an eighth rift, lost in the feedback noise of the other seven. You need to warn them. You need to do anything other than stand at the threshold, gawking into the other plane like …

He may never have looked this closely before. Inside the rift Adrian saw a sulfur-clouded version of Monument Valley: tall, tan rock formations painted red by a tarnished sun. The rift was small enough (2.5, maybe) that its exhale was minimal, still Adrian felt sunburned by standing here. But his sinuses filled with what he could only think of as brimstone.

Father James says Dad is going to Hell.

His childish fear the day his father died, now seeming a real and present danger.

He looked up and saw the Legion. Adrian's father, Eldon Porter.

"Dad?"

Arm extended, under red and blowing skies twenty feet

inside the rift. He wore no helmet, and yet his skin had not blistered. He was breathing just fine, without oxygen or a rebreather. The extended arm waved a hand slowly.

Come to me, the gesture said. *Come join me in this terrible place.*

"Dad!"

Beckoning hands. Beckoning fingers. Eldon was doing just fine inside: no heat, plenty of air.

Again Adrian looked back, to where the sane world and his responsibilities lay. He had a job to do. People were counting on him. He needed to tell someone about this — anyone.

But how, without walking away? The entire site was loud with rift-breath and moving equipment. Even if he yelled, nobody would hear him.

And his father, seeing Adrian's disinterest, was walking away.

"DAD! COME BACK!"

Farther. And farther. The air carried a shimmer; soon it would be impossible to see him at all.

He entered in a rush, failing to watch where he stepped.

The heat inside the rift hit him all at once, making his intruding leg feel like it might burst into flame and ash off. Instead that leg dropped hard to the red rocks inside, landing on an ankle-breaker: a capture tube, not a filler rod casing, as if the fiends were using them to collect samples of the real world, like Brennan collected samples of their world ... and the Zen Element inside.

Why were capture tubes inside the rift?

What was someone trying to capture?

But those were only partial thoughts, lost in the miasma. As Adrian's foot struck the tube, he lost his balance and toppled backward.

He landed hard, tailbone to rock, head rapping hard enough to daze him.

Adrian fell unconscious with his bottom half inside the rift and his top half outside, as a corp of voices rushed to grab him.

6

THE MORGUE

A tall, bald man appeared like an angel above him.

"Can you sit up?"

The answer was no. Adrian was having a hard time fathoming existence.

"Let's try sitting up," the man decided.

A hand slid behind his upper back. Another went across his lap, holding him in place. He found himself upright on a metal table that had its own echo.

Or so Adrian thought, until he realized the entire room was that same brushed aluminum.

A familiar figure turned out to be standing nearby: Denny Brennan, of the cross-Brigaded forensics team.

"Rift," was all Adrian could say.

"Yes, rift," agreed the bald man. "And wasn't that a surprise."

"You got your head, Porter?" Brennan asked.

"I ... I'm not sure."

"That's good," Brennan replied, as if Adrian had answered *Yes.* "Sorry about the digs. You were attracting too much attention on the main floor. We had to move somewhere more private."

Now Adrian recognized it. They were in a hospital morgue, and he'd opened his eyes on an autopsy table.

"'Attention'?"

"'Adrian Porter, knocked flat when he tried to take out an unreported rift all by himself,'" said Brennan. "That's the way Ray spun it."

Ray. Yes, of course it'd been his brother to take advantage. Adrian remembered finding the eighth rift, then entering it like a colossal dumbass.

He remembered slipping on something, falling in non-heroic fashion, then presumably being rescued by the people he'd heard coming before he lost consciousness.

Ray must have been among them. Ray alone knew he'd sent the Brigade's Anchor Stitcher to fetch his rebreather pronto, so when Adrian didn't come back quickly enough, Ray had come to scold him.

Tried to take out an unreported rift all by himself.

Yes, that sounded like a Ray thing to tell the press. It would give Adrian a wash of heroism and fame in their famously acrimonious relationship, and Ray wouldn't like that, but it was still better than the embarrassing truth: that Adrian had done something incredibly stupid and anti-regulation, then fallen flat on his ass because he was clumsy. And again stupid.

"I saw my dad."

"Let's not be dramatic," said the bald man. "It was a bump on the head."

"No. I mean: *I saw my dad.* He was there. I watched him enter the rift."

Brennan shook his head. "It was someone else, Adrian."

"I saw his face."

"I did too," said Brennan. "The day he died. Let's just say

that as the investigating coroner's representative, I was quite sure he was dead. I can be more graphic, if you insist."

Adrian swung his legs to one side, then hopped down to stand and lean against the metal table. He suddenly didn't want to be on it, given what Brennan was saying.

"He walked right into the rift," Adrian insisted. "Whoever it was."

"Wearing a rebreather?"

"No. No helmet, either."

"Obviously that's impossible, Adrian. I won't beat you over the head with it. Just use your brain for a second."

Adrian wanted to insist, but he knew what this must look like to Brennan. He might as well report his fellow Stitchers using molten lava as a hot tub.

"Tell us about this, Mr. Porter." The bald man held up a cylinder, like a tear gas grenade.

"I'm sorry. Who are you?"

"Adrian, this is Special Agent J. Dixon," Brennan said. "I believe Captain Kaur wanted you to meet."

"You're from Spread and Containment?" From what Adrian understood of S&C agents, they weren't terribly well-regarded in the department. Killjoy rule-enforcers, like HR reps with teeth. *Internal Affairs of the Brigades* as some Legions put it. Or, *Traitors to the men and women who put their lives on the line every day.*

"That's right," Dixon said.

"What's the J stand for? *J. Dixon.*"

"'Just Wonderful,'" Dixon answered.

"I just want to know what to call you."

"You can call me 'Special Agent Dixon.' In fact, you know what?" He seemed to think, as if considering granting a favor. "I insist on it."

"Did Kaur tell you about the spread?" Brennan asked.

"Maybe?" Adrian wasn't sure how much he wanted to say, heretical as it sounded.

"Did he tell you there've been incursions outside the Gore Point."

It wasn't really a question. It was an answer to Adrian's implied query, which was whether or not he should admit the bizarre and start playing ball.

Adrian nodded.

Brennan continued. "At first we didn't understand how it was possible. One Gore Point. Many rifts, but all within the radius of the first epiphenomenon. For more than fifty years, that's how it's been. For fifty years, we've known exactly what to expect from all of this. Circumstances never varied. Rules were never broken."

He held up a hand, then ticked off fingers. "All rifts inside the Point's dead zone. Rifts open until Stitchers close them. One rift per repellance. And of course: Only one class of fiend per rift."

Brennan said the last one pointedly, looking Adrian hard in the eye. The look said, *I believe you. I've believed you, about what happened to your father, for a while now.*

"All of those rules, now falling one at a time," added Dixon. "Today we saw eight rifts in one place, and although it's not widely known among the Brigadiers, three of them — including the one you found — were technically outside the Gore Point. I know Kaur told you we've seen rifts close without anyone closing them. The rifts themselves seem capricious — almost as if they're testing an opening more than opening all the way."

"Today felt like a test, too," Brennan said. "No, we haven't seen any rifts expelling more than one class of fiend. As far as I know, that's only happened once. But line up eight rifts and you get the exact same thing. Eight rifts could produce eight classes. Without tight control over each rift, fiends coming out of any of them could have intermingled. *Then* how would we have contained them?"

"Let's get back to this," Dixon said, again holding up the cylinder. "I assume you know what this is?"

"It's a capture tube. It's used to collect Zen Element."

Dixon nodded. "You were mumbling that there were a few of them."

Adrian nodded. "Yeah. There were."

"Only this one was found. You'd fallen on it. If there were others, they either walked away or someone took them. What do you make of that, Mr. Porter?"

"I don't make anything of it. I hit my head."

"Your brother came for you. He was there a good thirty, forty-five seconds before anyone else arrived."

"Wait," Adrian said. "Are you saying you think *Ray* took the other tubes?"

"Maybe you can tell me. What do you know about Zen Element?"

"That it powers our weapons. Our welders."

"It comes from their realm, but mostly from their bodies. You render a fiend's corpse, Zen is what you pull from what passes for their blood. The details are technical. Maybe only Lieutenant Brennan's people understand it. All that really matters is that it produces its own energy."

"You know the first law of thermodynamics?" Brennan asked.

"No."

"Well, Zen breaks it. The element is essentially a limitless power source, if you have enough. It's also a mutagen. Alters biological matter in a way that we thought was chaotic at first, but some of my lab's work suggests it could be guided. Maybe that's even how two different classes came through your father's rift in oh-four: Classes can't survive other classes' conditions, but maybe that was a mutagen at work; maybe one kind of fiend transformed into another somehow. Who knows? All I can say for sure is that the medical implications of Zen Element are immense. The weapons and tech uses are *already* immense. But you know that. I understand your lady friend works at GEN."

"Okay ..." Adrian said.

Again Dixon indicated the capture tube. "That single tube, if it was completely full, would probably fetch one, two hundred thousand dollars to the right buyer. Maybe more. I understand that Ray had some significant medical expenses this year."

"Ray doesn't have any medical expenses."

"Not for himself. For his mother."

Now Adrian understood. Mom had had a rough year. Cancer and kidney issues, striking in a hideous one-two punch, were debilitating in more ways than one.

"You mean *my* mother," Adrian said darkly.

Brennan moved to intercept, verbally putting himself between Adrian and Dixon. Using a make-peace voice, he said to Adrian, "Nobody's accusing Ray. He was there first, but we know the two of you spoke before you headed off to get your rebreather. But the fact is, you articulated multiple tubes and we only found the one underneath you. They had to go somewhere."

"Somewhere else," Adrian said, staring at Dixon.

"Somewhere else," Brennan repeated. "Maybe it was the other Legion you saw. Maybe he ran off with them."

Adrian considered his options. His story was four shades of nutty, and that atop Adrian's reputation as already being a disciple of insanity. Right now the most tangible facts were Ray's presence and the missing capture tubes.

He needed to pick his battles, and place blame where it belonged ... meaning not on his brother.

"That's probably what happened," Adrian said. Then: "Why am I here?"

Dixon interposed. "You're here because the theories you never let go of are starting to jibe with the real world, and we don't think any of what's happening now is an accident. Fabricated rifts. Experimental protocols, like tests. Missing Element. And a whole lot of coincidence. Mr. Porter?" He shook his head. "I don't like to admit needing anything, but right about now this department could badly use your help."

Adrian saw what he was saying. "I'm only staying in Fortune another week or two. I'm transferring out. I need to get away from Ray. Get away from all this Hell."

"I suppose that's your call, but I'd be remiss if I didn't tell you that what we've found so far might actually help shed some light on your father's case," Brennan promised. "The case you've been pursuing ever since he died."

The famous Porter Brothers. At least one of them remembers what their father stood for.

He'd make it up to Laurel.

She'd hate him for a while if he stayed, but after what Brennan said, it's not like he had a choice.

"It's not just an outbreak, is it?" Adrian asked.

Dixon shook his head. "It's happening on purpose. What we're dealing with, I'm afraid, is a saboteur."

7

SUSPICIONS

Laurel kicked him out. For a little while. After the fight died down and the raw emotions beneath their quarrel came to the fore, he dared to ask her how angry she was.

They had each staked their positions, each immovable. With a chance to understand what had happened to Eldon on the table, Adrian couldn't back away; he'd admitted to himself how firmly he'd bought in while driving home that night.

But Laurel reached her breaking point. She had a tough facade, took care of herself even when nobody else would, and was the most hard-as-nails woman Adrian had ever met ... but she was still human, and broke when somebody dropped her.

It wasn't lost on Adrian that he'd vowed their departure a day ago, and promised harder than ever this time. His latest broken oath was far from the first, and she had been plagued by demons of her own and *needing* to leave the city for too long now.

It also wasn't lost on Adrian that Laurel loved him. That's what made it hard for her. Otherwise she could leave Fortune all by her lonesome. She had come to this place on her own, and eventually lost the spark from her eyes under such an unrelenting darkness. She had to get out of here before the spark fizzled out for good.

But despite all of that, she stayed. Because she loved him.

They lived at an impasse. Both had to stay in Fortune and both had to go.

Laurel decided to wait for him a little longer, hoping — and the guilt conveyed upon him by her decision held the weight of a thousand bricks.

"I don't know how angry I am." She seemed to mean it. "But I need time. And to ... not see your face for a while."

Her hurt was somehow worse than fury. Adrian had grown used to not just her presence each night, but also to the aura she projected. Laurel was a yoga and feng-shui type of woman. She had a small fountain in the living room that gurgled peacefully like a brook. His own disused apartment, which he shared with Ray out of financial necessity, had atrophied into something filthy without him. As a believer in randomness and chaos, his brother saw no value in keeping order.

For the first night back in his old place, Adrian felt condemned to a flophouse where he still payed rent. He spent the entire next day — the one he'd earned by losing his Sunday and after a near-concussion — cleaning in long kitchen gloves and a mask to filter the fumes.

Pizza everywhere.

Grime from the dodgy stove made aerosol, caked like dirty Vaseline on the ceiling.

He booked back-to-back shifts so he could sleep at the station. He'd traded Ray's disgusting perfume for the reek of chemical cleaners. It needed time to settle.

Life around the station was the same as ever. Except that

after hearing what Brennan and especially Dixon had to say, it felt entirely different to Ray.

Whoever's opening these rifts, they know how it all works, Dixon had told him. *But hey — don't take my word for it. Look through the files for yourself.*

So Adrian had taken the offered files home, and after disinfecting the apartment, he'd pored over them.

Adrian had never considered how much he knew without even realizing it. The experience of observing riftfare from the outside was a little like trying to teach someone to drive.

A well-experienced driver didn't think about pressing the gas pedal slowly but evenly, about cheating at a stop sign before turning right, about the complicated dance required when changing lanes, so it was hard to remember that amateurs didn't know those things.

People used to driving got in their vehicles and went, easily losing track of all the tiny things they needed to know before they could start.

Same for riftfare.

Ray didn't think about *how* he swung his Rollard. He just swung it. Yet Legions took Stitcher training and Stitchers took Legion training, and because of it Adrian knew how nuanced Rollard work could be. You didn't swipe at anything with a dorsal plate; those, you had to stab at the joints. You jabbed right and parried left when facing folts and pillagers because despite being from different fiend classes, both had enormous right claws like a lobster but almost no power on the left.

Directions were reversed for boolies, scrubs, and halfheads, though — not because of disproportionate armament but because all three became dizzy easily if forced to overcompensate on their left sides.

And that was just Rollard work. Each weapon the Legions used worked differently from the others. There were subtleties even within uses, too: You shot Zen rounds from a Paulson Rifle at anything from the gallance class, but experienced Legions knew that the slower-moving lob rounds from a Paulson should be fired up to arc down rather than shooting straight, meaning that fighting the tallest gallance demons was almost like shooting the sky itself.

Stitching was its own nest of complicated snakes. Officially, Stitchers thought only of "close the rift," but there was a lot more to it: a coordinated, multi-person effort on all but the smallest gashes, requiring work from both sides at the same time.

Reading through Dixon's files, the Special Agent's notion struck Adrian as obviously true: Whoever was opening new rifts understood riftfare like a professional.

The aurora colors of the supposed-saboteur's rifts, if viewed with one of Brennan's forensic machines, suggested the presence of Tullehmite. Stitchers wore a small reservoir of Tullehmite behind their rigs on every job. Some rifts were unstable; they expanded and contracted once they were open, making them harder to stitch. Dosing an "unruly" rift with Tullehmite made it behave.

So what did it mean that the saboteur seemed to be using Tullehmite? To Adrian, it meant they knew rifts *could* be unstable, and therefore took precautions to make their rifts solid.

The files were full of things like that: small details that nobody other than those in the business knew about rifts and the work of battling them. It smacked of an inside job. This wasn't some random person who'd stumbled on a cache of Zen Element, catalyzed it, and managed to open a sloppy rift like setting off a bomb. The internet could tell you how to open rifts if you had a shit-ton of a Federally-controlled substance and didn't care what happened when you set it off, but that's not what this was.

No. This was someone who knew rifts the way they knew their way home at night. The saboteur had nuance and precision. The rifts never grew out of control and were always tidy to fight off and close down.

To Adrian, it felt like testing: creating orderly battles for the Brigades specifically to find out what the Brigades could handle and what they couldn't. Like eight different-class rifts in one place, for instance.

Brigade One — Ray and Adrian's Brigade — had responded to every one of the rifts Dixon believed a saboteur had opened. Only two had engaged more than their single Brigade. One, being the first Brigade, handled most of the real riftfare inside the Rampart because it was closest to the Gore Point.

The other Brigades — dozens in number, but mostly in outlying districts — were more like deputies to the real workhorse. Brigade One alone worked with GEN. And they alone had stockpiled Zen Element under heavy, and always accounted-for security.

The saboteur is one of us, Adrian thought the next day, considering Dixon's files and all he'd learned, sitting in the common room among the poker tables and pool table, among a dozen of his milling fellows. *A Legion. A Stitcher. Right here in One — maybe in this room right now.*

He was sure of it. To someone as steeped in riftfare as Adrian (and *nobody* was more steeped than the Porter Brothers), the saboteur's hallmarks were a fingerprint. But *whose* fingerprint?

"You're up," said Harrison Kim, pointing his pool cue at Adrian.

"I'm not on deck," he replied.

Adrian couldn't appear more unavailable. He was in the plushest of the station's chairs, pretending to read a book so his newly suspicious eyes and churning mind wouldn't give him away. He'd always liked it in the station, but the place felt poison today. Almost everyone in the department was still a friend and brother-in-arms. But somewhere inside the organization, one of them wasn't.

Was the saboteur here now? Was it Kim?

Adrian felt unsafe in his safest of spaces.

Harrison Kim, Adrian thought as he looked up from his chair, running through facts like some sort of distrustful actuary. *Third-most kills among Brigade One's Legions behind "Black Widow" Dee Scott and of course Ray in first place. Harrison hates rifts. Hates fiends. His little sister was ripped limb-from-limb by an escaped halfskull when he was seventeen, before riftfare figured out containment. Harrison would never open rifts on purpose — he'd die before loosing more of those bastards on the world.*

"Look," Harrison said. "It's not a big deal. I can find someone else to play."

Adrian realized that his face was surely suspicious. The way he was looking at Harrison (at everyone, really) was sure to raise these warriors' antennae. "No. I want my turn."

He racked. Broke. No balls fell into pockets. Adrian counted, then counted again.

Sixteen pool balls. Seven stripes, seven solids, the eight and the cue.

It was the only way he could focus on the game, and he wanted very badly to focus on the game. Playing pool around the station house was as normal as things got. And Adrian, who still desperately wanted to leave with Laurel after the mystery got solved, was extremely eager to feel something normal.

"Seriously," Harrison said. "You okay, man?"

"Yeah. I'm fine."

"You sure? I heard you took a pretty good bump on Sunday."

"He's fine," said Ray from across the room.

"Whatever." Harrison circled the table and sank three balls in a row. "So what exactly happened out there? I heard you tried to take on a rift all by yourself."

"No." Ray was playing poker. Barely even looked up.

"No?" Harrison asked.

"Hey," Adrian said. "I guess if *Ray* says it was nothing, then it was nothing. If *Ray* said it."

"I didn't say it was nothing. It wasn't nothing for *me*. You had it easy. *You* just had to fuck up and go to sleep. *I* had my hands full trying to save your ass. Of course, you missed all of that while you were getting your beauty sleep."

"It's a good thing you were there to save the day."

"Exactly."

"Like always."

"Exactly," Ray repeated.

"Got to be the hero. Got to impress everyone."

"Is there something you want to say to me, Baby Brother?"

Adrian wondered why he was picking a fight. Probably because he was angry at whoever was betraying him and had no idea who it might be. He felt like a sucker, acting the same as ever and being nice to everyone, certain that some asshole was laughing at his gullibility.

Dixon's suggestion at a sour apple among the people he leaned on most was beyond destabilizing. Adrian wanted to lash out, but didn't know where. So where was safe? Who could he always mix it up with, talking shit and getting his fists sticky with blood? His answer was always the same.

"Nothing, Ray. You just stay where you are, being great."

Ray stood. Dee, beside him, put a hand on his arm. Stitcher Matt Baker was there, too, also interposing himself between Ray and Adrian.

Matt had known the Porters longer than anyone and knew

exactly how they were. He was a twitchy kid even as an adult. Believed he was doing the Lord's work — literally, in this case.

Ray pushed through, now just two feet away with his big, manly chest out and his thick, bulky arms like pythons at his side. Adrian wasn't even the most handsome between them. In addition to his Hulk physique, Ray had the cover-model face. It had never been fair.

Adrian had come second, already subjugated, second-favorite from the start. Even their mother had chosen. Who took care of Mom when the chemo made her sick? Adrian. But who did she call for help? Ray.

"Oh, sit down, hero," said Adrian as Ray tried to make himself intimidating.

"Talk to the captain about that rift you found?" Ray asked.

"The captain knows."

"Really? Because I heard they took you to that prick from Shitting and Cunting."

"I see what you did there. It's pretty clever. Because those two words start with S&C. Tell me some other words you learned from the big kids that start with S&C."

"Not Kaur," Ray went on. "Not your CO inside the Brigade. Are you still a Stitcher? Or you some sort of a rat?"

"I don't know, Ray," Adrian answered. "Just so I can be sure I understand the question, would I be ratting-out your stealing Legion boots to use for hunting in this scenario? Or is this more of a 'Ray keeps telling the commissioner that he deserves more pay because he brings the most sponsors' sort of an argument."

A few people rumbled, though Adrian didn't hear their words.

Ray really had been trying to get a raise on the basis of his awesomeness. He'd told several politicians that he did more than any two other Legions, and therefore should earn at least double.

"How's your love life, Adrian?"

"Fuck off."

Ray moved closer. "Still peachy? Or is the beautiful Laurel moving on to greener pastures? I heard you really pissed her off."

"None of your goddamn business."

"Maybe I'll give her a call. It was straightforward when we were together. She knew who I was, because I had a spine. I wasn't always yanking her chain the way her next 'boyfriend' did."

Ray stepped even closer. Adrian put a hand on his chest and Ray smacked it away to inch forward one more time.

"Of course," Ray said, "it wasn't my *chain* that *she* yanked."

Adrian had heard enough. Ray outweighed him by thirty pounds, but Adrian had always been a smarter fighter. Ray was brute force. He just had to strike smart and stay out of the way.

Adrian tackled Ray, slamming his lower back into the pool table. They overbalanced; Ray's shoulders slapped balls and sent them flying off the felt.

Ray pushed him away, paused, then did his own tackling.

Adrian hit the rug, and then Ray punched him in the gut.

Air left Adrian's chest. He pivoted hard and threw an elbow into Ray's jaw, causing something to give.

"WHAT THE FUCK IS GOING ON IN HERE?" boomed Captain Kaur.

Ray had a fist back, preparing to smash it next into Adrian's eye. He stared his brother down instead, for a very long, on-the-floor moment. Then he stood, but did it by spearing Adrian's side with his knee.

Matt Baker extended the hand Ray didn't, helping Adrian to stand.

"Porters," Kaur barked. "My office. NOW."

8

THE DYNAMIC DUO

Kaur closed the door. Adrian considered a proactive apology, but the captain's face told him to keep his mouth shut. Ray even seemed to have gotten the message. Kaur hated *any* breach of Brigade camaraderie, but outright fighting made him steam at the collar. It would be worse with the Porter Boys, of course, media darlings that they were.

"First things first," Kaur said. "You two are goddamn clichés. Twice in a week now I've seen you measuring up, and both times it's been over a woman. The *same* woman. What year do you think this is?"

Adrian and Ray sent their eyes away — anywhere but looking at each other, anywhere but looking at Kaur.

"I hear you two fighting over Laurel Gantry or any other petty, locker room bullshit again and I will castrate you myself. You're not only embarrassing my gender; you're embarrassing yourselves. You have examples to set, you stupid assholes. Every person here is a protector and role model whether they like it or not. Lest I remind you, more than half the population of this city *literally* sees us as the only thing keeping Hell from their doorstep. You're responsible to those people. If I *ever* get *any* feeling that you're disrespecting that responsibility, you're out of here. I don't care who you are. I don't care who your father was. I don't care, Ray, if you've got your own line of razor blades so everyone can look as handsome as you. Your job here ends, and that'll be all she wrote for the famous Porter Brothers. Nobody's going to give you sponsorships for sitting at home watching game shows. You're just grunts to me, you hear? Both of you. And you're disposable if you keep being assholes instead of assets. Do we understand each other?"

Both men nodded.

"I can't hear you."

"Yes, sir," they said in unison.

Kaur inhaled, exhaled, then took a moment to stand before sitting behind his desk.

"You two," he said, shaking his head a little. "You're both like him in very different ways. When I was Stitching, your pop hogged all the glory. Nobody knew what Stitchers were yet, and Eldon wanted to make sure it stayed that way. We were janitors; Legions were the heroes. But he was smart. Too smart for his own good. He was always sneaking off just like you, Adrian. Thought he knew better than the brass."

"He did?"

Kaur nodded. "Did a lot of good with it, too. Your father is the reason we know there's only one class of fiend per rift. He's the reason Stitching exists, even though he wanted us kept in the background. And he was close with S&C before there was S&C."

Kaur eyed Ray; he must have heard the Brigade rumbling about Adrian's visit with Dixon. "He started rift forensics. Not personally, of course. He wasn't a scientist. But at first, when the military was in charge, it was the case of a man with a hammer thinking everything's a nail. Generals and colonels wanted to bomb the rifts. Just keep hitting them with ordinance until they laid down and behaved. Your father was curious, though, and he started to see nuance that bombing didn't explain. He was full of unpopular theories. You didn't know his private reputation. He wasn't as loved by his company as the wider world believed. Certainly not as revered."

Adrian knew this was going somewhere. He resisted the urge to speak, and tossed Ray a look that suggested his brother do the same.

"You two are a pain in my ass. *You* don't know how to quit," Kaur said, looking at Ray. "And *you* don't know how to sit still and take orders. Unfortunately, that's exactly what I need most right now."

Ray and Adrian traded a look. It almost sounded like Kaur was going to bring Ray in on the saboteur case, but that couldn't be; Kaur had specifically said to keep Ray out of it.

"Public opinion has taken a nose dive over the past few days," Kaur continued. "I don't normally pay much attention to polls, but I sort of have to when a pissed-off citizen's group shows up on the mayor's doorstep. Word's leaked about the increased number of repellances we've taken lately, but word's *also* leaked somehow that even all those repellances aren't keeping up with rift incursions. We're in a tricky spot. The Feds don't fund the department enough to handle our load, and some people think that's because the Feds are conducting their own experiments — a bit more invested in Zen development than is widely known. More than half of what we get comes from sponsors."

Kaur indicated the patches sewn onto both men's uniform shirts: Beast, Old Spice, Colt, even Dairy Queen.

"Sponsors want spectacle. They want that Ray Porter splash and that Adrian Porter Sherlock Holmes intuition, and more than anything they want to see the two of you working together. You argue, you bitch at each other, but officially you're a team. One that battles demons, keeping the whole world safe. Doesn't matter how much of that is true. What matters is that makes it on-air. But with this citizen's group and the drop in public opinion ..."

Kaur sighed.

"It's the kind of thing that goes from bad to worse. People think we're not doing a good enough job — they don't feel safe; maybe they see a few mosquito-sized fiends buzzing around their kitchens soon, who knows — and sponsors pull out. Sponsors go, the show goes, then there's no way to sponsor us at all. We become cops if that happened. Police without powerful enough weapons to do our jobs. I didn't ask to be a showman, but that's what I became. So now I'm in a tough spot: Ray and Adrian Porter are half my problem, but the brothers might be the only way to get out of a different problem. I'm sure you can imagine how much it pisses me off."

"What's going on, Cap?" Adrian asked.

"I need the two of you working together."

"We already—" Ray started.

"Directly," Kaur interrupted. "Front and center. I need the two of you, and *just* the two of you. It kills two birds with one stone. Highlighting the *goddamn fucking Porter Brothers* gives the people what they're looking for. They want the drama, as long as in the end you're working as a team. PR thinks that if we focus the cameras and the narrative on you, we can increase sponsorship rates. That would let us build out some of the halo Brigades, so it's not just One on all the jobs near the Gore Point all by our lonesomes. GEN says they can equip us with better and stronger weapons — and a new '4D resin,' Adrian, that Stitches better and faster than what's in your filler rods right now. We need money for that. Whoring you guys out can get us that cash, if you can refrain from killing each other."

"What's the second bird?"

"For dramatic purposes, we're going to need you guys on some of the usual repellance jobs. It's powerful to see you taking out big fiends from wide rifts, and closing them up. But mostly, I'm moving you to a new detail. Something you can accomplish with just one Legion and one Stitcher."

"*One* Legion?" Ray asked.

"You've probably heard the rumors that we're getting more rifts than ever." Kaur's eyes darted briefly to Adrian, making clear that he wasn't telling Ray about the saboteur or rifts outside the Gore Point on purpose. "Anything up to a one-five can be handled by a single Legion."

Ray laughed derisively. "You want *me* on 1.5s?"

"Anything sub-two only seems small when an entire Brigade shows up to deal with it. We've seen halfskulls and halfheads in rifts as small as one-one. Lower than that and you mostly get rovers and dragonflies, but one-five still makes good TV. When I was Stitching, we had a macerator poke through a one-four rift."

"'Poke through'?"

"Head and shoulders. But that's the part that breathes fire."

Ray rolled his eyes. Fighting a pinned fiend was a little like fighting a man locked in an old-school pillory, accepting the jibes and taunts and thrown tomatoes of the townspeople because he was unable to move.

"I've already talked to the commissioner. This is happening. It's a showy, crowd-pleasing way to address the new smaller-scale proliferations we've gotta deal with anyway. The Brigade needs a mobile, highly responsive two-person unit and our PR needs a boost. Try to see this as an opportunity. Your job is basically to draw all the attention away from the rest of the Brigade and keep it for yourself. I'd think you'd like that, Ray."

"What about me? I'm already ..." Adrian had to couch how he said this. "I'm already on an investigation."

"What investigation are *you* on?" Ray asked.

Adrian just watched Kaur.

"Nothing changes," the captain continued. "Report as normal. The only difference will be your assigned jobs. You'll be on camera even more than usual when you're deployed, but once you're back at the station, you'll do ... Well, you'll do the same things you're already supposed to be doing."

Ray seemed unsatisfied by that answer. He seemed to sense a hidden deal between his brother and the captain, but Kaur fell silent.

Fight with Ray, then report to Brennan and Special Agent Dixon.

It made Adrian wonder if there was a third purpose in mind, reporting back more on his brother than anyone else.

But nobody could possibly suspect *Ray*, could they?

"So are we all in agreement," Kaur asked, "or are you fired?"

"Agreed," they said.

9

IF

"Level with me," Ray said.

"Not now," Adrian replied.

"Wait. Look."

Ray stopped as they were navigating around stacked file boxes in the back hallway, using body language that made Adrian sure he'd grab him by the arm. Instead, his obvious restraint — a clear-as-day sense that Ray was resisting his usual impulse to master his brother by force — was somehow more disarming.

"I know you're pissed at me."

"I'm not pissed at you, Ray. This is our normal. This is how we are."

"You're just so goddamn righteous. You make me want to hit you, over and over again."

"This ... This is great, Ray. This is why I'm not pissed at you. All the lovey-dovey. Just stop. You're embarrassing me."

"It's like Kaur said. I got Dad's fight. You got his brain. You think things out. I just *do* them."

"So?"

"So tell me the truth. What do you know about what's going on?"

He couldn't tell him about the saboteur; that much had been made abundantly clear. Maybe he could cheat on the rest. Maybe there were things he could tell Ray — things Ray would probably find out anyway, on Kaur's new and special assignment.

"Rift incursions are up. I told you that on Saturday."

"Yeah. But I was drunk. There's more than just new rifts. I saw you in there. Kaur was just stating the obvious. We wouldn't be on new duty if it was just 'more rifts.'"

Adrian considered his brother. Theirs was, in Adrian's experience, an entirely typical fraternal relationship. They hated and loved each other in equal measure. They wanted to murder each other while unfailingly having the other's back. Their session with the captain had blanched the sting of their earlier quarrel. Ray always took easy, infuriating jabs like a playground bully. It was all he had. Adrian should have some understanding. He should find a way, if Ray let him, to be the bigger man.

"When's your watch end?" Adrian asked.

"Noon. Yours?"

"I'm already off." Adrian didn't want to be at the apartment, where his mind would keep reminding him Laurel was estranged and for now he was all alone.

They looked at the up-ahead wall clock.

"Ditch ten minutes early," Adrian said, "and meet me at Sophomore's for a beer."

"I saw Dad," Adrian told his brother.

"Dad's dead."

"I know. I saw him anyway."

Adrian waited. Normally Ray would mock him at this point, but his brother had called this summit; Ray knew he needed to be nice if he wanted Adrian's help. Which in itself was strange. Ray was still the more powerful of them in terms of popularity: It was *Ray* that people loved; Adrian was merely his foil. By all accounts, Adrian should be in more trouble between the two of them, but it was clear to Ray that he wasn't — that Baby Brother was involved in more than he was letting on.

They could keep that imbalance, or Ray could take Adrian seriously for once. The struggle not to dismiss Adrian out of hand was very real.

"Did you catch when Kaur said that Dad had some 'unpopular theories'?" Adrian asked.

Ray nodded.

"I have some idea about what they were. One was what he called 'primordial form.' He thought that maybe the fiends only took shape *right before* they came through the rifts. We'd see a hellbringer come out of a rift, but before you had a hellbringer, it was just ... I don't know ... a pile of 'unformed fiend goop' or something. Kind of like stem cells before they specialize."

"Really?" Ray asked.

"I'm not sure that I believe it literally, but I don't think we have the whole picture. That's probably what you meant when you asked me to level with you. Kaur knows I share Dad's interest in research. And like Dad, I think there's more happening on the other side than we see come out on this side."

"Is that why you're working with that agent guy from S&C?"

"Yeah," Adrian lied. "That's what S&C does. It doesn't just

try to stop the spread. It also wants to understand what's happening."

Ray studied Adrian's face, probably trying to figure out if there was more to his brother's partnership with S&C.

"What else did Dad believe?"

"He thought rifts could be opened using Zen Element, before anyone even considered the possibility of opening more than what showed up naturally. Obviously we know that's true today. He thought that rifts were one-class-only because of random chance. It was like an opening rift rolled a die. Like some crazy quantum choice. Mindless creatures, following instructions. Becoming what the fiend ahead of them became."

"Are you just telling me this because I didn't know? I saw the way you and the captain kept looking at each other. Do you think this has something to do with the new rifts?"

"I do." Adrian nodded. "Remember how I thought rifts were opening outside the Gore Point?"

Ray replied carefully. The last time this came up, they had almost come to blows. "Yeah."

"Dad didn't think there was any specific reason for rifts to appear where they already had. A lot of people think the Gore Point is just a 'thin place' between our worlds, or dimensions, or Earth and Hell ... whatever you believe, and for that reason the Gore Point is where all rifts have to happen. But you know Dad. Hell, you know *you*. What do you always say, Ray? 'Everything is random. Chaos is the only constant.' Random incursion struck him as a logical follow-up to primordial form. Fiends become what the fiend ahead of them becomes if primordial form is a thing, so all fiends coming from any given rift are the same class. For the same reason, rifts show up inside the Gore Point only because that's where all of the rifts have always been."

"But you think that's not happening anymore," Ray said.

"I don't think rifts are *exclusively* forming inside the Gore Point any more. Our entire detection and battle system is based on those assumptions. Rifts happen in a specific place and the fiends that come from them are predictable and uniform. But if that's not true, then what if *none* of it's true? If rifts can form outside the Gore Point, what's to say we won't start seeing them with multiple classes?"

"That's quite a leap. Maybe it's you just trying to find a pattern like you always do."

"Not at all. It's the very essence of chaos. The very essence of randomness. That's how evolution always works: For a very long time, new babies are all basically the same. But then, through some random event, a baby is born with a new trait that gives it an advantage. This isn't my philosophy or your philosophy, Ray. It's both."

He sat with that, sipping his beer. Ray had asked what Adrian knew, and now he was getting it. The subject had gotten heavy and hard to sort out.

"You don't really think it was Dad inside the rift," Ray said.

"I don't know. I keep thinking about the rumor Matt's dad told me back when we were kids. About how some Legions crossed rifts."

"I don't see how that's possible." It was an upgrade; usually Ray would flat-out say it was wrong, then call Adrian an idiot.

"To tell the truth, I don't either. I just ..."

"What?"

"Nothing."

"Ade. I asked. I won't laugh at you. Just say it."

Adrian exhaled. "I just get the feeling it was messing with my head. Taunting me."

"Messing with ... Wait, you mean the rift? *The rift* was taunting you?"

"Their plane, or something inside, I don't know."

"They're roach holes. They don't 'taunt.' They infest."

Adrian thought but didn't reply. Dad was far too much like Ray to believe there was order to the rifts in the biggest picture, but Adrian was the pattern-maker. Like Mom, he tended to see meaning where Ray saw none.

And yet, *taunting* didn't only imply order. It implied *consciousness*. Did he really think a rift had been out to get him? How would that even work?

Adrian considered the capture tubes. The answer to all of this was simple enough, but for some reason it didn't ring true. He'd seen the saboteur and profiteer on Sunday — not their father and not a fiend.

So why couldn't he believe it? Why did his head insist that even if that much was true, the bigger truth was something more?

"I guess you're right," Adrian said. It wasn't worth the argument. Or the philosophical debate.

"Is that all?"

"All I know?"

"All that's relevant. If it's just going to be me and you on a lot of repellances, you have to stop holding out on me."

"I don't hold out on you," Adrian said.

"*Really?* S&C. Tell me about them. Tell me about this guy Dixon."

"What about him?" Adrian asked, stalling for time as he realized he'd walked into a minor trap.

Ray had only been playing innocent. This right here was the crux of what he'd wanted to know all along. *Nobody* liked S&C. Everyone in the Brigade had looked sideways at him today — because Adrian, now that he was putting two and two together, was quite sure Ray had told them all who'd taken Baby Brother away after Big Brother saved him.

Went with the rats, did he? Too cool for the Brigade, was he? Looking at Ray now, Adrian could almost hear the whispers.

"He's a special investigator," Adrian said.

"What's he investigating? Us?"

"What's that mean: *Us?*"

"Come on. S&C is basically Internal Affairs. Cops to watch the cops. The Brigade is built on trust. You go into a scrap, you have to know you can trust the person on either side of you. I trust the other Legions and Stitchers with my life. Do you know how it looks, when my own brother sides-up with the guys who think we're crooked?"

"Nobody thinks anyone's crooked."

"Interesting," said Ray. "Couple of the other Legions were asked about stores of Zen Element. Seems they should be asking the Stitchers, seeing as you're the ones who carry a million bucks' worth of it around on your backs every job."

"Who asked about Zen Element?"

"Your friends at S&C. They think we're stealing it."

Again Adrian thought of the capture tubes. But nobody knew about the capture tubes, did they? Only one had been recovered, and Dixon had it.

Adrian protected his facial expression, knowing how easily Ray could read him. "Stealing it from where?"

"Not actually stealing. 'Skimming' would be more accurate. The Element recorded at repellance sites apparently isn't lining up with the amount making it into GEN's vaults. Ten grams harvested from the dead fiends on site, but only nine gets deposited. But how could a Legion steal Zen? We just kill 'em. Stitchers are the ones who go in after."

"Not to harvest the bodies."

"I hear it comes from the rifts, too. But what do I know? I'm not a Stitcher. I'm just a meathead Legion."

Adrian verbally backed away. He didn't like this quiet ambush. He hadn't wanted a fight. "Are they sure?"

"Maybe ask Dixon. Or maybe you don't *need* to ask."

"Now hang on a second ..."

"I know you're through with Brigade work. I was talking to that weird Erika woman at my party. She says that packing up and leaving town is all Laurel talks about. I'm not saying you know more than you're letting on. I hope you know better than that. Dad basically built this department. He *is* riftfare. I guess it's your choice if you want to turn your back on this life. It's a hard one; I get it. But I hope you've got enough honor to not turn on *us*."

Ray took a breath before he continued. "I'm going to ask you once and only once, Adrian. Is Spread and Containment investigating the first Brigade? And if so, are you spending every breath you've got to tell them *NO*, that the Legions and Stitchers are your family and they'd *never* steal? *Never* turn rift-fare into greed? Are you telling them they can shove their suspicions up their asses ... or are you a rat, selling out the men and women who risk their lives to protect this place just so you can get yourself some kind of golden fucking parachute — enough pension, maybe, to buy a *goddamn sailboat?*"

"Watch yourself," Adrian said.

Ray held his gaze for a few seconds, then leaned back. "Hey. No worries. If it's not true, then we're good." Then his smile turned down at the edges as he added, *"If."*

IO

RIFTMAKING

S o it went, for a while.

Ray stayed true to his nature and worked as much as Kaur would allow him to. Adrian did the same, because he didn't trust his mind when alone. By the time Laurel finally invited him to move back in (he'd packed only a suitcase), work at GEN and at the Brigade had ramped up enough that it was no longer a question of being alone; it was a question of too much fiend work and not enough time.

Adrian had no other choice. Both brothers found themselves on a regular 1.5 shift rotation: twelve hours on and twelve hours off, every day.

Several of Adrian's hours most days belonged to the forensic investigator. Brennan and his research assistant Erika Dale (who did most of the actual work while her boss did the thinking) were thick with new theories they wanted Adrian to verify, test, or debunk. He'd become their pet Stitcher: a man from the front lines who knew not just the theories of riftfare, but their nuance as well. They'd considered all of Adrian's theories, alongside what he remembered from his father.

Ray raised eyebrows every time Adrian went to work with Brennan's department — knowing it was kissing cousins with S&C these days — but had thus far settled for only giving his brother knowing glances.

Remember your loyalties, those glances said.

Dixon, meanwhile, did some sort of pattern-matching, statistical magic with the department's records of Element stores, trying to figure out how much Zen had gone missing at what times. He compared the days that had shortfalls (less Element put into storage than should have been collected on the days' jobs) against Brigade shifts, trying to determine who was on duty most consistently when Zen went missing.

So far Matt Baker was the only person whose pattern was remotely suspicious, but to Adrian that only proved Dixon's method wasn't working. Baker had no use for Zen, and none of the money you'd expect if he were selling it. His family was gone, he lived in a dump, and could not possibly network himself into a black market buyer. Baker was also a weird kind of idealist when it came to riftfare. He'd become more of a zealot since his father died two years ago and mostly regarded his work as religious, not at all for-profit.

"My job is to keep the Devil behind bars," Baker had once told the cameras, and of course the show's producers had loved that.

"It's not Baker," Erika Dale said after Adrian told her what Dixon's statistical analysis had uncovered. "I'd know if Baker was up to something. I've known him most of my life. That's why I always keep an eye on the guy."

"Meaning you trust him," Adrian said.

"Meaning I don't." Erika seemed genuinely confused. "That's like saying you trust your mother."

"I trust my mother."

"Well, yeah. I hear she has cancer."

"She does."

"If she's got cancer, you can trust her."

"If ... What?"

"I miss mine," Erika said. "But at least we're in the same club. 'Moms with cancer.' I guess we're more alike than different."

Adrian didn't agree. Erika couldn't be more different from him if she tried. She struck Adrian as quirky to the point of absurdity. She also struck him as the kind of person who'd show up to work in pajamas.

"While we're here, I have a question for you," Adrian said, "about the saboteur investigation."

"You should talk to Denny, then. Or the agent from S&C."

"It's not about the investigation itself. It's about the sabotage."

"Still sounds like a question for them."

Just ask, already. She's weird. "You think someone's opening these rifts on purpose."

Erika shrugged. "That's right. Wouldn't be sabotage otherwise. The capture tubes you found suggest that the reason they're doing it is—"

"I'm not wondering about the reason. It's what you're all presupposing that I don't understand."

"What are we presupposing?"

"That it's possible to intentionally open rifts in the first place. My family's been in riftfare from the start, and I've never heard of rifts as being under anyone's control. It's like I'm a storm chaser, and you keep wondering who's creating all these tornadoes. I've always thought rifts were a natural phenomenon."

It's how everyone on the Brigade thought. It was also why it'd been so easy to keep Dixon's secret about a possible saboteur. Nobody would ever think they were looking for a bad egg because they'd didn't believe that bad eggs were possible. If Adrian had stood up in the common room and announced that Dixon was looking for a rift-opener, everyone would have probably laughed in his face.

Erika's expression had changed. Adrian decided she was probably thinking, but it was a pained sort of contemplation. She didn't look like she got out much. Or saw the sun. Her skin seemed thirsty for pigment.

"I have to make a call," she said.

Adrian assumed that was all the answer he was going to get. She'd pick up the phone, order a pizza or something, then forget he'd asked a question.

Instead, within two minutes she'd returned. He'd begun browsing one of the lab computers, open to a list of safe protocols for using the Element. He'd never before realized how widely Zen was used, particularly in tech and medicine. Apparently it could cause human cells to differentiate and de-differentiate, meaning that when treated with Zen, lung cells could become blood cells could become brain cells could become hair follicles.

Someone in a lab outside the Rampart had successfully turned a rat's kidney into a second heart. The rat had died soon after.

"You want some water?" Erika said, returning.

"I saw a coffee pot. Is coffee an option?"

She went into the lab's kitchenette, looking around corners as if Hide and Seek was a game she and Brennan regularly played. But the lab was empty except for them.

She handed him coffee. It was from the boiled-down pot, thick as sludge and ice cold. "I had to make a call. I'm sorry."

"Hey. You do you."

"I mean, I had to call Denny. Denny had to call Dixon to be sure."

"Sure of what?"

"That I was allowed to answer your question. You're right. Only a few people know that rifts can be opened on purpose. We let *that* cat out of the bag and you know how people are. They'd start making YouTube tutorials. Adding riftmaking to *The Anarchist's Cookbook*."

"It's that big a threat?"

"Well, you do need Zen, and it's not easy to get your hands on. Everyone's heard stories of a neighbor who found a dead fiend in their woodshed or something, or even a live one, but you can't just run a fiend body through a food processor and suck out the Element. It's in their blood, and no good once the blood starts to clot. So you have to be fast, and you basically need a mortuary setup handy. Even then, it has to be centrifuged-out, molecularly distilled ... not simple at all."

"So it's not a DIY operation."

Erika shook her head. "The Zen being used to do this must be coming from the departmental stores. Or GEN stores. If you suspect anyone at GEN, let me know."

"You technically work for GEN."

But that did open up new avenues for investigation: Laurel, unlike Erika and Brennan (whose unit was adjunct and had two bosses), worked at GEN and might be able to snoop around for him now that they were living together again, and back on tentative terms.

"Anyway," Erika continued, "it's kind of technical. Almost nobody would have any idea how to open a rift even if they had enough Zen — and an instruction manual showing them exactly how to do it."

"Why not? If they have instructions ..."

"It's nuanced. You ever make homemade ravioli? Like from a pasta maker?"

"Um ... What?"

"My mom used to do it. There's a special way you have to crimp the edges to seal them. Do it wrong and they just open up when you put them in hot water. But all the instruction my mom ever had for me was, 'Erika, just crimp it.' When I couldn't do it right and my raviolis just flopped there, wide open, that's all she'd say: 'Just crimp it. Just do it better. Just do it *right.*' Opening rifts is like that. You have to be someone who lives with their hands in the dough. Someone who you can just tell, 'Find the midline.'"

Right up until halfway through that last sentence, Adrian was barely listening, already trying to figure out how to extricate himself from Brennan's antisocial assistant and query her boss instead. But his head jerked up at the word *midline.*

Finding a rift's midline had been the last thing Adrian mastered in Stitcher training. It was a fantastically subtle thing — a little like poking a thread through the eye of an invisible needle.

"The saboteur is a Stitcher." The field of people Adrian was silently betraying had just shrunk.

"Not necessarily." Erika shrugged. "It could be anyone with access with Stitcher training, available in software all Brigades keep on hand. Denny thinks you'd have to be strong. If it's a Stitcher, it's not a wimpy one."

Adrian was making lists in his head.

Apparently, so was Erika.

"Personally, I think it might be a Legion. Like your brother."

II

INCOGNITO

When Adrian was at the station, less and less of his time was idle. Most days boasted a big, full-Brigade call, plus he and Logan's two-man unit was soon put on duty.

Ray's reaction was complicated. On one hand, it was as Kaur predicted: Ray liked to be the star; and showboat for the cameras; Ray liked being half of the reality show's entire cast whenever the crew followed them instead of the Brigade. On their two-man repellances, he didn't have to share a molecule of glory with his fellow Legions or Stitchers. He had to share it with his brother, but everyone knew Legions were the badasses and Stitchers just sort of came along.

But on the other hand, Ray disliked being singled out, even as much as he loved it. The public had always made favorites of Eldon Porter's famous sons, but now the department had shifted to make clear that Ray and Adrian were definitely the most important among them. They were Teacher's Pets, and everyone resented the Teacher's Pet.

The Porters suddenly had special new uniforms with even

more sponsor patches on them. It seemed to all the other Legions and Stitchers that when time for pay raises came around, the Porters were building a case to take home more than everyone else.

"I know for a fact that you tried to get a raise above everyone else before all of this started," Adrian said after they left one day, leaving too many gazes staring at them.

"They think that *I* think I'm better than everyone else," Ray replied.

"You *do* think you're better than everyone else."

"Yeah. But now they know I know it."

Not that it was entirely about fame and glory. Kaur's funding dilemma was just the way he'd said: It *was* important for the riftfare docuseries (simply called *Brigade)* to stay wildly popular in order to keep ad placements and sponsorships high, and Ray's personal popularity *was* a big part of drawing eyeballs to the show and keeping them there. But the bigger reason for their two-man unit's creation became the *real* reason right away.

A two-man team could be fast.

A two-man team could handle many small jobs in a day, and that was great because that was exactly the kind that kept appearing everywhere.

A two-man team could also be discrete if it lost its reality-show tail. This was something Adrian explained to his brother on Day Three, when the TV crew left them alone and followed the rest of the Brigade to a 5.8 rift opening just inside the strange forest.

"Wait," Ray said, looking at the GPS. "They gave us the wrong address."

"It's the right address."

Ray looked closer. "This is in Findale Commons. The Gore Point is the other direction."

"Yep," said Adrian.

Adrian spilled half of his available beans then, expanding on knowledge Ray already had (that the rifts were proliferating faster and faster) without revealing the thing nobody else could know (that there was a saboteur — maybe even one of their Legions). He told Ray the middle ground, the impossible fact that wasn't all the way to heresy.

"Outside the Gore Point …" Ray repeated when his brother finished. "You really think rifts are opening in the city?"

"Brennan does."

"Inside the city," Ray repeated, using his *just-let-me-make-sure-I've-got-this-right* voice.

"The city. Suicide Flats. Suburbs. Remember the big repellance with eight different rifts?"

"Hard to forget that one."

"A few of those rifts were technically outside the Gore Point."

"They were inside the dead zone, though. And it's inside the Gore Point."

"They were in rock screes, where nothing grows anyway. The Gore Point's boundary is well-defined by Brennan's office. Sometimes the dead zone goes all the way to its border. I always thought of it as a big circle."

"That's what it is. A big circle."

Adrian shook his head. "Not on a map, it's not. It looks like Norway's coast: all fjords and inlets."

Ray digested this, even though Adrian was sure his brother had no idea what a fjord was. The point was made. Then made again later, when they arrived at an ordinary suburban address in an ordinary suburban neighborhood.

Adrian was already seeing the patterns: Whenever they were sent out without the TV crew, they were also sent in plainclothes, driving an unmarked van. Their Legion and

Stitching equipment was in the back for those jobs, hidden inside a touring band's roadie case. They'd been told to open the garage using remotes the department had coded for them, then roll the case inside and close the door before unloading.

"It still looks suspicious." Adrian had cracked the roadie case and was putting on his armor and welder, making sure he had a full complement of filler rods.

Ray was donning weapons, looking like Thor. Because there was no rearward Legion line in a job this small, he would have to battle the first wave with his Rollard *and* equip himself properly with distance weapons appropriate to the rift's class to finish the fiends off.

To make it possible, GEN had provided a multi-function Legion weapon they'd never known was in development. Its individual functions packed a fraction of the punch of (for instance) a real Gom or Rattler, but given the size of the rifts they'd be facing, it should be enough.

Adrian would then do double duty, moving in as a rear-ward scout before acting as Stitcher, watching the fiends Ray dispatched using his Rollard to determine the rift's class.

"What looks suspicious? The weapon?" Ray hoisted the thing. It was stout and fat with cylinders around the middle like chambers in a giant revolver. Like something from a video game. "The cameras have seen the weapon."

"Not the weapon. I mean two guys pulling up to a house in an unmarked van, then wheeling a big-ass cabinet into the garage and closing the door. Two *familiar-looking* guys."

Even Adrian, as the less-famous Porter Brother, had been stopped by autograph-seekers in the supermarket most times he shopped.

"You didn't notice? Nobody's here."

"Obviously nobody's here. They sent a drone. Salted a perimeter last night. Dispatch called them pretending to be

Fortune Natural Gas. Neighbors will probably think we're a couple of FNG techs, come to fix the gas leak."

Ray was shaking his head. "I didn't mean nobody's in the house. I meant nobody's on the *street.*"

Adrian frowned. The garage had a small window. He peeked out and saw that Ray was right. It was a sunny Monday evening. There would usually be men in hammocks and loud families in their backyards. Parents pushing strollers. Kids drawing on the sidewalk and riding their bikes.

"I assume it was a very big 'gas leak,'" Ray said.

Adrian didn't like it, but couldn't say why. He kept thinking of isolation protocol in paranoid, government-conspiracy movies. Agencies with three-letter acronyms kill a few birds and cows, then scare the residents into leaving so a troublesome area could be cleared.

If that sort of thing was really what had happened here — if *that* was the reason nobody would see the Porters come and go — Adrian had to wonder if things were worse than he thought.

It was starting to feel like they were their own cover story: *Ray and Adrian Porter, too well-known to act in secret. So let's make them bigger than before. Make them their own star-studded unit. Two out of three jobs, the whole world will know what they're doing, but nobody will see their real purpose — that third job — because of it. Showboat on one end, then quietly close rifts where rifts shouldn't be while all of that day's eyes stayed fixed on the Brigade.*

The small rifts that Ray and Adrian closed alone inside the Gore Point ... were those jobs even necessary?

Was it possible they only did the "understandable and normal" repellances specifically as a distraction to their real job?

Ray finished gearing up. Adrian, with rebreather in tow just in case a rift-entrance was necessary, had been ready for a while.

"We're in a house," Ray said. "Now what?"

"Supposedly the rift is in the living room."

Ray didn't move.

"The living room," Adrian repeated.

"I heard you. I'm trying to figure out how the hell a rift would open inside someone's living room."

Adrian had wondered the same thing when Denny Brennan issued the assignment.

Brennon had explained his theory: Although a saboteur seemed to be opening rifts, he or she wasn't personally opening all of them. It seemed to be a critical mass situation. The more rifts were opened, the more rifts *wanted* to open. The saboteur appeared to be weakening the boundary between planes. Rifts that opened this far from the Gore Point came as a result of that frailty.

It gave Adrian the creeps: a feeling that at any moment, at any time, the bottom might drop entirely out of this world, plunging everyone into the other. It would be the mother of all rifts: the reason the Minghai Scale's top end was technically infinite.

"Come on," Adrian told him.

They were operating on scant information. Maybe that was because there *was* no more information, or maybe Adrian's paranoia was true and in addition to full-neighborhood coverups, darker forces were conspiring to keep the Porters in the dark as well.

How had the rift been discovered — by the department before it was seen by the residents?

What was known about the rift? When had it shown up, how big was it — all the intel they usually had?

The early rift, before it opened, had to be subtle or there

would have been an uproar. The pre-rift now — pregnant with pulsing energy, clearly about to open — wasn't subtle at all.

It looked like a fire had been set in the center of all this middle-class mediocrity, only the flame consumed nothing. It simply hovered in the air, burning in many colors.

Ray held his meter to it. He nodded, then pocketed the thing. "Seconds away. Get behind me. Same as we did the last ones."

Yes. Same as they did the last ones. All of their two-man missions before this had been very different (public instead of on the sly, surrounded by cameras, and of course all within the Gore Point), but protocol was exactly the same.

The rifts were always small (this looked like low ones, maybe a 1.3), so they simply stood close with Ray in front and Adrian in the rear, the brothers taking the place of the more typical two full lines of Legions. Tighter quarters, but identical methods applied.

Seconds away. It's always seconds away.

Adrian hadn't noticed the perfection of the department's timing until he and Ray had started fighting rifts alone. In the past, spotters rushed ahead of the Brigade to secure and monitor the scene, the spotters in turn responding to ... Well, Adrian had no more idea what the spotters responded to on a typical scene than he knew how the department had learned about this one.

Full-Brigade repellances had chemistry and choreography, so it was never a surprise when the execution moved like clockwork. But on these smaller jobs (especially ones with no crew or onlookers), the clockwork felt strange.

Rifts seemed to open with minimal warning. Until the final minute or so, it wasn't an exact science. And yet not once did Adrian remember waiting more than ten minutes post-prep for a rift to open. Not once had he heard of a rift opening before they were ready.

The sole exception was the rift he'd seen on Sunday, but it had opened along with the others. They just hadn't known it was there.

They wait for us, Adrian thought.

He didn't have time to think anything else.

There was a crack like the sundering of a branch.

Then the aurora burned brighter, the eye opened, and all Hell broke loose.

12

THE PORTHOLE

Ray was ready. After pocketing the Zen meter, he'd unholstered his Rollard.

He stood holding it like a broadsword, one foot ahead of the other like a gladiator preparing for battle.

Adrian was less ready. His thoughts were a storm, all the things he'd taken for granted striking him as strange. They had remained in the living room for less than sixty seconds. The rift, supposedly, had begun to show last night on whatever instruments dispatch used to monitor such things. If he and Ray had arrived a single minute later, they'd have missed the opening. Then what?

The appearance of an anomalous rift was bad enough, but the incursion of fiends into a residential area would be far worse. It had been more than a decade since a fiend escaped a rift unseen, then entered the population center. It was the only reason people still lived in Fortune. Seen from the inside, the Rampart seemed more like prison than protection.

With so much on the line, why hadn't they been sent to the

house an hour ago? They could have sat and waited. Played card games until the rift finally decided to open.

Either that, or it would have opened an hour earlier. Have you ever waited? *Even once?*

But then the crack came and the eye lifted its sideways lid. The cloying reek of sulfur wafted from the opening on a small breeze, not the roar of a furnace. Ray waited for the first emergence and Adrian waited behind him. He had a small, laminated set of flipping pages strapped to his left arm. Once his brain stopped yapping, Adrian put his focus on the rift, waiting to see what Ray would start killing. Waiting to look up the fiend class in his laminated pages, so he could tell Ray which setting on his weapon would do the job.

Don't screw it up. He can re-equip the little weapon if you call it wrong, but it's tiny, with hardly any ammo.

His hands shook. He was nervous. Anxious about making a mistake. He had no idea why; he'd never been this jittery on a job before.

The countless unknowns were unnerving him.

Both those he could see, and those he could sense. There were too many questions now. So many miracles to riftfare that now struck Adrian as a little too coincidental.

"Here they come," Ray said.

The things that emerged were not human-size. The first of them looked like small, fat dogs with no front legs or faces. They waddled half-upright like turkeys to compensate. Concentric circles of wide holes where their necks should be, with only darkness inside. Like a dried-out lotus blossom.

A blow from Ray's Rollard cut the creature neatly in half.

It stopped moving, oozing yellow phlegm.

Three more came behind it. One stopped, started to shake, and emitted a vibrating sort of warble. The kind of sound that was building up to something: a pitcher winding up for a fastball.

Ray must have thought the same thing because he slaughtered that one first, before its warble could finish. He parried as the remaining creatures lunged, swiping one with the fork side of his weapon and then striking down to impale the other.

"Talk to me, Ade."

They were coming faster now. The rift was small, same for its discharges. Flipping through his book, uncharacteristically rattled, Adrian thought again of the fiends as swarms of insects. Mindless things obeyed instinct. They came in swarms: nature trading smarts for sheer numbers.

More of the half-dog things came. Then long, undulating ribbons with teeth; those had to climb up from the floor of their plane and over the rift's lip to land on the homeowners' wood floor. They left slime trails behind them. Ray was keeping up, but only barely. At their earlier two-man jobs (official and inside the Gore Point), the flow had been slower.

"Adrian? Come on, man — tell me what I'm fighting!"

But Adrian couldn't find the doglike things in his reference book. He'd never seen the ribbon things before. Every once in a while the Brigade would run across an unusual class, but in those cases there were rearward-line Legions on the job of figuring it out.

Today it was only Adrian. And these creatures were all new to him.

"Adrian!"

"I ... I don't know! I've never seen any of these fuckers before!"

The flow was coming faster. They were taking too long. Fighting fiends was like plugging a hole in an actively leaking dam. Plug the hole immediately after taking your finger from it and all's well … but wait too long and the dam around the hole weakens. Water pours faster than you can bail it.

Ray and Adrian were at that stage already: second and third waves lining up behind the first, and only one man with a hand-to-hand weapon here to stop them.

One of the dog things had started thrumming like the earlier one. Ray fought toward it, slicing ribbon fiends into shreds, but the flow was too fast now; he needed an energy weapon and Adrian hadn't yet decided which to use. The creature's siren reached its peak, and as it did, a pressure wave exploded out from it.

Ray rocked on his feet. Adrian was blown backward, crashing into a clear-doored cabinet full of glassware and china. Lamps fell and picture frames blew over. The pendulous light fixture above swung so hard, it slammed into the ceiling it had been bolted to, twice.

Another dog-fiend started to vibrate and warble. Unsure how to reach it, Ray picked up an ashtray and hurled it. He somehow hit his target, but the creature didn't fall or shake with impact. Instead, the ashtray vanished inside one of the black-bottomed holes on its front, gone without a trace.

The room was growing hot. More fiends came, and brought their heat with them.

"ADRIAN!"

Adrian flipped faster, heart in his throat. Something finally stopped him.

He saw a beast like the half-dogs, only the colors were different. The arrangement of holes was smaller, and on either side of that feature was what looked like dark black eyes. It was wrong, but it was the closest he'd seen. He ran his finger down the plastic-covered page, past WALKERS to CRAWLERS. There he saw pictures of something that was again like the squirming ribbons … but again not quite.

"Osiris," Adrian said. "I ... I think it's an Osiris-class rift."

"You *think?*"

He nodded, trying to convince himself. Maybe he was right and maybe he was wrong. Either way, they were out of time.

"I'm sure," he lied. "*Osiris.* So ... Paulson. Use the Paulson!"

Ray wasted no time. While Adrian stammered, he'd already moved the Rollard to just one hand and raised the multi-weapon. He rolled it one position to release the Paulson Gun attachment, and pulled the trigger.

The fat little weapon spit the distinct purple traces of Zen rounds. They were specific, not a wide-band killer like Rattlers. Ray had to hit every fiend at least once to kill them, but fortunately once was enough.

He sprayed the area in front of the rift. Then the rest of the floor, where they'd spread as they came. Some of the ribbon things were slithering up the walls and two of the dog things had hopped two-legged onto a standing piano, picking out a discordant melody.

Ray handled them too, laying much of the home to waste in the doing. None had escaped. They'd gotten lucky. Faster species *would* have been able to flee. There would be Hell to pay then, almost literally.

Thirty seconds later Ray was breathing hard, looking back at Adrian with wordless accusation: *We'll talk about this later.*

"Go," Ray said. "Close it."

Adrian shuffled past Ray, dancing on tiptoes to avoid the field of fiend corpses. A rendering crew was surely on its way, prepared to enter the garage once Ray and Adrian had vacated it to clean the mess and collect the Element.

They'd wonder what happened. On jobs this small, Ray should only need to kill a few fiends. Five, maybe ten. There were close to a hundred in this room.

Adrian assessed the rift. Its concavity was intact, so there'd be no need to enter the rift and start a seam from the other side. He found the midline faster than normal, making up some time. The wrist-worn computer he wore just up the arm from the flip book showed him a simple closure plan that Adrian had already computed on his own.

He flicked the nozzle of his Element welder from its stowage clamp, checked the filler rod charge one final time, and prepared to begin his suture.

But then he saw something. Inside the rift.

"Jesus," Ray said. "There's someone in there."

Adrian scanned the other plane's floor, making sure the next wave of fiends hadn't yet arrived to swarm them. Then his eyes moved back to what'd stopped him. It looked like a Legion.

Just like the other day, when Adrian had seen his late father.

Ray extended a hand. "Give me your rebreather."

"You want to *go in?*"

"That guy's not wearing a mask. He's going to suffocate."

"Then I'll go."

"Don't argue with me, Adrian. If you had the stones to pull someone out of a rift, I wouldn't have had to be the one to say it. Hurry!" He gestured more urgently with his hand.

"You're not heat-shielded! An asbestos coat isn't protection enough to—"

But wait. For a half-blip, Adrian swore he saw sunshine.

"Goddammit, Adrian, that's one of our people in—!"

Adrian held up the back of his hand to shush his brother. Then he pointed with the other hand. "Wait. Look closely."

Ray did. After a few seconds, he saw and gasped. "There's *more* people in there?"

Adrian nodded. "A Brigade's worth."

The silhouettes were hard to see at first, but unmistakable once noticed.

Beyond them, though, was something else. Adrian used his finger to outline a wide area around the people: a contrast border where brighter air met the rift's red darkness.

"And look," he said, tracing the border again for Ray. "When the sulfur clouds clear, you can see a shape around them. Do you see it? It's oblong, like a watermelon."

"*What's* oblong?"

"The rift that they're fighting on the other end."

Ray turned, his gaze half-uncomprehending.

"Christ, Ray. Those people aren't *inside* the rift. They're *beyond* it. I think we're watching a repellance from the inside out. I ... I think we're looking into our rift, then out through another one."

The brothers went silent. Now that they'd seen the shapes and made sense of them, the picture was plain as day. They could make out two lines of Legions: frontward and rearward. Faint in the distance behind them, they could even see Stitchers waiting for their turn.

"My God. It's us," Adrian said.

"What?"

Adrian nodded toward the rift. "That's *our* group. Brigade One."

"No."

"*Yes,*" Adrian said. "Look at their shapes and sizes. Tell me that's not Ollie on point." It was hard to mistake Ollie Davis; he was six-eight and as wide as the average person was tall. "I think the short person with big hair standing beside him is Dee."

Ray considered while Adrian kept peering into the double-ended rift. He'd never seen a Legion line from the front the perspective of the rift itself. It was spellbinding to watch them work. Between slashing at the fiends that came at them, Ollie, Dee, and the others moved with a flowing motion Adrian had never noticed before. They kept brushing one hand along their sleeves and the fronts of their asbestos heat jackets, then moving the hand behind them before reaching back out to re-grip their Rollards.

Was it something Legions were taught to do when facing rifts — a little dance to confuse the fiends coming at them? Ray broke his curiosity by speaking.

"Jesus. That *is* Ollie and Dee. I think that's Harrison behind them. But ... they're way across town! The rift the Brigade went after is at the center of the Gore Point!"

Ray and Adrian's home unit had deployed thirty or forty miles away, and yet through the double-ended rift they appeared less than a quarter-mile distant. Brigade One's rift was a monster — six-five at least, maybe nearing a seven-oh. Big enough for Ray and Adrian to see the sun-lit sky behind them, throwing the foreground fighters into silhouette.

If the rift wasn't so big on their end, the Porters would never have seen them. But now they had, and now they knew: There was more to the nature of rifts and the other plane than anyone understood.

A goose-over-grave sensation raised the hairs on the back of Adrian's neck.

This wasn't random. There was order here.

Ray was wrong; rifts weren't simple chaos.

He almost wished they were. Adrian's was a puzzle-solving mind, and mostly it worked in the background. His forebrain didn't always know what his deeper mind was busy concluding ... but conclusions it had been drawing, and for a while now.

Adrian didn't like the feel of what it seemed to have

decided. He didn't like the feel of what struck him as yet-unarticulated, but obviously true.

The hellbringer that had killed their father, appearing in a rift it didn't belong to.

Eight rifts in one place, as if it were a test for the Brigades.

Rifts opening only once the rift-fighters arrived and made ready.

Strange fiend-variants from an established class here, far from where rifts normally occurred.

The saboteur. The boundary weakening beneath all of them. Rifts that opened and closed on their own.

It felt like a behemoth in the shadows, waiting to strike.

"Close it, Ade," Ray said, backing away. "Close it now."

Adrian didn't need to be asked twice.

13

SECRETS AND DANGER

Ray's phone rang back in the van.

Inspector J. Dixon. Denny Brennan's forensic equipment had identified the rift through means unknown, so those same means must have told him and Dixon that the rift was closed. They were ready for their report ... and *what* a report Adrian had to give.

He was about to raise the phone to his face when a rough, scar-hardened hand laid atop his wrist. He looked over to see Ray looking into his eyes.

Adrian had never seen fear on his brother before. Didn't even know that Ray could experience the emotion. Not this particular brand, tinged with something else. Something worse.

"Don't answer," Ray said.

Adrian denied the call. He waited for reasons.

"What will you tell him?" Ray asked.

"I'll tell him what we saw."

"About the mutant Osiris fiends. About seeing into one rift and out of another that's nowhere near us."

"It could be really important. Brennan's team has some unconventional theories."

"Unconventional like Dad's?"

Adrian nodded.

"Tell me."

"I can't tell you. You know I can't."

"What's this all about, Ade? This whole thing with S&C and the agent and you being some sort of a special envoy to the forensics department."

"I'm not a special envoy."

"Why did they want you to work with them? It's not an insult. I swear it's not. I'm just asking the question. You're a good Stitcher, but you're still just a Stitcher. They're brass. Nobody else has been called up to the big leagues. Why only you?"

Adrian considered the story. He could tell Ray some of it.

"Kaur wanted me to help out. Some of my theories are things they'd already been thinking."

Ray nodded. He still didn't look like himself — like the cocky asshole the world knew him to be. Instead he looked tentative. On eggshells. Almost like someone afraid of being beaten.

"You mean theories like incursions happening outside the Gore Point."

"Right." Adrian nodded.

His brother had seen a rift in suburbia. As far as secrets went, that one was already out of the bag.

"Dixon's not involved in that, though," Ray said. "I'm asking why Dixon would want *you*."

"Dixon is S&C. S&C stands for *'Spread and C—'*"

"I know what it stands for. But I think we both know that S&C has two halves. There are the scientists and agents. One cares less about spread and more about the way spread is being contained. Agents are Internal Affairs."

"And?"

Ray looked toward the house. They'd left a huge mess inside: fiends to be taken away and rendered, but also a lot of smashed belongings. Adrian wondered how the department would handle the family's homecoming. Would they try to replace what was askew or broken and act like nothing happened, or blame the destruction on another force, like a tornado that materialized inside their living room?

"Tell me the truth, Ade. Are you working with them to spy on us?"

"Ray, I'm not a—"

Ray waved his hand aggressively. He wasn't just dismissing what Adrian had been about to say; he seemed irritated that the distraction was even a factor. "I'm not calling you a rat. I understand why S&C agents exist. I'm not questioning your loyalty. I just want to know if this is an investigation. If S&C is after Brigade One."

Adrian barely understood the question. "Why would they be after the Brigade?"

Again Ray went silent. He seemed to be deciding if saying the troubling thing he had in mind was necessary. "You know the federal budget's been cut. Over and over and over."

"Of course. It's half the reason we're on this detail. Every once in a while Brennan and the others need a pair they can trust to take care of these kinds of jobs quietly so people don't panic, but most of the time our job is to be The Famous Fighting Porter Brothers onscreen for more sponsorships."

"What you don't know is that the Legions took a bigger pay cut than was reported. Brigade One's Stitchers were cut by ten percent. Legions were cut by thirty."

"But that's—!"

"It's okay." Ray raised a hand. "We did it on purpose. You know Ollie adopted Jamie's kid after Jamie was killed. A lot of department kids aren't as lucky. Ollie's tied into it. He found out the department planned to slash funding for the orphan program entirely, so he asked us to take the hit. There was no question. We all agreed."

"You should have asked the Stitchers! You didn't have to take it all on by yourselves!"

Again Ray raised a hand. "Don't be a martyr, Ade. One of us had to earn to help pay Mom's medical bills. Shannon and Abid both got Zen burns on that July job that the medical program isn't covering. The Legions are healthy for now, so we took the bullet. You weren't told because nobody wanted to have the argument we're having right now."

Adrian let it settle. This was far from the usual arguments he had with Ray.

"Point is, people outside of Fortune can't really understand how bad things are here. It's not really their fault. If you live outside the Rampart, the notion of fiends coming into our world from somewhere else is academic. Maybe we protect the planet too well. There are no Gore Points outside of the Rampart. Nobody sees it. Nobody wants to pay to fund a problem nobody feels they have. So the feds cut funding. Just one more way to balance the budget. They know we won't quit. They know we'll make do. But Ade ... *We* have families, too."

Adrian was starting to get an inkling of where this might be going. He thought again of Mom's treatments, and how little of the cost insurance ended up covering.

"That weird way we saw the Legions moving," Adrian said. "The thing where they ran a hand down their sleeves after every Rollard swing. They're collecting Zen dust, aren't they?"

"I know it's illegal."

"Illegal. *Dangerous.*" Adrian felt his temperature rising, but wasn't sure which emotion to feel. "Where do you put it? In a fanny pack?"

"Baker's dad knew a lot of guys in R&D. Matt rigged a storage unit he says is pretty secure and we all wear them on the backs of our belts. Rollard kills always create backsplash, so all you have to do is wipe down your coat and rub your hand across a pad on the device behind your back to make deposits. We pool what we have after every repellance, and divide it evenly. Lee Barnes knows someone in the rendering crew who gave us a few old capture tubes to transport it safely. We even found a guy willing to pay us for whatever we collect."

"Shit, Ray! That stuff can be turned into—"

"—face creams. Fireplace starter logs," Ray interrupted. "Nothing weaponized. It has to be refined for that. But if you tell Dixon what you saw today, he'll know. S&C already thinks we're dirty. If word comes down that we're dealing black market Zen to keep the lights on ..."

The phone beeped with a new voicemail. Dixon would be wondering why Adrian wasn't responding right about now, eager for his report.

"Please, Ade."

Adrian's jaw firmed.

"The world isn't always as black and white as you want it to be. Sometimes the right thing comes in shades of gray."

Adrian looked hard at his brother. "They *have* asked. Not about the Legions, but about missing Zen Element." He was treading turf he really shouldn't share with Ray, but anger was fueling him. "You're asking me to lie about the one thing I'm most supposed to tell the truth about. God*dammit,* Ray; what am I supposed to do with this? Either I rat you out or I handicap an investigation that might end up meaning everything. To everyone. Which should I choose?"

"Tell me."

"I *can't* tell you!" Adrian snapped. "And right now, I don't fucking *want* to tell you."

"Then tell me this ..."

Adrian waited, not wanting to give him the satisfaction of engaging.

Ray finally finished. "Are you still my brother?"

14

MOLE AND EPIPHANY

hy did they want you to work with them?

Nobody else has been called up to the big leagues.

Why only you?

"Adrian? Did you hear me?"

Adrian blinked away his brother's voice, which kept circling inside his mind. He should have filibustered on this debrief with Brennan and Dixon and cleared his head. Physically, the three of them were in Brennan's lab among the clank of glassware and hum of forensics machines with assistants and scientists buzzing around in the background ... but mentally, Adrian was still in the van, hearing Ray's shame and silent accusations.

He'd already given his report. He'd admitted to everything except for the sweeping motion he'd witnessed from the Legions. He wasn't sure if he'd made the right choice. Theft of Zen was at the heart of this saboteur project, and the fact that the Legions were skimming *raw* Element didn't put them in the clear. Supposedly refining Zen was extremely difficult and impossible to do efficiently at small scale, but that didn't mean it wasn't happening. What if the Brigade's actions were enabling the saboteur? Adrian ignored the notion for now, but kept it on file in case the revelation was required someday.

With the report finished, only Ray's insinuations stuck with him. Adrian *was* just a Stitcher, so why *had* Dixon called him up into this little brain trust? Adrian was considered a Boy Scout, and was close to the Brigade. That made him the perfect mole.

Was that all Adrian was to them? Ray said S&C had been watching Brigade One from the start. Did they really want Adrian's opinion and his totally-standard, not-actually-that-impressive "expertise"? Or had they instead recruited a tattletale?

"I'm sorry. What?" Adrian asked.

"I was asking about Tullehmite," Brennan said.

"Captain Kaur would be a better person to ask about the Brigade's chemical stores."

"Captain Kaur is not part of this investigation." Dixon tapped one finger with his hand flat on a lab bench, causing his large ring to count the beats while he rubbed his bald head with the other hand. They were almost nervous gestures in a man who didn't show his anxiety. It made Adrian remember what Dixon had hidden from him. His words were telling. Not that Kaur *wasn't involved*, but that Kaur was *being excluded*.

The captain had sent Adrian into this back when it was still only about investigating unusual spread. Little had he known he was sending Adrian out to help S&C tie the Brigade's noose — netting Kaur, who led the suspicious Brigade, right along with it.

"I don't know if we keep Tullehmite on hand," Adrian said.

"Could you find out?"

"All supplies are under lock and key."

"What if I gave you a key?" Dixon was a hard man, used to

barking orders and being obeyed. He held more power than he'd admitted, if he could go behind a Brigade chief's back, giving grunts access to forbidden materials.

"I don't know. Maybe."

"'*Maybe,*'" Dixon repeated, as if it was a response worth mocking. Then his tone changed. "Try."

"It might matter," Brennan said.

The investigator's eyes ticked between Dixon and Adrian as if trying to soften the blows to maintain peace. Brennan was a good man. Adrian had always liked him. He liaised with GEN, which was civilian and for-profit in nature, but his loyalties were always to the department — including to its star, Brigade One. Dixon's words tried to split the difference: Yes, finding out about the Tullehmite was important, but they needn't be disrespectful about it.

Brennan continued. "The paradox tells me something. Tullehmite is like a control rod. It stabilizes rifts and hence makes them safer. But we're talking about sabotage. We're talking about someone making more rifts, which is the *opposite* of safe. My assistants' work all shows that our person is using Tullehmite. It burns in the aurora with a distinct spectral signature. It points to a *methodical* saboteur. This isn't someone who wants to smash and grab. It's someone with a methodical mind. Someone who wants control. You need access to get Tullehmite ... and the key Mr. Dixon just offered you isn't the only one out there. There's a key hanging in Captain Kaur's office. Anyone could break in and grab it."

Adrian noted his careful words. Brennan had added his last sentence so Adrian wouldn't think he was accusing only Kaur. He'd simply said "anyone" instead of "anyone in the Brigade" to open the possibility that it was an outside party: a late-night burglar, perhaps.

"I can try to look at the stores if you give me a key," Adrian said. "But in the meantime, don't you want to hear my thoughts about the patterns in the new rift openings?"

"I'll get you a key." Dixon had zero interest in Adrian's thoughts. Only in his ability to look where Dixon could not.

"In addition to having access to Tullehmite," Brennan went on, "the saboteur would need detailed knowledge about opening and closing rifts. They'd need a motive. *Why* do they do what they do? It's like I said; using a retardant makes me think it's someone with a strong *reason* to do what they're doing, and controlled use of Tullehmite must be specific to that reason. Finding that reason will get us that much closer. Is this about money? If all you wanted was to collect Zen Element, you wouldn't want things to be messy. What's curious is that anyone with enough knowledge to do this should know how dangerous it is *to* do, even with Tullehmite."

Brennan shook his head. "No rift is a safe rift. So they'd have to be willing to lose whatever control they're trying to hold onto. If the planes shatter and rifts start opening everywhere because of their actions, they'd have to be okay with it. They'd be thinking, 'Profit from the world … but if that can't happen, burn it instead.' So we're looking for someone with a grudge. A malcontent. A little nihilistic. That about cover it? Anything I'm forgetting?"

Adrian nodded, mostly checked out on the conversation … but then something hit him.

Tullehmite was carefully controlled by the department, but there was another rare thing that Adrian himself had found on a sabotage scene that Brennan and Dixon seemed to have forgotten about.

Adrian, in fact, once found himself directly on top of it.

Capture tubes.

You couldn't get capture tubes on the open market, and capture tubes were required to transport both raw and refined

Zen Element. You needed a hook up to get them. You had to know someone for whom capture tubes were stock and trade.

Adrian hid the epiphany that struck him. He alone knew there was a saboteur *and* that Brigade One's Legions were skimming raw Zen Element. He alone knew the things he was keeping from the Brigade ... and the thing he'd earlier decided not to tell either Brennan or Dixon.

It wasn't the Legions doing this. Or the Stitchers. There was a third party that nobody was considering, and that party had access to all the capture tubes anyone could ever need ... and to Tullehmite.

The saboteur must be one of the renderers.

The crews that came to collect the fiend bodies and squeeze raw element from them.

Adrian ended the meeting early. He had a realization to share, but not with Special Agent J. Dixon.

15

WHISKEY

"Where's Ray?"

Harrison Kim was reading a magazine, and the first person to hear him. He looked up at Adrian's slightly manic entrance, then around the room to see if anyone else was closer to the door — if anyone else would answer Adrian.

Apparently Harrison would have to. "Where've you been, Adrian?"

"Where's Ray?"

"Out." Then a pause. "Where've you been?"

"What's it matter?"

"Laurel came by. She said you were supposed to be home by now and you're not answering your phone."

Adrian checked his phone. He'd gotten in the habit of putting it on Do Not Disturb while with Brennan and Dixon due to what felt like a Cone of Silence situation. He'd missed three calls from Laurel, and hadn't even thought to check.

Dee turned, twisting on the couch, legs forward and torso back to face him. "Yeah. Where've you been?"

"What? Who cares?"

"We had a real big burner today," Harrison explained. "Seven-point-two. You know climate change?"

"I'm familiar with it."

"This was the climate change of rifts. Some people are talking like it's hitting some sort of a critical mass. Like something's going on that's making the rifts a lot bigger than they should be ... *Where were you*, Adrian?"

Then Adrian understood. They knew he'd been talking to Brennan, and now rumor seemed to have circulated about his meeting with Dixon. If everyone in the Brigade was part of the theft Ray had described, then they all had theories as to why Dixon was around ... and about why the most Boy Scout of a Stitcher among them had been spending so much time with the new cop in their midst.

"I was on a job," Adrian reported.

"So were we," Dee said. "You should have *seen* how much Stitching this big mother took to get closed. Matt was the MVP. Took over your usual quarter while handling his own quarter at the same time."

"You know I'm on a special assignment." Adrian hadn't expected a need to defend himself. He was still in the doorway, still just trying to get directions.

"Yeah. For publicity, right? Help get some more sponsors." Harrison shrugged as if this was a fair answer. "But the camera crew was with us today. Weird, right?"

"Ask Kaur. He sent us off."

"*Us?*"

"Me and Ray."

"So you were with Ray."

"*Yes* I was with Ray!"

"Hmm. And now you want Ray. I guess just go back where you were, if you're looking for him."

Adrian's eye caught sight of Ray's pullover draped over the couch. Now he got the rest of it: Ray had been here by himself just recently — alone.

Maybe Adrian had been with him earlier, but it was the missing time between (when Adrian had been with Brennan and Dixon) that Harrison was apparently jabbing a finger at.

"Did you guys see the rendering team arrive?" Adrian asked.

"Yeah," said Harrison. "Did you?"

Adrian ignored it. "Who was there?"

"Allie. Steph. Roland. Why?"

"Do you know if they used Tullehmite when the rift was closing? To stabilize it?"

Nobody answered. Adrian wished he could just blurt his theory, but the room had its tendrils in everything and he had to understand it all before saying another word. For all he knew, Legions had been handing their skimmed Zen off to one of the renderers as the first-stage buyer. Best not to start throwing accusations and theories until he ran it by his brother.

"WHERE'S RAY?"

Matt — hero Stitcher, apparently — turned around in his seat at a desk where he'd been playing Solitaire. His voice was sympathetic, as if he'd noticed Adrian squirming on his hook and was ready to let him off.

"He went home, Adrian. Said he wasn't feeling well. Looked pretty bad, actually. What did you guys face today?"

Matt had spoken softly and with some pity, so Adrian answered only for him, ducking out of Harrison's gaze to move closer. "I'll tell you later, Matt. I swear I will. But I can't right now. I just ..."

"It's okay. Ray went home. You wanna talk to him before the rest of us, that's where you'll find him."

Adrian moved to go, unsure of how to take Matt's very specific statement.

"Adrian." Matt stopped him.

Adrian turned.

"He said he was sick. *Said.*"

"You told me that."

Matt finished. "But he took a bottle of whiskey when he left."

ADRIAN KNOCKED. No response.

He knocked louder. *"Ray."*

He heard something fall over behind Ray's apartment door. Something small.

"Ray. It's Adrian. Open up. We need to talk."

He shouldn't have said it like that. It sounded accusatory. The way the last hour had unfolded, Adrian thought he saw a change of mood around the station: everyone alarmed by sudden shifts in the rifts and riftfare, everyone apparently at least a little concerned that Adrian might be on the wrong side. So he said what he'd actually meant to say, knowing the negative weight *We have to talk* carried for most people — Ray included.

"Ray. I figured something out. I need your help. To catch some real bad guys."

Still nothing.

"RAY!"

Another sound inside as Adrian banged on the door. He thought of what Matt had said, imagining Ray passed out on the couch after drinking to forget. Like Dad used to do. Drinking was said to quiet the demons, but that was almost literal for the Porter men.

Adrian fished the keychain from his pocket, then picked out the key to Ray's apartment. He'd never given it back after moving in with Laurel again.

The edge of the door struck the small table beside the door where Ray threw his wallet and keys. The only thing on the table now was an empty beer bottle lying on its side. The bottle rocked as the door brushed it. The apartment was otherwise quiet.

"Ray?"

The living room was dark with the blinds pulled. Blacked out because Ray had been working odd shifts lately with all the recent overtime, occasionally sleeping at night like usual and other times needing to catch naps during the day. The swinging shifts had knocked him a little off-kilter, turning him irritable. He'd been drinking more. Blustering more. That's the second reason it felt important to tell Ray his news: to erase any fear he had about Adrian ratting him out to Dixon, sharing confidential realizations instead.

Even Dixon hadn't heard Adrian's theory about the saboteur's identity. Maybe the brothers could work out the truth on their own. Find the renderer causing all the trouble without S&C's help. If the brothers could do that, they could take it to Kaur first, Brennan second, and Dixon last.

Adrian wasn't sure he liked Dixon. Knew he didn't appreciate being a pawn. This news would be relieving to Ray. Maybe even make him happy. But he wasn't on the couch drunk as Adrian had expected.

"*Ray?*"

He checked the bedroom. The blinds were open in there, spilling dusty sunbeams into the room. The sheets were rumpled, no one under them.

Adrian frowned. He got his phone and tapped Ray's contact

to call him. He'd tried on the way over and gotten no answer, but that felt normal because Matt's parting words suggested Ray was probably drunk. He wasn't a bar drinker, or an outdoors drinker. If none of his friends were having a party, his apartment was the only place Ray would drink to drown any sorrows.

So was Matt wrong? Before Adrian went off to meet with Dixon, Ray said he was going to the station house, and yet he wasn't working nor ditching work at home to drink.

The call rang once. The second time, Adrian followed the sound and located Ray's phone on a kitchen table littered with books, under a sheet of written-upon paper, full of math and what looked like chemical formulas.

Adrian frowned at the paper. And at the books. Neither seemed like his brother at all.

The top book was called *Hell on Earth.* Ray flipped it over and found a subtitle: *How Plane-Closing and Rift Warfare Threaten God's Kingdom.*

Adrian's eyebrows drew closer together. Ray wasn't much into God and Hell. He said that neither existed, both were mankind's attempt to make sense from the senseless.

He looked down. What appeared to be a photocopied map had been sandwiched between books, visible now that Adrian had removed the top one. He picked it up, studied it, then frowned.

It looked like a map drawn by someone insane. There were a lot of real names and places around Fortune (town hall, Springfield Meadows Plaza, Gerhard Park), but in all the wrong places. Like someone had cut a real map into pieces, then rearranged the puzzle.

Thinking saboteur thoughts, Adrian looked to see if he could locate Findale Commons: the spot of that job in suburbia —the one with mutants in the rift.

He found it, but just like everything else it was in the wrong place. Instead of bordering Sycamore Avenue, Findale Commons was sandwiched between High Street (way across town) and the Gore Point's black lake … which, on this map, wasn't inside the Gore Point at all.

He pushed the map and *Hell on Earth* aside and looked at the next book in the stack, called *The New Alchemist's Handbook.* Glancing at the dust jacket, it seemed to be a fringe publication done mostly DIY. An update to the 1980s Satanist craze, informing a new generation of weirdoes on how best to summon the other side.

Apparently you were still supposed to draw pentagrams on the ground and light candles, but sacrificing goats had fallen out of fashion. Satan's front door was always opening these days. The book was all about how to ring the bell, invite the big guy in, and generally attract the devil's attention.

"The fuck?" Adrian said to himself.

The door opened behind him.

Adrian dropped the book, spun, and faced the newcomer with wide eyes and an unconcealed expression. Of course it was Ray.

"Ade?"

"Oh." *Breathing too fast. Slow it down.* "Hi, Ray."

"Hi." He stepped forward, inspecting his brother. "Why are you here?"

"I was looking for you."

"I was out." He looked at the door. "Did I leave the door unlocked?"

"I have my key."

Ray took a few more steps, now actively puzzled. "You just … walked in?"

"I thought you might be passed out."

Ray's head tipped. His eyes flicked toward the books, then at Adrian's face. Then he noticed the phone in Adrian's hand.

Adrian gave it to him, but jostling woke the screen. On it, Adrian saw the missed call he'd just placed, but there was a second notification on the lock screen. A voicemail from a name Adrian recognized: a refiner named Cerina Dell who worked on most Brigade One jobs.

Why was Ray talking to Cerina? Adrian had never so much as formally met her.

"You left your phone."

He took it, but still looked fazed.

"I know. That's what I came back for." Ray slipped the phone into his pocket, and Adrian noticed he was holding a plastic bag.

"Saved me a trip anyway." Ray handed the bag to Adrian.

Inside was a wooden box that seemed to contain a bottle of whiskey — the same bottle, presumably, that Matt had seen him take from the station.

"That's for Laurel's Dad. I was headed to your place to give it to her."

"You're getting whiskey for Laurel's dad?" Adrian asked.

"We got along. Remember? We did a lot of fishing. That's an 18-year-old Jameson. It's his favorite and it's his birthday. What the hell's wrong with you, Ade?"

He had been stock-still and wide-eyed since Ray's entry. Barely taken a breath. He'd forgotten how well Laurel's father had liked Ray — something he only knew from the other end. When Laurel stopped dating Ray and started dating Adrian instead, Paulie Gantry's disappointment was obvious. Ray was a real man in Paulie's eyes. Adrian struck him as soft. Now Ray was giving him whiskey. Maybe Adrian could give him flowers.

"I have something to tell you," Adrian said.

"Okay. What?"

Ray turned long enough to set his keys and wallet on the table by the door, and Adrian again read the titles of his books — along with a scrawled paper full of strange chemistry.

Adrian moved away. He didn't want Ray to know that he'd seen them. "I ..."

Ray waited.

"It's nothing."

"*Nothing?*"

"Look. I have to get back." Adrian moved toward the door. Why was he so unnerved? They were just books. About the end of the world. About bringing Hell more to the forefront of life on the planet.

That plus numbers and equations, as if Ray had spent a lot of time figuring things out. Ray didn't usually figure things out. Ray acted in the moment.

And if it all fell apart? Ray usually figured that was okay. If the world was going to burn, then so be it. Everything was random. Everything was chaos.

Except for Mom. Her medical bills were orderly, and Ray — even more than Adrian — said that he'd do whatever it took to pay them.

Family mattered. Not much else.

"Ade. You came here to tell me something. Just fucking say it."

The words almost formed on Adrian's lips: *I know who the saboteur is. I figured it out, but I didn't tell Dixon or Brennan. It's someone who needs money. Someone who doesn't want the rifts they open to get out of control ... but if they do happen to get out of control and the whole thing collapses, that's okay, too. Because the person's a malcontent.*

Someone who's gotten a little disenfranchised with life lately. Someone who thinks they got a raw deal. Someone who believes in mixing things up because everything is chaos anyway. Someone with easy access to capture tubes. Someone who knows riftfare inside and out because it's something they do every day of their lives.

Then following that: *It's someone on the rendering crew.*

But Adrian wasn't sure he believed that anymore. "It was just a question."

"Okay. Ask it."

"It's a secret."

"Ask it, Adrian."

"I need something from the controlled substances room, but nobody can know about it," he improvised. "I heard there's a key in Kaur's office. Have you ever seen it? Do you know where his key is?"

Brennan had said it was *hanging right there.* Surely Ray knew. Surely everyone knew, if all the Legions had turned out crooked.

"Sure, but you won't be able to get it. Cap takes it with him whenever he leaves. He lets you use his office all the time, Ade. Why the hell are you asking *me* how to get his key?"

"No reason. Sorry." Aiden pushed toward the door. "Thanks anyway. Look. I've ... I've got to go."

His heart hammering. His thoughts racing. Ray was just staring at him, suspicious of everything.

"Ade!"

Adrian stopped with his hand on the door.

"You okay?"

"I'm fine."

"You get spooked today? Is that what this is?"

Adrian blinked. It was a perfect excuse for his current behavior. "Yeah. The mutants. The way it almost got out of hand. It kind of fucked me up."

Ray nodded slowly, seeming to believe him.

"You need that key for something secret? Something

important? One more thing you can't talk about with me, but can talk about with the agent?"

"It's not for Dixon. I swear it's not."

Ray took his keys from the end table, then peeled one off of the chain. He handed it to Adrian.

"Controlled substances room," Ray said, meaning the key. "Don't tell anyone I have a copy."

16

TELL ME

Adrian left the whiskey on the kitchen table.

Laurel came home from work, kissed him on the cheek, then ignored him for an hour while he dissected spreadsheets on his computer. He'd had to ask Dixon to pull some of the spreadsheets, but had somehow managed to do so without revealing what he knew.

Dinnertime came. Laurel came out, briefly rubbed his back and pecked his cheek, then moved into the kitchen.

Adrian heard plastic rustling. Then, "Is this yours?"

He looked up. She'd pulled the whiskey from the bag. Its box was nice: a pale wood of some sort, shot through with red like cedar.

"Oh. Yeah. It's for your dad."

She was still looking. "Shit, Ade. This is an 18-year-old Jameson. You can't afford this."

"It's from Ray."

"*Ray* can't afford this. It's like two hundred bucks. For a father-in-law he's never going to get. Where's Ray getting enough money to splurge like that?"

"L." Adrian waved for her to come over. "Come over here a sec. I need your brain."

"The rest of me comes with it." She wrapped an arm around Adrian, but he didn't seem to hear the joke. From the side of his gaze, he saw the affectionate smile fall from her face. She became dire, feeling his mood. "What?"

"You do statistical analysis and stuff, right?"

"No."

"But you work with numbers! At GEN."

"Yes, but not statistical analysis. We're more about atomic weights and electrical charge capacity and—"

Adrian slid what he'd been working on so it was in front of her on the table. "Tell me I'm crazy."

She pulled her reading glasses from her pocket and slid them on. "You're trying to requisition something?"

"It's a record of requisitions. For Tullehmite, from the controlled substances room at the station."

"Don't you only work with it from tanks?"

"Yes. But after we Stitch a rift, our tanks are recharged and recorded electronically. This is for unmetered tanks."

"Who needs unmetered Tullehmite?"

"Just … Take a look at this. And this." He slid her a second paper. "See the discrepancies?" He'd highlighted the places where Tullehmite seemed to have gone missing on the first paper, which he tapped. Then he tapped highlights on the new paper: Ray's work shifts. "Do you see a pattern?"

Instead of considering the answer, she turned to face Adrian while considering his question. She seemed to know at least the heart of what he was really asking. What Adrian was really trying to prove.

"What's going on? Do you think your brother—"

"Do you see a pattern," Adrian repeated, tapping the papers.

She blinked, then studied his work.

She looked up, removed her glasses, and said, "Yeah. I see a pattern. Are you sure about this?"

Adrian nodded once.

"Ray's stealing Tullehmite," she said.

"I think he might be."

"Why? He's a Legion."

"To stabilize rifts."

"That's your job, not his. Why would he care about rift stabilization? How would he even know how to do it?"

An excellent question, and one Adrian had wondered most of the way home. But then his mind had turned to the books he'd seen on Ray's table, and once he got home he'd looked up the text of those books online. *The New Alchemist's Handbook* in particular turned out to be a step-by-step guide to inviting the Devil over for dinner.

Among its advice: *The planotropic derivative Tullehmite will make your Satanic invitations much easier to control, but it is extremely hard to come by.*

Instructions for gaining that control using Tullehmite had followed anyway, just in case any budding anarchists were able to get their hands on it.

Adrian must have looked nervous. Uneasy. Out of sorts. Because Laurel again encircled him with an arm when he didn't respond.

"What's bothering you, baby? Tell me. Maybe I can help."

Adrian admitted what Dixon had told him about the saboteur, and that Ray turned out to fit Brennan's profile of the saboteur exactly — right down to motive and means.

Adrian told her everything.

17

THE ECHO

Adrian spent the next two days trying to figure out how to handle the situation. A two-day delay in revealing what he knew about his brother was unforgivable considering the stakes, but seeing as only he and Laurel were aware of the situation, there was nobody to critique their restraint.

Adrian needed to stall while he grappled with his discovery, so he told Dixon that the key he'd provided for the controlled substances room turned out to be wrong: that particular duplicate didn't work in the lock. He'd been ready for a lot of bluster to follow (to keep Dixon from demanding Kaur open the room for him), but Dixon was a little more afraid of the riftfare department than he'd been letting on.

Strictly speaking, S&C was out of their jurisdiction. Strictly speaking, it would require proper channels to demand entry to Brigade One's controlled room, and Dixon didn't want to take those channels lest he ruffle too many feathers. So when his key "didn't work," Dixon was out of ideas. He believed Adrian that Kaur must have changed the lock. Apparently that was something the captain was allowed to do, and Dixon couldn't officially do dick about it.

"We can't just sit on this and not take action," Laurel told him. "If rifts are really happening outside the Gore Point …"

"I know." Adrian didn't need to be told how dangerous it was. One man-made rift, even inside the Gore Point, could weaken the entire plane — especially if it was one of the weird ones that sometimes closed on its own, or birthed mutants of known fiend classes instead of normal fiends.

That might cause new rifts to form on their own. Rifts were like perforating paper: Each new rift made subsequent rifts a bit more likely to rip through the fabric of everyday life.

"If Ray's really behind this …" Laurel said.

"Then I'll watch Ray."

The sabotage couldn't be happening often, and it couldn't be easy. So, as much as Adrian could without drawing attention, he researched the business of artificial rift-opening. More than difficult, it almost sounded impossible.

Opening even small rifts took a ton of Zen Element, and that was paradoxical because Ray's goal in opening new rifts was to *gain* Zen, not *spend* it. And whatever he was doing surely required time and solitude. By being around Ray as much as possible, his hands would be tied. Adrian could buy himself some time before deciding what to do.

Should he turn Ray in to the authorities? Or shut his brother down himself?

Adrian hated every possible answer.

It was Laurel's idea for herself and Adrian to fake a fight, then turn their "separation" into leverage. It was more than believable; they'd fought often enough. Laurel wrote the script. One night when Ray was over, Adrian would mention that he'd been working with Dixon on a long-term problem and Laurel would blow her top. She'd waited long enough to leave

Fortune, she'd tell him. She'd waited and waited, hoping Adrian would decide to put her first for a change instead of always choosing his job.

When the time came to perform their stage play in front of Ray, Laurel was barely acting. The irony was, even now Adrian was choosing his job over her. Bickering over her own desire to leave had been Laurel's idea, but that didn't mean she didn't feel every terrible thing she said to him.

After the fake fight, Adrian told Ray he needed to move back in. The brothers became roommates again. Adrian slept little, and did so only when it was clear Ray wouldn't be awake for hours. He stayed closer than normal on full-Brigade jobs, and watched him with hawk eyes when they went off on their own — with or without cameras.

There wasn't much to see. Adrian tried to talk himself out of his deductions, rationalizing that Ray *wasn't* the saboteur because he wasn't acting any different than normal.

Ray was *always* superior. Ray *always* claimed to know what was best for everyone. Ray *always* thought he alone had hung the moon — and as always, Ray kept declaring that if the end came, it would come.

There was no order to the world.

Laurel said, "Watch him close, if you really think he might be innocent. If another rift opens where it shouldn't be, you'll know whether or not he caused it."

So Adrian watched and waited, unsure of what he believed.

The biggest rift of the year came on the afternoon of the third day, but it happened inside the Gore Point where rifts usually opened. It was, however, entirely unexpected: no forecast metrics whatsoever. The sound was the booming of thunder. The rendering cacophony of a planet opening underneath them.

The Brigade was dispatched to the black lake, which

Adrian learned later now contained no water at all. A crack in its bottom had drained the thing.

It was the first time anyone remembered a rift opening under the rock. They got lucky. The sound broke the crust above the rift, turning the lake's water into a fountain of aerosolized steam as it drained into the hot world below.

If the rock covering the rift *hadn't* broken, the fiends would have burrowed through slowly and swum to the surface. The lake would have taken days to drain through burrowed holes, making closing the rift damn near impossible.

Fiends would have run rampant. Fortunately, the Brigade was dispatched post haste, still with a chance to reach the Point before the fiends came too thickly to fight off.

"Hang on." Kaur grabbed Ray by his shoulder as they rushed toward the trucks with the others. "You guys aren't going with everyone else. Dispatch has another special detail for you two. No cameras. You know the drill."

Ray and Adrian knew the drill just fine by now, but ironically *Kaur* didn't. Despite the captain's setting Adrian up with Brennan and Dixon in the first place, he'd thus far been denied knowledge of everything that followed.

It infuriated him, the way his star team kept being assigned new and unknown places without his foreknowledge or permission. Kaur knew only that when special calls came, Ray and Adrian were ordered to the unmarked vans.

He had no idea where they went next, nor what they did. Adrian was loyal to his captain. It was hard not to tell him about their missions ... just because.

So while the others rushed toward a massive lake-bottom rift that topped 7.5 magnitude, the Porter boys were secreted to a quiet private hospital on High Street where a secondary new rift awaited.

"Excuse me," said a slim and short man as they tried to

pass the reception desk. "I assume you're not here to see a patient."

Ray and Adrian looked like Ghostbusters in their gear. It wasn't subtle. This was their fourth covert exercise, and until now they'd assumed the site would be cleared as it had been every other time. But the hospital was staffed and operational, as if they had no idea a rift existed in the building. Which they probably did not.

And if that was the case, then the brothers definitely weren't supposed to tell them.

Adrian mumbled. The small man stood with his arms crossed, clearly bothered by the intrusion.

"Ade," said Ray.

Ray gave the man a hang-on-a-sec look, then turned to his brother.

Ray urged Adrian's gaze down, to where he was hiding a magnetometer.

"What?" Adrian said.

"Look at the signature. There's a rift here, but it's not the one we were sent to close."

Adrian looked. Ray was right.

This wasn't the rift they'd been briefed on, but the magnetometer's display was clear: Correct rift or not, there was obviously *something* inside the hospital. They had followed its energetics to get here. Maps were pointless, because for security reasons they were only ever given coded coordinates. Adrian had been driving, assuming the rift shining at his instruments from inside the hospital was the rift they'd been sent to close. He hadn't banked on two in the same neighborhood.

Adrian's secure phone blipped. He looked at the screen. "It's dispatch. They're saying we're in the wrong place." Then as if speaking to dispatch: "Yeah. We figured that out."

"But there's a rift here. Look at the meter."

Adrian looked again. "The meter measures *energetics*. Usually we'd follow rift energy to find the rift. But ... can there be energetics without a rift? Maybe that's what's happening inside the hospital — just energy, no rift."

"How?"

"Maybe the real rift is somewhere else and the signal is bouncing around. Showing up here as an echo." It sounded ridiculous. He was trying to fit this absurd situation into a logical container.

"How could a signal bounce into a completely different building?"

Adrian waited for Ray to figure it out. Just days ago, they'd seen through one rift and into another that was nowhere nearby. Denny Brennan's tech had had a theory about that: Physicists still didn't agree where exactly the fiends' dimension *was*, so guesses abounded.

Was the fiends' world *behind* ours, like a second layer of reality?

Or maybe somewhere else entirely, still in space and time, but the rifts acted as transdimensional doorways?

Nobody knew. So Erika Dale had said, *Maybe the paired rifts are actually right next to each other on their side of the veil. Maybe they only seem far apart on our side. Maybe from their perspective, the topology makes perfect sense, and it only appears weird to us.*

If that was true, echoes could happen pretty much anywhere.

"Gentlemen?" said the small man, clearing his throat to reclaim their attention.

"Run up and check out what's here," Ray whispered to his brother, so the hospital administrator wouldn't hear. He changed the magnetometer's display and now had a map up. He showed it to Adrian.

"Broad spectrum view says there might be rift energy coming from a boarding house three doors down. Dispatch thinks that's the one we want. You stay here and I'll go there. Call me and I'll come back if you find a rift. Don't approach it yourself."

It was a sound plan, but it also sent Ray toward the real rift, and his brother needed watching.

"I'll go to the other rift," Adrian said. "You handle what's here. The energy is stronger here, so if fiends are going to emerge, it'll be here first."

Ray didn't like that, and for no good reason. He insisted on heading toward the other building. Which he'd already identified, even though there was no address on Dispatch's orders and Adrian didn't know this part of Fortune at all.

Why was Ray so sure about which building had 'the real rift'?

Come to think of it, on the drive in, he kept trying to tell Adrian to go down the block, not to this hospital. As if he knew where the rift was all along, and was surprised the energy seemed to be here.

Because he's the saboteur. Don't you dare let him go to the other location by himself, not when he might be the guy Dixon's been looking for.

"*Ray,*" Adrian said while the small man crossed his arms and looked on with irritation. "You stay here. I go to the boarding house. That's how we're going to do this. Got it?"

Ray stared at him, annoyed and seemingly angry. The worst of Adrian's brother stared out from furious eyes — furious at being challenged, maybe furious that his plans were going awry, and Adrian would find the rift he'd caused without him.

This is good, Adrian thought as Ray stared him down. *This might actually clear him. If there's a rift ALREADY open in the boarding house, how could Ray have opened it? What I find over there just might get Ray off the hook. Prove he's not our man, like I want to believe.*

Still Ray glared at him.

"I'm doing this for you, asshole," Adrian whispered.

Before Ray could ask what that meant, the Dispatch tablet chirped again, wanting to know why no one was moving.

"Fine," Ray said. "I'll check upstairs, but I'm not going to find anything. Dispatch doesn't know what they're talking about, and neither do you."

Adrian wasn't sure if he wanted Ray to be right, or for Ray to be wrong.

18

THE SLASH

They moved to conversing by walkie talkie.

Dispatch was an obnoxious back seat driver, working from beneath layers of departmental camouflage and unsure of what exactly it was doing other than "what the metrics and bosses told them to do" in an instance like this.

The walkies, unlike the tablets or the in-van radio, only connected the brothers. They were the ones out here risking their necks on secret missions they couldn't so much as tell people about, so as far as Adrian was concerned, this was their business by now and their business alone.

"I shook Mr. Belvedere," came Ray's voice over the earpiece. "Heading up by the back stairs."

Adrian could hear his feet on concrete steps. His voice was clipped at both ends, somewhat short on breath as he climbed. "Coming up on three. My meter still says the rift energy is still coming from the fifth floor. Which works. Mr. Belvedere said the fifth floor is empty right now. Budget cuts."

Adrian had double-timed down the street. By the time he

reached the front door of the boarding house, his instruments had gone haywire. Not only did there seem to be a ton of rift energy inside the building, it was *weird* energy. The meter read it halfway as a rift, halfway as a lightning storm.

He knocked on the front door twice, then realized it opened on a foyer, not anyone's apartment. It wasn't locked, and neither was the door to exit the foyer and enter the hallway full of first-floor apartment doors.

"Where are you now?"

"Fourth—" A breath. "—floor."

Adrian, alone in the hallway, raised his meter and moved it around above him like a man searching for a cellular signal. He could hear a television playing in one of the low-rent apartments and a baby crying in others. The plumbing dripped audibly like downspouts after rain.

What the meter told him became even weirder. The strongest energy was coming from the direction of the small hospital at which Ray was doing his recon: still inside the building, but only on that *side* of the building.

Stranger still, Adrian got the strongest signal from the ceiling's corner. If his meter was a gun, he'd be aiming it at the hospital's fifth floor, where Ray was headed right now.

Adrian frowned and checked the meter. He wasn't reading a rift on the second floor of the boarding house. He was reading one that seemed to be between floors, half in the first floor apartment and half in the one above it.

What did it mean, that Adrian could line up both signals: the strong rift signal inside this boarding house and whatever echo Ray was chasing? Was that how the echo worked? It started here, and radiated straight out and up like an arrow, piercing the fifth floor of the taller building down the block?

Adrian didn't like it. There was too much guesswork. Last time they'd nearly been overtaken because the rift spit out unusual versions of typical fiends, and this time the rift was doubled like a hologram. They shouldn't be on these jobs alone, and none of this should be a secret.

Riftfare was changing, maybe because of a saboteur and maybe because of something else — something deeper, the way his father would have theorized. Keeping it quiet was a bad idea. Fortune had hundreds of trained rift fighters, but they sent only two of them after the newest and weirdest developments. In a recipe for disaster.

"Ray, where are you? Are you at the fifth floor?"

The walkie was silent.

"Ray. Come in."

Nothing. It might be the interference. Instead of seeing a *point* of planar disturbance as was typical in most rifts, this oddball situation looked more like a *line* of disturbance.

The energy was electromagnetic and high frequency. Adrian was no engineer, but a line of energy like that struck him as being like an antenna. Maybe it was screwing up communications. Making it hard for Ray to hear him, or for Adrian to hear Ray.

He stepped back, away from the door that seemed to contain the problem. He'd heard people moving around inside. How was that possible? Not only had the area not been cleared; the occupants apparently hadn't noticed or cared.

Today's big rift had opened without the warning they usually had for such openings. None of it was standard. All of it gave Adrian the willies.

"Ray. Can you hear me?"

He heard garbled static, little else.

Adrian moved forward again, then knocked on the door. He'd have to bluff his way through this. He couldn't admit what felt an awful lot like a coverup.

Sounds indicated someone approaching the door from the

other side. Adrian was deciding what he'd say when he realized he'd forgotten something vital. They'd both had their gaiters on upon entering the hospital: neoprene sleeves that created a seal once masks were lowered. So the hospital manager hadn't seen their famous faces. Adrian raised his gaiter just in time, covering nose and mouth.

A woman with curlers answered the door, holding a sleeping infant. She didn't greet him. She stared, seeing this weird, fully-equipped alien on her doorstep.

He had fished out his ID, and flashed it — just enough so she'd see his authority, but not that he was a Stitcher.

"Sorry to bother you, ma'am. I'm with Public Works. There's a gas leak somewhere in the building. We think it might be inside your apartment."

She looked around, seeing Adrian alone.

"I'll need to come inside, ma'am."

"Baby's sleepin."

"He can keep on sleeping, ma'am. I'll just need you to step out into the hallway while I check your lines." He peeked past her. "Is there anyone else inside?"

"My husband. Who're you again?"

"Public Works. We think there might be a—"

"—gas leak. I heard ya. There ain't. I ain't smelled no gas."

"I still need to check it out, ma'am."

The walkie crackled. Aiden heard something on his brother's end, words or interference, he could only guess at what Ray might be doing.

"I ain't gotta let you into my home."

"That's true. You don't. But the mains in this area don't use scented gas. Natural gas is odorless by itself. You wouldn't necessarily smell a leak."

Adrian waited for her to challenge him.

Instead she half-grunted and said, "We'll stay in the living room."

It would have to be good enough. Fortunately his story held; he donned a rebreather to look convincing and the gas hookups were on the outside wall, away from the living room, approximately where he detected what might be a rift.

"Ray. I'm in," Adrian told the walkie once he was alone again. "Can you hear me?"

He waved his meter around, finding the point of maximal energy. Just inside the utility room, high up near the ceiling. There was no visible phenomenon. Not so much as an auroral glow, nor the faint pops of light preceding a rift that were sometimes called fairy lights.

"No rift. Strong energy, but no rift. And it's directional." Adrian took a quick measurement — strange, because there was nothing but air to measure. "It's not a single point. It's a diagonal line of rift energetics measuring approximately one foot. The 'one foot' contains about eighty percent of the energy here, but it then directs outward, seemingly at where you are, diminishing exponentially. I'd say we're looking at the pre-formation of a Lango rift, except with an exceptionally long tail. Probably why you're seeing the echo high up in the other building. Do you copy?"

Still nothing. Was Ray getting any of this?

"Ray. I can't hear you. I'm switching to passive so I can at least see if the connection is open."

Adrian pressed a button on the walkie. A low, baseline hummed in his earpiece. Now Ray's microphone would be locked open. The sound of nothing meant the rift was likely jamming the signal. If heard something, it probably meant the signal was only jammed at Adrian's end.

He heard footsteps and the shuffling of gear.

"*Ray.* Ray, do you copy?"

Nothing. Ray was on blackout. Probably walking. He'd left the stairwell, presumably. After losing contact with Adrian, he'd probably decided to scope the site of the building's rift energy.

He heard no hurry in Ray's movements. So he'd likely come up just as empty. But what did it mean, that a line of rift energy spanned this diagonal line of space far from the Gore Point without opening a rift?

None of it fit, the way the multiple rifts and the seeing-through rifts and the mutants from the earlier rift didn't fit.

The meter beeped. Adrian raised the device and scoped the section of indoor space he'd scanned moments ago.

"Ray, if you can hear me, the energetics are changing. The line is filling out. Eight percent of the total energy is no longer here, in a one-foot length of space. It's about sixty percent now. I think I'm seeing more and more energy building on your end. Ray. Ray?"

It was pointless. He could hear Ray fiddling with something, but his brother still hadn't said a thing. If he could hear Adrian, surely he'd be trying to respond.

His fear was boiling. He wasn't a Legion, and yet the line of empty nothing he'd found in the utility room had ceased being an unfamiliar pattern and become one he almost understood. A rift was forming. Adrian had no Rollard or energy weapons.

What's more, the rift itself wasn't focused in the way they usually were. Instead of threatening to rip a *hole* into this world, the fiends' side now seemed likely to open a big, long *tear* instead.

The meter showed a rising swell of energy flowing to Ray's end of the forthcoming rip. Now the fifth floor of the hospital was glowing white-hot, the entire works threatening to sunder from end to end.

They hadn't found two rifts after all, and they hadn't found one proper rift plus an echo. Instead they'd found both ends of an enormous tear — a slash through the world instead of a dot.

There had never before been a rift that big in history.

"Ray. *Ray!*"

Adrian backed out of the utility room, heart slamming, yelling for his brother.

He could still hear Ray's movements on the other end of the walkie, but he heard no signs that Ray was taking precautions or running away. Ray's footsteps and the slow rattle of his equipment was measured — even relaxed.

Why? Ray should be staring at a hot eye of power right about now, glowing with a brighter aurora than what Adrian could see coming from the apartment's back room.

He should be backing off, same as Adrian.

Arming up, like his brother could not.

The family was agape, now staring at their brightly-glowing utility room. The woman and a dull-eyed man stared at him, halfway understanding.

"Out," Adrian said. *"Run!"*

They ran. There was no bluster this time.

Adrian made for the hallway and stopped, watching the man, woman, and baby flee into the street. They weren't alone. The light was growing exponentially, the rift's aurora now penetrating walls and even brick.

The outer wall was starting to shake, its molecular cohesion soon to give way.

Others in the boarding house were awake and aware now, but not all of them.

"RAY! RAY, DO YOU HEAR ME?"

The walkie-talkie sparked. The batteries popped and began to leak acid. Adrian raked it away, letting it fall to the floor. The earpiece wire dangled, so he raked that away, too.

Now he was alone. Unarmed, and about to face the biggest motherfucker any full Brigade had ever seen.

Adrian couldn't swallow. His eyes were permanently wide. He had absolutely no idea what to do. Back in the early days of riftfare, it must have been like this.

There were no Legions at the start; escaped fiends made their way through the small mountain town where Fortune now stood with little opposition. A few of the smaller ones were taken out by enterprising ranchers with machetes and axes, but anything human-sized had its run of the land.

In the end a military minigun had cut them to bits. Even after Eldon Porter established the Legions, rifts remained open as long as they wished. Legions became guards, tasked with killing whatever came out at all hours.

By comparison to the good old days, riftfare now was almost safe. Or at least, the kind of "safe" that held as long as nobody looked too closely.

But if this rift opened, everyone inside the Rampart would remember how things had once been around here. *Anything* could come through a rift this big. They'd have to send in the army. They'd have to evacuate who they could, and nuke the city.

Adrian ran to the wall and pulled the fire alarm. A shrill bell began to bray, and the apartments came alive.

For a few heartening seconds, Adrian thought things might be a little okay. But then the rift began to open from some-where outside.

The wall split as if it wasn't there. The ceilings and walls above, robbed of their support, began to fail with it. A huge chunk of rebar-reinforced concrete ripped from the roof and fell through first one floor and then the other.

Adrian barely managed to dodge it.

He pulled his sidearm for the first time. Even Stitchers

carried M9s in hip holsters just in case small fiends broke through the Legion lines, but Adrian had never known a Stitcher to need one. Now it was the only comfort he had. The only defense. All that stood between this place and oblivion were a handful of 9mm bullets.

And more often than not, fiends didn't die by destroying the brain or vital organs. According to GEN, fiends *had* no brains or vital organs. They were neural nets and distributed systems of lymph sacks. That's why Rollards made the best manual weapons. They cut a creature's body to pieces and stopped it from coming.

People now trapped above began to scream. Adrian could hear children.

There's nothing you can do to stop it. Save whoever you can.

It gave Adrian a purpose. He ran for the stairs.

But then the rift ripped the rest of the way open, and the sound was so loud he thought his head had sundered. It was like standing next to a bomb. He heard only a low ringing, and the mumble of a faraway world.

The rift shifted the brick. It opened holes in the building's interior walls, and through those walls children and adults crawled to freedom. Except for one frightened child he could still see on the second floor's mezzanine, frozen in place by the sight of the horror before her.

The massive rift yawned wider. Its hot breath blistered his skin. The roar was a freight train that never stopped coming, making Adrian glad for his lost hearing. He could only sense the onslaught instead of being crippled by it.

He made for the wide staircase. He had to get the girl.

But then a huge piece of plaster and lath detached itself from the ceiling in a spiderweb of cracks. It struck Adrian's back and shoulders, knocking him down.

He tried to rise but found himself pinned. There'd been joists in that fall, and they were leaden on his body.

The girl was still up there. Maybe six years old. Holding a teddy bear so closely it was almost part of her, almost like another limb. The stairs were starting to crack and moan now that so much of the building was breaking. Soon the whole of it would collapse.

(ade)

He could tell the sound of someone calling his name was loud in the real world, but Adrian's hearing had been temporarily obliterated. The plaster fall had ripped his coat; his arm was out from beneath the rubble like something on display. Blisters from the rift's heat were already forming. His eyes moved skyward as the world swam; he could see the little girl blinking into the inferno, wallpaper fifty feet from her starting to catch fire.

(adrian)

Almost with an exclamation point. Too quiet, from Adrian's point of view, for a shout.

But shouted it was; Adrian's head jerked toward it and saw Ray rushing in through the asunder front door, pulling one of the two emergency fire shields all of them wore from behind his back to cover Adrian's exposed arm and face. He had the second blanket out already, barely pausing, rushing up the crumbling steps to the mezzanine.

It was surreal to watch. Adrenaline had staunched the pain Adrian felt sure his body was feeling, so he was able to follow Ray up the stairs as someone casually interested. It was a heroic TV show on mute. Hard to get too excited without any soundtrack.

Ray snatched the girl, wrapping her entirely in his second blanket. No protest; she didn't even seem alive while standing there wide-eyed. Ray had her seconds later: a burrito in shiny foil.

The lower half of the big central steps finally gave way. Ray went as far down as he could, ignoring the reality that the rest could go at any time. He chose his spot and jumped toward a fallen pile, barely saving himself from a spill.

He rushed out with the girl and was back seconds later. He held a piece of metal that, when he used it to lever-up the joist that had pinned Adrian in place, was hot enough to cauterize the paint.

Once clear of the building, Adrian looked from the ruined boarding house with the crowd of evacuees outside, over to the hospital they'd been in earlier, now sheared at the top. An enormous red hole into another dimension spanned the space on a diagonal, each of its ends at a place one of the Porter brothers had been not long ago.

The heat was so intense, Adrian could see the air warble from a wide swath in front of it. Two buildings between the hospital and the boarding house were now burning.

Adrian checked himself, surprised to find himself standing. If anything had broken, it wasn't his back or neck. He was bleeding everywhere, and his arm had blistered like a bad sunburn now that the blanket had fallen away. He could feel heat on his face; some of that had probably blistered as well. His hearing was still humbled, but starting to recover. He could hear the roar of the thing now, and Ray when he spoke.

"You okay?"

But Adrian didn't care about that. Not at all. Nobody agreed where the rifts led to, but never before had he more firmly believed they led to Hell.

"We have to get back up there!" Adrian yelled, hearing his own voice as if through thick balls of cotton. "Give me your weapon! You'll have to use the Rollard!"

But before Ray could remind Adrian how ridiculous that was — one Legion and one Stitcher against the largest ravages this world had ever seen — sirens came from the rear. They screamed past the brothers, immediately unloading for battle.

It was every single Brigade left in Fortune. All of the Legions and Stitchers other than their home unit, which had already been dispatched.

For a while, Adrian watched them fight. It was not simple. Or easy. But the old rules held, and only one class came from the rift, and with enough Legions and Stitchers it ended the day closed.

By then medics had surrounded Adrian, making him sit so they could tend to him. Two broken ribs. Multiple contusions.

As far as the sundering of worlds was concerned, Adrian had gotten lucky.

19
HOW AND WHY

Denny Brennan stopped Adrian in the hallway. "We're having lunch today. Me and you."

"All right," Adrian replied.

The forensics man was holding his good arm — the one that hadn't been burned to blisters. The other, though, was healing well. Same for his ribs, even though only two days had passed. Laurel had pilfered an experimental Zen ointment from GEN and it was working like a charm. He'd heard that the Element could change — even heal — human tissue better than any conventional treatment, but hadn't believed it until now.

The stuff really was a miracle.

"But don't say that," Brennan told him. "Say you're having lunch with Matt Baker."

"Nobody has lunch with Matt. The guy is too weird."

"Exactly. He's also off today. Tell people anyway. I don't want them looking for you."

Adrian did as Brennan requested, but wasn't entirely sure why. People didn't hang much with Matt because they usually ended up getting a sermon — and it wasn't even the kind that sermon-appreciating folks enjoyed. Original Sin was in overdrive these days, according to Matt. Everyone was to blame.

But Adrian's words did the trick. Nobody asked to go along or wanted details. He was officially out of everyone's mind for a few hours, and that was a feat in itself. The massive downtown rift had finally put Fortune back into the forefront of mainstream news after decades bubbling along, mostly forgotten in the background. At first people had been aghast that Hell had a front door in Utah, but then they got used to it fast.

The big rift was now enough to scare CNN and MSNBC. If rifts could open in populated areas, who was to say New York wasn't next?

But of course the press needed a hook, and of course the hook was the Porter Brothers. Ray and Adrian had been besieged with interview requests for 48 hours straight. Disappearing, for the likes of Adrian Porter, was not easy. Declaring intent to have lunch with *persona non grata* was apparently the best way to do it.

Adrian and Brennan didn't actually eat. They drove to GEN, then entered Denny's second office through the back door. Nobody else was there. The entire wing seemed quiet.

They sat and Brennan looked Adrian hard in the eye.

"I'm going to talk straight with you, Adrian. You ended up on our special little task force because Dixon knew you were in good with Kaur and he wanted to use you. The Brigade respects that you're not showy like Ray and the other Legions. Dixon told Kaur that my office was interested in your theories, but that's not true. We figured this out a long time ago. You were supposed to be a source of information. Like for the controlled substances audit, if he'd had the right key to get you in."

Adrian nodded. It felt good to hear Brennan confirm what he already knew. Or honest, at least.

"I like you. I think you're smart. I actually wanted you on a similar task force a while ago. You take initiative. You have a forensic mind. It's actually more impressive that you realized there'd been incursions outside the Gore Point than us realizing the same thing because you were doing it without instruments to measure rift energy. How did you even do that?"

"I see patterns in everything. It sounds quaint, but my mom taught me there's a reason for everything. Meaning to everything." A teaching Adrian had absorbed, but not Ray.

"Then tell me what you make of what's happening. What 'patterns' have you seen emerging over the past few weeks?"

The room was half laboratory, half office. One side looked like an accountant lived there. The other side looked like something in a sci-fi flick. Seeing Brennan here, in his element, with such wide and worried eyes was disarming. He'd always struck Adrian as a diehard stoic. He was probably late fifties, wrinkled in a distinguished way, with a mouth that rarely smiled. Right now he was leaning forward, elbows on his knees.

"I ... I don't know."

"Adrian. I have to tell you something. It requires that I trust you. I know who you are and I know who your brother is and I know who your father was, but what I'm about to say could still cost me my job. I'm going behind Special Agent Dixon's back to be here."

Now the secrecy made sense. Adrian had gotten used to thinking of Brennan and Dixon as a unit, but they weren't at all. Brennan worked first for the department. He stood on the first Brigade's side and would stay there even if the Zen-skimming scandal fell under the spotlight. Brennan advocated for the Brigades, and believed they were all heroes, and that they deserved to be more than a sideshow and budget line-items for the government.

Dixon was the hatchet that cut through all of that. He never minded the department bleeding. His job was much easier with someone to blame — whether they were the best person to blame or not.

"What is it?" Adrian asked.

"Dixon has no idea who the saboteur is. He doesn't even really know if it's someone in your Brigade."

Strange, because that been the operating assumption from the start. It's why Adrian had been recruited as a mole.

"He has suspicions," Brennan said, reading Adrian's face. "But that's all they are. He doesn't like the press always fawning all over your Brigade. Especially over you and Ray. He just sort of thinks that anyone as big and loud as you guys *must* be up to no good."

Brennan shrugged. "It was fine. Until anything concrete came up, his prejudices would stay put. That's why I didn't protest when you were brought in. It was half my suggestion. I don't know if Brigade One is the bad guy or not, but nothing would come down without solid proof. Maybe discrepancies in the Tullehmite stores would have given it to us; I don't know. I'm a man of science. I believe that nothing is true until it can be demonstrably shown. That means your group is innocent until proven guilty. I wanted to find the saboteur and end this, my way."

"Thank you," Adrian said.

"But things have changed. You've only seen the public side of the uproar. It's much, much worse from the administration's side. People are scared. The government wants answers. It's all a big blame game right now. I spoke with Dixon a few hours ago. His plan is triage first. He wants to settle things down, *then* find the truth. Do you understand what I'm saying?"

Dixon was feeling the heat, so he needed a scapegoat.

When Adrian nodded, Brennan continued.

"He's going to pin this on Brigade One. As a whole. He's known for a while that Zen has run short on their jobs for the past year or so, and thinks it's because someone is stealing it. A *lot* of someones. He's building a poor-man's Rico case against your unit, Adrian, and using it to blame the new rift variants on you. On all of you. There will be arrests."

"But that's not true!" Adrian blurted.

It was partway true; that was the worst thing. According to Ray, Zen *had* been going missing: The underpaid and unnecessarily-endangered Legions had taken it upon themselves to give everyone a covert raise.

And the saboteur *was* in Brigade One; the missing Tullehmite stores suggested the possibility and the events of a few days ago practically proved it.

Adrian had reviewed his meter's logs over and over since. The rift had clearly opened not from his own end, but from the end Ray had been closest to. Adrian had heard his brother doing something on the fifth floor before it happened.

The optics were terrible.

But for Dixon to call it a conspiracy? To lump every hard-working, death-defying Legion and Stitcher in the entire Brigade together as disgraced criminals — thieves, terrorists, casual murderers — was insane.

"Truth doesn't matter anymore," Brennan said. "If he takes down the first Brigade and this keeps happening, he'll just say it's because he didn't get all the bad apples on the first pass. He'll blame the system. The department. *Then* how well-off will things be? We're already understaffed on riftfare workers. They'll end up dropping bombs inside the Rampart. Declaring Fortune lost."

"What if that doesn't close the rifts?"

Brennan actually laughed. "I don't see how it could. Ever have a rip in your couch? Ever try to patch that rip by blowing it up? But who am I to say? I'm just the man who's studied all of this for my entire life. I'm just the one with the best idea of how to deal with it. Nobody outside of GEN — and especially my department — has any real inkling of what we're dealing with here. So, level with me, Adrian. Do you think it's just about keeping on fighting? Is this thing linear and unchanging ... or are you seeing *patterns* suggesting there might be something new on the horizon?"

That gave Adrian a chill. *Patterns of change* was exactly what he'd been sensing ... and not for the better. He'd wondered about rifts opening outside the Gore Point, but didn't think that was all the saboteur's doing.

Going all the way back to his father, there had been unsolved mysteries of riftfare, and collectively those in charge of fighting them tried to ignore it. The official line had always been: *Close the rifts and destroy what comes out.* The collection, refinement, and innovations (plus profit!) from Zen Element were secondary. There was no discussion of evolution. No discussion about whether there might be more to rifts than exterminating fiends like bees from a hive — or whether the nature of the rifts themselves might be slowly becoming something new.

"You're seeing the same things, aren't you? The shift inside of them?"

Brennan nodded. "I've always thought there was more to it than what we can see. Everyone who works for me feels the same. Most of our experiments are based on the premise that this could evolve — that we need to *understand*, not just destroy. I worry that what Dixon has in mind could take us to a tipping point. We demonize the people who keep the rifts safe, then dismiss the rifts as another thing we can ground out to keep on living life as usual. But how often has that strategy worked in America's past? In *humanity's* past?"

"Why did you call me in today?"

Brennan gave Adrian an *I'm going to be honest with you* look. "I think you know more than you're letting on. I don't blame you. I don't say everything I know, either — especially not to J. Dixon."

"Sir?" Adrian asked.

"I think you know something about the saboteur." Then, when Adrian started to protest, Brennan violently waved a hand to cut him off. "It doesn't matter! Don't tell me! I don't want to know. I didn't ask you here because I want a name. I know you're too loyal to hand it over, even if you have it — not if you think you can solve this problem without being a rat. So I'm offering you a way out."

Adrian waited.

"Don't tell me *who*. I need you to figure out *why*, then tell me *that*. I'm at the limit of what I can learn using all this equipment." He waved a hand around the lab. "Knowing *who* just plugs a hole. Holes can re-open. If, instead, I can figure out *why* the saboteur is doing this, maybe we can solve this for good."

"How?"

"There are two sides to every story, Adrian. It's an unpopular way to think, but maybe what's behind the rifts doesn't have to be at odds with us. What if the saboteur had found a way to communicate with — well, maybe not with the fiends, but with the rifts they come out of? Zen Element has already helped us in many ways. I even smell it on your burns, healing you faster than anything else the hospitals have. So what if it doesn't have to be all blame and bombs and force? What if this can be handled more subtly?"

Brennan leaned in. "And what if, by understanding *why and how* the saboteur is doing what he's doing, we could stop them at the source? Is it better for us to punish someone for doing this to us ... or is it better to understand how, so we can make sure nobody else can ever do it again?"

He looked at Adrian for a long time, his eyes asking if they understood each other.

I know you're protecting someone, Brennan seemed to say. *Find out what they're up to and why, and they can stay free. I can make it so their sabotage won't be able to hurt us anymore. Because it's either my way or Dixon's way. A solution ... or an apocalypse.*

Adrian shook his head. "I don't know who is doing this."

Brennan didn't break eye contact. He didn't believe that for a second, but it didn't matter.

"But give me until tomorrow," Adrian finished, "and I'll find out how and why."

20

PLANS

"Jesus," Laurel said. "So it's true."

They were at her apartment. Still really Adrian's place, if he wanted to live there. The playacting, at being broken up, was in deference to Ray. Back when Adrian thought he was the saboteur, before he basically *knew* it.

Adrian was supposed to keep his eye on his brother, and yet still Ray had managed to shake him. Gone to the top of that private hospital, then done whatever needed doing to open the rift that changed everything.

He nodded. "I think it's true."

"*Think?* So you think there's a chance Ray might be innocent?"

"I don't know. I want to believe it. But you should have heard Brennan. He's always so diplomatic. Always trying to say the right thing, while also getting across what he believes to be true. He didn't outright say that Spread and Containment knew the Legions were stealing and selling raw Zen Element, or that Ray was the saboteur. But it was *me* he wanted to talk to."

Adrian shook his head with the memory.

"When I started to open my mouth, he stopped me like he didn't want to know. Didn't want to hear me say it, because then he'd have a responsibility to tell someone. But who would know better than Brennan? He's forensics. He and his team understand rifts more than anyone, at least from an investigative point of view. His team went into the rubble after the downtown rift. Ray was up there for a long time doing *something*. I could hear him. Brennan confirmed it from street cameras. He's a bloodhound. I wouldn't be surprised at all if he already has a case. If he just added the other day's evidence to the pile. Hell, he probably knows about the Tullehmite. He'd know if Kaur changed the locks on the controlled substances room. So yeah. It seems open and shut."

They sat with that for a while. Ray had always done things his way. Bullheaded like their father, always believing his choices were the right choices and that those who didn't understand should stay out of the way.

Ray was the nihilist. Ever since Laurel left him, he'd talked like his best years were behind him. He drank too much. He had access. Motive. And the Tullehmite logs were a glass slipper fit to his shifts.

But what was a person to do, when someone they loved turned out to be a bastard? Nobody had died when the big rift opened, but they easily could have if Adrian hadn't evacuated one building and dumb luck emptied the other. The other Brigades arrived with Legions to fight and Stitchers to stitch just before the first wave came. Ray was almost a killer. His ends — whatever they were — justified the means.

"Why?" Laurel asked.

"That's what I have to find out. Brennan essentially told me that he won't say anything about Ray — about *anything* he might know involving Brigade One — if I can figure out how and why he's doing it. He wants to understand what's really happening with the rifts. If we don't understand, anything Dixon's actions cause could just make it worse."

"'Understand what's really happening with the rifts,'" Laurel repeated. "That's different from 'understand Ray's motivation.'"

"I think he was implying trial by fire. There's only so much his forensics team can do safely, to study rifts. The biggest lessons come from mistakes. From things that could go wrong, and therefore can't be attempted by anyone responsible. The saboteur is doing a lot of forensics work that the Brigade can't do."

Laurel nodded. She was quiet for a while.

"What?" Adrian asked. "What are you thinking right now?"

"I was thinking that you don't even know the right questions to ask. You're a rift-closer, not a rift-studier or a rift-opener. The best way out of this — at least in the short term — is to give Brennan the best information you can, right? The more you can tell him — the more you can fill in gaps in what he already knows — the better the outcome ... again in the short term?"

She hadn't needed to say "in the short term" a second time. Adrian understood her meaning the first time. So far, Adrian had his fingers in his ears and was saying *NYAH NYAH NYAH I CAN'T HEAR YOU* about the larger situation: namely, the fact that Ray Porter was a psychopath.

Maybe Brennan could keep Ray from being prosecuted for his crimes, but was that really for the best? Was Adrian planning to just keep on keeping on with Ray, ignoring what his brother had done?

"Yeah, that's about right," Adrian said, again blissfully turning his back on the long-term.

"If that's the case, then *we* need some questions answered first."

21

THE PERFORATION EFFECT

Laurel's argument was simple: The more they knew before Adrian confronted Ray, the better and more specific answers they'd get from him. The question wasn't really, *What's wrong with Ray that he'd done this?* so much as, *What was Ray trying to achieve by doing this, and is it working?*

Both questions reduced to "why," but the second would help Brennan find his answers. The first would help diagnose Ray as either mentally ill, or a criminal.

Adrian agreed that knowing as much about the topic as they could beforehand was a good idea, but also that they couldn't ask Brennan, or any of the specialized Stitchers, or the rendering crew he'd initially thought responsible, to provide the information they needed. Those people could all help, but they were indiscrete or otherwise off-limits.

He just wasn't sure about the choice of person Laurel had in mind: her GEN coworker and Brennan's weirdo protégée, Erika Dale.

"I'm not really into water," Erika told Adrian now.

He stopped with the glass halfway filled. He turned off the

tap. He'd asked if everyone wanted a drink of water, and both Erika and Laurel had said yes.

"She says 'water' in reference to any liquid," Laurel whispered when Adrian eyed her.

"So, like, motor oil."

He'd been kidding, but Laurel nodded. "And acid. I keep waiting for her to offer Denny acid to drink by mistake."

Amused but also a little exasperated, Adrian asked Erika what kind of water she'd like. She said anything without peanuts in it was fine. Then she told him about several of her other allergies, including shellfish.

He gave her Pepsi. "No lobster in there," he joked. "Unlike Coke."

She stared at him. Laurel kicked him under the counter.

"Laurel says you're doing some sort of an internal report on rifts and Zen Element," Erika said as she suspiciously sipped her Pepsi water.

Adrian looked at Laurel, who'd apparently told Erika this. She shrugged and Adrian nodded his okay. It was a good enough cover story.

"That's right. I wonder if you could run us through the basics. Stuff the lab's found out, not just what's commonly believed."

If Erika found this request strange or a violation of departmental security, she didn't show it. "Good. Because 'what's commonly believed' isn't always right. I mean, Law of Attraction."

Adrian decided not to ask. He wasn't sure if Erika was saying that the Law of Attraction was believed by everyone but was clearly false, or that nobody believed the Law of Attraction but it was clearly correct. Adrian had problems with both arguments and thought he should just let her go on.

"So, start with closing rifts?"

"Actually," Adrian replied with another raised eyebrow at Laurel, "maybe you could talk about *opening* rifts."

Then Adrian waited. That information was *definitely* confidential. Only a handful of people knew that Brennan had brought Erika into his lab in the first place because rift-generation theory was one of her specialties. Laurel had told him that Erika's work involved the opening of tiny, artificial rifts in the lab: a topic that intensely interested Brennan. She probably wasn't supposed to tell anyone outside of GEN or Brennan's division about that, but Adrian was her boyfriend and loose lips hardly applied.

Instead of balking or acting secretive, Erika blossomed at the question. It was familiar territory, after all — unlike water and misperceptions about spiritual laws.

Erika spooled off information too quickly to follow after that — something Laurel had warned him from her previous interactions with Erika might happen. To prepare, he'd turned on his voice recorder earlier and hidden the phone in his pocket. For now he only worried about finding new questions to ask — possible loose threads to tug on.

There was much Adrian hadn't known. For one, opening rifts specifically with the goal of harvesting Zen didn't make much sense, because the amount of Element required to open a rift paled in comparison to the amount that naturally spilled out from it.

It also paled in comparison to the splashed-back amounts the Legions must be getting from fiend blood. Most Zen came from rendering the bodies of dead fiends, and the sizes of the rifts tended to be proportional to the number and size of fiends that came out of those rifts. Small rifts spilled a few small fiends, which when harvested would contain a small amount of Zen Element. Big rifts spilled more fiends containing more Element, but they required a lot more Element to open if the means were artificial — something Erika allowed as possible, but shied away from saying had ever actually happened.

What's more, the "actualization energy" (her term) required to open a rift was exponential. Opening a 2.0 rift would require *twice* as much Element as a 1.0 … but a 3.0 rift took *four* times as much as a 1.0, and so on.

Fiends grew in linear fashion. On average, a 4.0 rift would only generate four times the "fiend biomass" as a 1.0 despite taking *eight* times as much Zen Element to open.

It sounded like a losing proposition to Adrian, if the goal was to get more Element out of a rift than the saboteur put into it.

Knowing that desperate times called for desperate measures, Adrian decided to tell Erika the saboteur theory so he could ask questions along those lines, offering it up as a hypothetical:

Let's just say, for the sake of argument, that some of the recent, atypical rifts were atypical because they didn't open naturally. Let's JUST SUPPOSE there's a bad guy out there who's been opening them on purpose.

It was a gossamer-thin ruse, but Erika didn't seem to see through it. She answered the questions that followed without emotion, as if it really was only hypothetical rather than something her boss, Adrian, and Special Agent Dixon already believed to be true.

At the peak of this, Adrian asked her why anyone would open a rift as large as the one that had spanned across four buildings a few days ago. It would take an insane amount of Zen Element to do such a thing — far more than anyone could hope to get from the fiends that came out of it.

Nobody would ever do it for profit because the math didn't work out, right?

Erika's answer surprised him. "Well, so far we're ignoring

the Perforation Effect. Should we be considering the Perforation Effect?"

"What's 'The Perforation Effect'?"

Erika picked up a pad, but didn't write on it. "My theory is that our plane maps to the fiends' plane in a predictable way. It's not widely accepted."

She ripped two sheets from the pad. On one of them, she wrote OUR PLANE. On the other, she wrote FIEND PLANE. Then she laid OUR PLANE atop the FIEND PLANE and resumed.

"Some people think that *this* is true, where their plane is 'under' ours somehow, so that everything matches up. If you punch a hole in our world, then travel a mile and punch another, those holes are a mile apart, in the same direction, in *both* worlds. Because everything maps one-to-one. Make sense?"

"That's not how it is, though." They all knew Aiden had seen proof to the contrary: the rift he'd seen *through*, proving that nearby holes on the fiend plane could be miles apart on the ordinary plane.

"Right. So the prevailing theory right now is that rift locations are random or otherwise unpatterned in terms of mapping to both planes."

She tore the FIEND PLANE into many small pieces, then dusted the pieces onto OUR PLANE with her fingers. The result looked like confetti.

"In that theory, rifts connect our plane to theirs, but in a nonspecific, unpredictable way. You could punch a hole right here and end up in their version of Chicago today, then punch another hole in the same place tomorrow and end up in their Los Angeles."

Adrian nodded, though he found it bizarre to consider Fiend Chicago and Fiend Los Angeles.

"But now consider this …" Erika brushed away the torn-up bits of paper, then ripped a new sheet from the pad and wrote FIEND PLANE again. Then she crumpled it into a ball. She took the intact OUR PLANE sheet from the first demonstration and wrapped it around the wadded-up FIEND PLANE sheet like an outer shell.

"This is how I think it works. If you peek inside, you'll see that there are a bunch of places where the outer layer — *our plane* — touches the inner, crumpled up ball — *their plane.* You'll also see that a lot of places where one plane *doesn't* touch the other. There are spots where the inner ball is too folded up to touch the outer sheet, and there are places where the inner ball isn't a perfect sphere, so nothing is touching the outer sheet. But look. The spots where they touch don't change. The two planes *do* map to one another, but not with the geometry you'd expect."

Adrian mostly got it. She was saying that the fiend plane had a predictable and stable relationship to the ordinary plane, but that the one was all jumbled up relative to the other.

Both planes made sense if you moved around inside only one of them, but rifts between them worked like warp holes if moved through more than one.

"So what's 'the perforation effect'?" Adrian asked.

"It's something people used to talk about a lot, but stopped discussing when the old model of planar topology fell out of favor. At first, everyone thought our planes were like two sheets of paper laying on top of one another, like I showed you a second ago. The worry was that because the worlds were tied together, enough holes would be like perforating the paper, and weaken them both."

Adrian nodded. He'd considered something similar.

Erika continued. "What *really* bothered people was that 'perforation' would be a bigger problem for the weaker plane than for the stronger one. I could give you a lot of numbers and measurements of electron volts, but trust me: we're pretty sure that our world is tissue paper and theirs is cardboard. Or plywood. Or metal. So, if you lay out a sheet of metal with a piece of tissue paper over it and you apply pressure to both, what happens?"

"Shit," Laurel said.

Adrian looked over. She worked in development, not research, and apparently hadn't known this theory.

"Right," replied Erika. "The tissue rips but the metal doesn't."

Now Adrian understood. Enough small rifts could pave the way for the mother of all rifts.

"The non-local model of planes, which your little incident seeing through two non-adjacent rifts helps prove, mostly stopped people talking about perforation," Erika told him. "There's no way to 'perforate' planes that don't really map to each other in a stable and regular way. But remember how I said my theory isn't widely accepted? The wadded-up paper with the other paper wrapped around it?"

Adrian nodded.

"People who don't believe that theory have forgotten that the perforation effect is a real thing. I can measure it. I *have* measured it. Any rift 'exhales' trace amounts of Zen. It just comes out in the air that exudes from an open rift. Not very much at all. It's a very specific, very consistent amount, and it's always proportional to the size of the rift. If you open a rift of a certain size, let's say you get 'one unit' of Zen coming out of it on the air. But open *two* rifts and you'll get a little *more* than two units. Open *three* and the discrepancy is even bigger. After about five rifts, if you open them close to each other, you'll see enough Element coming out that it will look like six rifts are open instead of five. Get the picture?"

Adrian's mind was spinning. "So if there was a saboteur …"

"Theoretically," Laurel interjected.

"If there was *theoretically* a saboteur — if that's the reason there's been so many rifts recently — they might be counting on this 'Perforation Effect' to get more Zen out of them than they put in?"

"Well, let's not get carried away. The rifts would have to be close to each other for that to work. The only time that happened was at the quarry."

Yes. Adrian remembered that vividly. The time he'd found an eighth rift on his own, and watched a Legion walk right into it, thinking the man was his father at the time.

"We measured effluence at the quarry," Erika continued. "The effect was noticeable but nothing to write home about. If those rifts had been artificially opened, someone spent a lot more Element to do it than they'd ever get out."

"What about the other rifts we've seen? The ones even outside the Gore Point?"

"Brennan would tell you they're too scattered to act as perforation. If they're part of a grand plan, it's something the department doesn't understand yet. But what else is new? The only way an institution ever accepts something new and revolutionary is when someone risks it all to show them the truth. Copernicus said the Earth wasn't the center of the universe and they burned him at the stake. We won't know for sure unless they all re-rupture."

"Wait. '*Re*-rupture'?"

"Of course. Even closed rifts remain weak spots. You didn't know that?"

Adrian shook his head.

"Nature's systems can be incredibly delicate," she explained. "It's like a perfectly balanced spinning wheel. One small change can throw off the balance. The whole system collapses."

"You said Brennan *thinks* they're too scattered," Laurel cut in. *"Thinks."*

Erika shrugged. "It depends on how the planes map to each other. According to the dominant theory — the one where there's no pattern of connection between the planes and it's all random — they *don't* map, so it's a non-issue."

"But in your theory, they *do* map, just not in a straightforward way. So if someone opened enough rifts ..."

"They have to be near each other to risk perforating," Laurel reminded him. "You've been on most of the calls, Ade. They're nowhere near each other. Those new rifts are all over town."

Adrian exhaled. There went that theory.

Getting more Zen Element out of a rift than you put into it required many rifts close together, perforated planes, and a hole so massive that the planes would bleed into one another — spilling all the Element anyone would ever need while simultaneously causing mayhem.

But that's not what the saboteur was doing, because his rifts were nowhere near each other. That put Adrian back at square one. Why *was* Ray doing this, if it was costing him Element instead of helping him collect it?

"Not necessarily," Erika said.

Adrian looked at her. She seemed to have stopped for dramatic effect. She was looking at both of them with big eyes, stirring her water-that-was-Pepsi with a naked finger for some reason.

"The rifts don't necessarily have to be near each other to perforate?" Adrian asked.

Erika shook her head, then corrected him: "They aren't necessarily all over town."

They had been standing around the kitchen island. Something about the way Erika said her absurd, paradoxical sentence made him want to sit down.

"What do you mean?" he asked.

"Who knows?" Erika said. "Viewed from the fiends' plane, those rifts might line up neat as can be."

22

THE HANDWRITING ON
THE WALL

*F*indale *Commons. High Street. The black lake.*

And there were more. Locations scattered all across town, and yet somewhere Adrian had seen them all together like soldiers in a row.

He slammed his fist on Ray's apartment door. He'd left the house so fast, it felt like a cartoon — like he'd left a shimmer of himself behind. He didn't know how he felt. Angry? Betrayed? Murderous? Disappointed? Even nostalgic, in some weird, we-were-boys-together sort of way?

Adrian wasn't even one hundred percent sure what he'd seen, or why it all felt so familiar. He remembered something glimpsed. Something dire. Something he'd seen in a pile of doesn't-quite-belong inside this apartment.

Books. Notes. And a drawing. It was all feeling, no specifics. And not knowing for sure made him more than frightened. He was mostly sure of what he'd come here for. Terrified that he'd be right.

Adrian raised a foot and slammed the heel hard just to the side of the knob. The lock was a feeble thing, and easily broke, the door rebounding hard and nearly striking him in the face as it came back home.

An old man down the hall opened his door and started to fuss.

"Get back inside and shut your fucking mouth," Adrian hissed, flashing his ID.

Adrian rushed to the pile of strange research, still where it had been last time.

Findale Commons. High Street. The black lake.

Where had he seen them mentioned? In addition to the books about Heaven, Hell, riftwork, and brewing anarchy, there were many stacks of papers. More than last time, as if Ray had been going through a buried part of the stack and brought them all to the surface.

Adrian rummaged around until he found the single loose sheet with all the chemistry and math. He scanned the page, frantic, but didn't see the words he was looking for. He'd been sure there were notes taken, because he'd puzzled over those places his last time here. But if not on the loose sheet, where? They wouldn't be in the books. They were fringe reference, not atlases. They weren't books about—

(The map!)

That was it. There had been a map the last time he was here, but it was all wrong. Adrian remembered thinking how jumbled and incorrect everything seemed to be, with a bizarro version of Fortune, where the local world was in the wrong place. It'd been like someone had wadded a normal map of Fortune into a crumpled ball.

He rummaged without care for another five minutes. Now that he remembered what he was looking for, his search had purpose. He flung books to the floor. Tossed papers into the air to seesaw gently back down.

But then Adrian found it, pulling it forth with victory as he stared, both satisfied and deeply disappointed to see that he'd remembered just right.

Fortune's names and places were all on the page, but jumbled all over.

Adrian brushed the rest of the table clear, then grabbed a Sharpie from the rubble. He slapped the map down, then put X's where he remembered rifts forming. Then he logged into the Brigade's public dispatch records and found additional rifts — many technically inside the Gore Point but farther from the epicenter than usual and many outside. Most of those, Ray and Adrian had responded to on covert detail, but he was surprised to see that after the public rift that'd caused so much trouble, *other* Brigades had also shared anomalous rifts they'd responded to … maybe one reason those other Brigades responded so fast.

The big rift occurred between the boarding house and the hospital, both on High Street.

The living room rift that had caused Ray and Adrian so much trouble had been in Findale Commons.

There was the rift that'd drained the black lake. That one, the full Brigade had taken.

The quarry. Quiet rifts in alleys behind libraries, in parks, and in a few backyards. There'd been a small one just behind Brigade Seven's garage and a minuscule one that a 78-year-old grandmother had somehow managed to seal by throwing Stitching gel from a scam-brand doomsday kit at the thing.

Beyond that were energetic anomalies that hadn't been reported as rifts because no rift had been found — or, Adrian now thought, because they had been peek-a-boo rifts that opened and closed without intervention, which he'd first heard about weeks ago now.

He stepped back from the map once finished. His dots made the rough shape of an incomplete circle. The only spot where the circle truly broke was around Devil's Castle. Rough terrain these days: part of the national forest before the Gore Point formed, now home to die-hard cabins mostly taken over by the suicide freaks who made their cultish home in the woods.

Adrian understood. The map wasn't jumbled, but the way Fortune must look from the other side: from inside the crumpled paper of the fiends' plane.

Findale Commons between the black lake and High Street.

They were far apart in the real Fortune, but rifts poking through at that trio of spots lined up perfectly when seen from the fiends' plane. Someone had gone inside a rift, then charted the city from inside. The saboteur's riftsites weren't random at all. They made a perfect series of rips in a row ... and it might only take one more incursion to complete the circle of perforations.

The area inside would collapse. Fiends would come, from all the rifts comprising the circle. There'd be all the Zen anyone would want once the smoke cleared ... after the dead were counted and the damage done. Even that assumed a hole that big could be dealt with — let alone closed — at all.

Brennan's words from last week came back to him: *If the planes shatter and rifts start opening everywhere because of their actions, they'd have to be okay with it. They'd be thinking, "Profit from the world ... but if that can't happen, burn it instead."*

Each rift made new rifts easier. He'd been stringing them together, not starting fresh each time. Opening rifts using the map must have been like ripping paper slowly. Once one spot was weak, the next tore easily.

"The fuck is going on here?" said Ray's voice from behind.

Adrian turned and saw his brother out of breath, big chest rising and falling. A stress vein had popped out on his forehead. The old man must have called Ray. Told him a burglar had entered his apartment, and that he should come home right away.

"Listen to me, asshole. Maybe Dixon's pulling your strings, but he can't protect you unless—"

Adrian didn't think. He dove. He tackled Ray to the ground, his shoulder slamming hard into the glass tabletop.

They fell into the hollow between the table and the couch, Adrian on top and Ray too stunned to best him.

Ray found his wits. He rolled, eking a long, wooden dragging sound from the shoved-aside table. He was on top for long enough to straighten his arms, but then Adrian kneed him in the testicles.

Ray crumpled; Adrian pulled himself away and upright, backing across the room in ready stance.

Ray crawled to standing, wincing.

"Ade ..."

Adrian searched. He saw the massive glass vase in the corner — the one Laurel had bought for them. Its base was two inches thick. A real concussion maker.

The vase was full of fetid, evaporated-down water because after the last flowers died, Ray had simply pulled them out and left the rest. Adrian dumped it onto the floor to his brother's protest. Then he held it up with both hands like a bat, which made Ray raise his palms to ward him off.

"Wait."

"You son of a bitch," Adrian said. "After all you said about honoring Dad's legacy."

"Adrian? Put the vase down so we can talk, Adrian."

He moved in and Adrian swung. The thing was clumsy and heavy to hold, so he almost dropped it when Ray flinched back.

While he re-gripped and reloaded, Ray's eyes grew wider. That had been a killing blow. Ray knew Adrian meant business.

"Ade? Listen to me. I'm your brother."

"Fuck you!" Adrian spat.

"Look. Look." Ray looked like a mime trying to push an invisible wall, hands out for pat-a-cake. "I don't know what this is about, but if you'll just—"

Adrian stepped in and swung. He'd never been so debilitatingly angry. He literally couldn't think. The betrayal was so deep, so great, it had unseated the whole of him.

He wanted to slash and burn; he wanted to scream and cry. Ray's apocalyptic work had undone all the good their father had done.

Eldon Porter, the hero. Ray Porter, the killer and thief.

This wasn't just his own life that Ray was messing with. It was Adrian's, and what remained of their mother's. It was Eldon's death. It mattered to every one of Fortune's citizens.

Right now Adrian didn't want to talk. He wanted revenge for deeds only halfway done.

The heavy vase made a powerful and deadly arc. Ray stepped out of its reach just in time, so instead of hitting him, the vase struck the tile chair rail and exploded like a bomb.

Adrian felt glass slice his hands. He felt them begin to bleed.

But only for a second because then he felt Ray's head spear him in the gut, forcing all the wind from his lungs.

They hit the naked floor this time, Adrian's back rolling over the rough form of dropped and incriminating books.

Adrian slashed out with his hands, but Ray had him pinned. He dodge and parried his brother's scratching claws.

"Stop it!" Ray said. *"Stop fighting me!"*

When the flailing continued, Ray sat tall over Adrian and hit him in the stomach again. Adrian had been clawing for air; now he thought he'd never breathe again.

Adrian sucked breath. Ray hit him again, and again, now more to make a point than hurt him. They were both a mess:

hair askew, faces more confused and hurt than angry now that so much energy had been lost to battle. It wasn't the first time they'd fought. But it was different. And worse.

"Stop it, Adrian! This is exactly what he wants! Don't you get it? Or are you that fucking stupid?"

Ray rolled away, eyes daring Adrian to come at him again. He sat sideways to Adrian, who was still gasping for breath. Ray heaved, trying to recover his own.

They were both utterly spent. There was nothing left in the room. No fight at all.

Ray flopped to one side. At first Adrian thought he'd collapsed, but he seemed to be reaching toward a pile of dry goods that never made it to the pantry and instead lived a satisfying life atop the kitchen table.

He found a plastic bottle of peanuts, opened it, and tried to eat some — presumably for energy or for something to do in all this insanity. But he winced as he bit down.

"Broke one of my fucking *teeth."* Ray shook his head at Adrian, then threw the open bottle at him. Peanuts went everywhere. They ended up down his shirt. In his hair. In his pants and in his pockets. "Asshole."

Adrian rubbed his jaw. His ribs.

"Me. You," Ray went on. "Always at odds. Always jealous of the other and always fighting. After Dad died, it was the two of us against the world. Don't you remember our pact? That we'd stick together, no matter what. *Blood. Family.* Don't you remember?"

"You're the one who broke it," Adrian said.

"Not me. You went first."

Something wasn't right about this. "Went? Where?"

"First Brennan. Brennan was okay. But what was I supposed to think when Dixon came, too? S&C? *Spread and Containment?* I never figured you for a rat."

"I haven't told anyone. Not yet." Adrian backed up to sitting, considered going at Ray again, then thought better of it. Ray was the superior physical specimen. This time Adrian wouldn't have the element of surprise to level the playing field. "I wanted to hear it from you first."

"I'm an open book, Baby Brother."

"Then tell me why you did it."

"You know why I did it."

"For money."

"Money *for Mom!*"

Adrian shook his head. He felt a drip and knew his lip was bleeding. "How dare you bring up Mom. This isn't for her. It's not even for you. Was I right about you, that you've always secretly wanted to die?"

"What?"

"Come on. The out-of-control drinking. The stunts you pull on repellances. You're always at the front. Always at the tip of the spear. It's like nine to five suicide. So you can go out with glory just like Dear Old Dad."

Now Ray looked puzzled. He said again, *"What?"*

Adrian sat up further. He was still angry, but holding onto it was getting harder. Adrian knew his brother like nobody else, and Ray wasn't a good enough actor to fake his lack of comprehension.

"I found your books," Adrian said. "I saw your map."

"So you know. Did Dixon tell you?"

"I figured it out by myself. Laurel knows. Nobody else."

"Not even Dixon?"

"Fuck Dixon." Adrian pulled himself into a chair. Everything hurt. "Brennan might know. Or be close to figuring it out. But he only wants answers. He wants to know how and why you're doing it, and he wants it to stop. He'll help us cover.

Somehow. But that doesn't settle things with me, Ray. I need more than they do."

Ray pulled himself up to a chair, a good ten feet between them. "Tell me what you think you know, Ade. Just spit it out."

"There's a saboteur."

"I know."

"*You're* the saboteur."

"Bullshit." He laughed a beat, then realized his brother was serious.

"The day of the big rift. It opened from your end, not mine."

"And you think that means *I* opened it?" He made a disbelieving noise. "Adrian. You've seen thousands of rifts open all by themselves. What makes you think this one had to be tickled with a feather?"

"How could you know about the saboteur, if it's not you?"

"From Dixon," Ray replied.

"You didn't hear it from Dixon. He wants to nail every one of us to a cross."

"No shit I didn't *hear it from Dixon,*" Ray mocked. "I said I *learned it* from Dixon. Fucking idiot leaves his briefcase in a locker when he's at the station."

"And you just happen to have the combination?"

Ray shook his head. "Kaur gave me the master key."

"Why would he do that?"

"Jesus, Adrian. Keep up." He waited, made a face, then answered the question: "To check up on you, asshole."

"*Me?*"

"Dixon cut Kaur out of the loop the second he got you working with him. Everyone knows S&C has been gunning for Brigade One. He doesn't like that we're celebrities. They might know something about the Zen skimming, but *fuck*, Ade ... Is it even really skimming? We *decontaminate* our gear. We don't give it to Rendering so *they* can scoop Element off of it. What we're taking was just going to waste. It barely earns us anything. So when you joined the task force investigating the Brigade ..."

"I'm not investigating the Brigade!"

They looked at each other. The truth was dawning on them.

They were *both* wrong.

"You're saying that Kaur asked you to spy on me. And to spy on Dixon. All because he thought we were trying to make a case against the Brigade?" Adrian asked.

"Yeah ..."

"But you know there's a saboteur."

"Yeah." Ray nodded. "It was in Dixon's paperwork."

"It's not you?"

"I'm a Legion! I fight this shit every day! Why would I sabotage anything?"

"If you knew there was a saboteur, why didn't you tell anyone?"

"*I told the captain!* Why do you think he gave me a key to the controlled substances room, so I could keep an eye on the Tullehmite supplies?"

The pieces were starting to fall. His fury was gone, obvious now as misdirected.

Adrian scrunched his brow, trying to think. Dixon and Brennan had put Adrian on the case of a saboteur he'd thought was his brother, and at the same time, Captain Kaur had put Ray on Adrian's case to make sure Adrian didn't turn rat and sink the Brigade.

They had both been quietly investigating each other.

"Wait. Why the hell was there a voice mail from Cerina Dell on your phone, if you're not working with Refining on the sly?"

"We've gone out a few times. You were the one who told me to move on and get over Laurel."

"But ... Ray. You have books about this. About rift theory."

"Kaur ran my theory up the food chain and Dixon stomped it flat. He said there's no saboteur, and basically threatened Kaur with insubordination if he raised the issue again. I couldn't exactly admit to peeking through his briefcase, so I started some poking around on my own. They're from the library. Pulled for me by the actual librarian. Jesus, Adrian. You didn't talk to Becky before deciding I was some sort of anarchist dickbag?"

"Then what about the handwritten notes? Ray ... *What about the map?*"

"Map?"

Adrian fished it from the floor. He held it up.

"Yeah. I saw that one. You want proof that whoever's behind this is a psycho, there's your evidence. It's like a strung-out junkie drew it." He squinted, looking closer at the paper in Adrian's hand. "Did you *draw* on it?"

"These aren't your papers?"

"Yeah. They're all my papers," Ray said, sarcastic. "Because I'm a science genius. Because I know calculus or whatever the fuck this is." He scoffed, picked up a sheet, then threw it at his brother. "For Christ's sake, Ade. They're not even in my handwriting."

Adrian looked. How had he missed that? The scrawl was close, but definitely not his brother's. "Then where did you get all of this?"

"It was in one of the other lockers. While I had the master key, I figured I might as well search them all. Found this stuff in one of the spares, where someone seemed was apparently hiding it. I came in when the station was mostly out on a call, on my day off, and Xeroxed it all because it looked like shit I didn't want disappearing."

"You didn't just take it?"

He shook his head. "I made copies to study. Left the originals." Then in an *I-shouldn't-need-to-explain-this-to-you* voice: "It's an investigation. You think I wanted to tip the guy off before we figured out who it was?"

"But you haven't told anyone what you found?"

"I told Captain Kaur."

"And *Kaur* hasn't told anyone?"

"No. Think for a second where I found it — in a spare locker in our very own locker room. S&C is already looking to nail us. Kaur and I have been trying to solve this on our own, and then *handle* it on our own, but we're out of our depth. It's *one of our own people,* Ade. *Someone in the Brigade* is the saboteur! We thought it was only right to try and handle it internally before giving it up. We were going to Brennan with what we knew after the big rift, thinking maybe we just needed to bite the bullet because it'd gotten out of hand. But Kaur wanted a few more days first."

With the air of a lingering question not yet resolved, Ray leaned forward and took the map from Adrian. "What are the dots you drew all over this?"

"Rift locations. Ones we think were opened by the saboteur."

"They make a circle." Ray put his finger on the gap. "Almost."

"And you said you weren't good at math."

"How the hell did that work out on this weird-ass map?" Ray asked, looking at the paper again. "These spots are nowhere near each other."

"I think they're close to each other on the fiends' side."

"The fiends' side?"

Adrian stood, dropping thrown peanuts like an avalanche and brushing more from his hair. He barely heard Ray repeat his words. Something had caught his eye: a doodle on one of the pages, exposed now that Adrian's search and their fisticuffs had thrown papers hither and yon.

It looked like a little lizard. A character he'd seen someone doodle before.

He snatched the paper, stared at the doodle, then looked at his brother.

"Ray. You said Kaur asked you to check the controlled substances room."

Ray nodded.

"Did you copy the Tullehmite log?"

"I took a picture of it."

"Show me."

Ray searched until he found the photo, then handed Adrian his phone.

He scrolled down to a line written by the person he'd been looking for — a Stitcher whose Tullehmite usage was already suspect, but that Adrian had decided — erroneously, it seemed — must be safe.

He looked back and forth, comparing the Tullehmite ledger entry to the saboteur's handwriting all around them. Then he looked at his brother.

"It's Matt Baker," Adrian said.

23

THE SEIGE

The response was not subtle. Nor understated. Nor coy.

Considering the fame often shone upon the Porter Brothers, it would have been a fitting end to the sabotage if Ray and Adrian had kept things to themselves and gone after Matt Baker on their own. The reality show that followed Brigade One in general (but the brothers in particular) would have loved it. The cameras would have pretended the crew wasn't there, that Ray and Adrian were alone.

There they would be, all by themselves, tracking down the rogue Stitcher without any help and in full disregard for protocol, the command chain, or safety.

But that's not what happened.

From the apartment, Ray did the most sensible thing and called Captain Kaur. Once he had Kaur on the line, the two of them called Denny Brennan together.

Adrian piped in from the background, saying, "Tell Erika thank you."

When Brennan asked what for, Adrian would only smile.

This was Erika's collar, if collars were given. She'd told him the stakes and Adrian had merely connected the dots.

Kaur helped; Baker was on a short, pre-planned vacation, but a lot of his stuff was still at the station. Turned out he wasn't dumb or sloppy enough to leave a can of Tullehmite in his locker, but Baker didn't know how to remove the stuff from his clothes. He was a Stitcher; he used Tullehmite legally every time he went on a job. Legal use would have explained a few sprinkles here and there, but a quickie forensics job from Brennan's people showed splashes. Resin covered a pair of gloves. A shirt's front. Most of a left boot. The stores had been pilfered over a long time — Baker had amassed more than a quart of the drops-strong stuff. Half of that seemed to have spilled on his clothes. Baker was heedless. And they had gotten lucky.

Ray and Adrian were halfway to the station house in Ray's car by the time Brennan was convinced. With Brennan on board and Kaur and Ray already in the loop (as well as the forensics team that'd done the work on Baker, and with half the Brigade turning gear inside-out for clues), there was no reason not to involve Dixon.

Dixon was S&C, and had pull to get things done that the others didn't. By the time they brought him in, S&C could no longer hang the Brigade. The shock and outrage of learning about the saboteur had already popped. Those above Dixon would see that Kaur and the others had acted responsibly. Yes, the Brigade had a bad egg. But nobody else was in on it.

And there was no evidence left of Zen Element skimming by the Legions. Someone had tipped them off that S&C was looking. That tipster's name might have been Darren Kaur — who hadn't known it was happening before Ray told him, but looked the other way while anything incriminating suddenly disappeared.

The Brigade was clean. The saboteur had been identified

and the correct authorities were on it. The station house emptied, every Legion and Stitcher wanting a piece of the man who'd gone out of his way to endanger their lives and the lives of Fortune's innocent citizens.

Only Ray and Adrian remained — and only then because Brennan forced the issue.

"We need to build a case," he told them as the station went quiet.

"We have a case," Ray replied.

"We have *evidence,*" Brennan corrected. "It doesn't become a case until it's all sewn together. There's a legal group. Advocates for the freaks who live in the dark forest inside the Gore Point. You know where everyone's headed, right?"

Adrian almost answered, but not with Brennan's intended response. Literally speaking, Matt Baker still owned his great-grandfather's cabin in what used to be Wasatch-Cache National Forest, and literally speaking, that's where he always took his vacations.

But "vacation" was only a rough approximation of what Matt Baker did for fun. He'd told the crew after prior "vacations" that he tended to go into a blacker shade of Walden and "just kind of exist in the woods for a while and pray." His version of a silent retreat, to clear his mind.

Pray was the operative word. Wasatch-Cache had been federal land before the Gore Point consumed it — convenient, because the feds hadn't needed Eminent Domain to take control of the land when the original rifts made it worth controlling.

When Suicide Flats first earned its name by becoming the "it" spot to go and die, everyday citizens had sought to patrol and prevent more deaths while advocacy groups claimed people should be able to head off and kill themselves wherever and whenever they wanted.

Federal ownership of the land made the Suicide Flats issue federal. Media turned it into a separation-of-church-and-state thing, meaning that if there was religion involved, the government would leave it alone.

That's how the vandalizing, goat-sacrificing freaks who moved into the forest became a religious order. And that's how the fastest way to weasel out of anything around the Gore Point became the mentioning of "God" ... or, in this case, "pray."

There was no doubt that Matt Baker was devout. In Adrian's opinion, he was far *beyond* devout — devotional to the point of troubling. He should have seen this coming. The craziest people often waved their crosses the hardest and loudest.

"We rush in half-cocked on this," Brennan explained, "and Baker will walk. And by 'half-cocked,' I mean 'anything less than a notarized photo of Baker in the process of opening a deadly rift.' I assume you still don't want to wait for his return to work, when he'll no longer be on federal land?"

Adrian and Ray traded a glance. The answer was of course not. Only one labeled site on Baker's inside-out map was in the finished circle — just one spot of interest in that missing arc. Devil's Castle.

Even if Baker didn't own a cabin there, the place would be perfect. With a name like that, there was nowhere better to blow Hell's gates wide open. Baker had probably planned for it to be the final domino all along, for poetic reasons.

"I'll take that as a no," Brennan said.

Dispatch was already tracking rift energetics, already agreeing that maybe something was going on out there. The way pieces seemed to fit, the mother of all rifts would soon open in the missing bit of Baker's circle — and that would open something that would make "the mother of all rifts" look like a baby. If they didn't take Baker now, before he opened his most recent (and likely final) rift from his place at Devil's Castle, they wouldn't take him at all.

Baker might never leave federal land again. The way Erika described things, the entire city might break at its dots and crumble into the other plane.

Hell on Earth, as it were.

"No," Adrian agreed.

"No," Ray echoed.

"So tell me …" Brennan removed a voice recorder and a pad from his pockets. "Tell me exactly how you figured this out. And if you can, gentlemen, tell me exactly how he's opening rifts."

24

THE SHOCKWAVE OF SUNDERING WORLDS

They were all-in.

That's what Adrian kept thinking with Brennan's cross examination behind them and the station quiet again — just the brothers, while Brennan ran off to analyze all they had told him.

Either the entire Brigade would come out of this triumphant or the entire Brigade would fall. Even the TV cameras had gone along to Devil's Castle, though everyone so far was refusing to tell the crews what they were all after.

It might be fine. Failure was likely to do more than ruin a reputation. It might just kill everyone in the Brigade. It might just fill Fortune with fiends, with no living riftfare workers left to take them down.

How long would it take for those fiends — even as brainless as they were — to shatter the Rampart and invade the wider world?

Even zombies eventually broke through a wall. And the rest of the world had no Legions. Or Stitchers. Even if new fighters could be trained quickly, with GEN and at least half of the world's Zen Element supplies lost to the void, who would equip those warriors to fight?

"There are no capture tubes. Matt didn't have any of them in his locker." Ray was using sterile tongs to sort through the locker, now quarantined in the captain's office. "You can't just stick capture tubes anywhere. They use some sort of weird magnet to hold onto the Zen Element you fill them with. Our contact was very specific about that. The station's footprint is all protected by an electromagnetic field that acts like a control rod. The storage devices we wore were temporary. We had to offload them right away. So if Matt didn't keep his tubes here, where's he keeping them? Damn sure there's no protection out in the woods where he is."

Adrian shrugged, then turned back to the TV. The reality show was doing something it'd never done before, with Kaur's permission. Instead of recording footage to edit later, the show was streaming live.

Kaur figured live TV would make things harder to hide and cover up. He had no intention of letting his Brigade and his people become scapegoats for some government plot.

"I don't know. Don't really care," Adrian said.

The teams had surrounded Baker's cabin. The lights were on and his car was out front. For the first time ever, the Porter Boys were the only ones *not* sharing the glory.

"Man. I wish Dad was here."

Adrian's head bobbed at that, too.

"I do wonder sometimes, you know," Ray went on while Adrian, absorbed in the onscreen action, tried to ignore him.

"I know I gave you a lot of shit, but honestly, it's always bugged me how things went down with Dad. Not that he died. Obviously *that* sucked. I just mean the way he was taken out by a fiend that had no business being where it was. I mean ... a hellbringer? That's just not fair. It'd be one thing if he screwed up, but Dad did everything right that day. Like a pro."

"Yeah," Adrian said. "It's unfair."

An armored SWAT team — accompanying the police whom the Brigade had, in turn, joined just in case the rift opened and things went bad — was now approaching the cabin's porch with a battering ram. They were suited in black, with matching helmets. To Adrian, they looked like wasps.

"It's funny," Ray said, "how things turned out."

"It is?"

Ray nodded. "When I was reading up, doing all that research you saw, I learned that the rift that killed Dad was considered a turning point. In some ways it was *the* rift. The first one where the Stitchers used filler rods made of Zen Element, not the shit they used before. I keep thinking of what Erika told you about 'perforation.' Supposedly that rift weakened the surrounding area and made later rifts possible, but only because it was open too long. If things had gone smoothly — the way repellances had gone before and have always gone since — they might have managed to close it for good. No hellbringer. No more rifts. No Gore Point. It would all just ... *be over.*"

Adrian frowned. Something had almost occurred to him, but he wasn't sure what it was.

"Lucky for them, huh?"

Adrian turned. The SWAT team had fallen back, seemingly because someone had seen movement inside. "What did you say?"

"I said it's lucky for them that Dad's rift happened to stay open a tiny bit too long. That the hellbringer came and delayed things just in time. Dad's Brigade might have been *this close* to sealing it all off, but that was the time when rules happened to not apply. Everything since is because of it. And *now* look."

Ray gestured at the world, but presumably he meant their present situation. "Baker is inches from blowing it all open. It's only possible because *one little thing* went wrong twenty years ago. Hell of a lucky break for the fiends."

For some reason, Adrian could only think of his mother. She always used to tell him that there was a plan for everyone and a reason for everything. All events had meaning; that was her usual refrain. It was why she only accepted certain treatments for her cancer.

In Mom's mind, if her illness was meant to be, there was a reason. If Eldon was still around, their mother today might be well but unhappy, because she would have traded health for her worldview. A sick mother no longer dominated by her anarchy-minded husband — another coincidental gift the hellbringer's unexpected appearance had given them.

"'Lucky,'" Adrian repeated.

He was just mouthing the word. Luck had been a hell of a thing in his life lately. In all their lives, really.

Luck that they always arrived at the rifts just in time.

Luck that, despite a seeming ability for multiple fiend classes to emerge from a single rift, it had only ever happened that one time in more than fifty years.

Luck that they'd stumbled on Matt Baker just in time.

Luck that they'd spoken to the right people and found the right information at the right moment, so they could be led to Baker in the first place.

Luck that although neither Ray nor Adrian had opened the big rift on High Street, they'd both been there — one perfectly situated at each end of it — exactly when it happened.

Luck — or maybe it was fitting coincidence — that Adrian and *only* Adrian had seen how rifts could connect to other rifts. That Adrian and Ray and *only* Adrian and Ray had seen a class of fiends mutated into new forms, as if they were on their way from being one thing to becoming something different.

A phrase came to him: *primordial form.*

Adrian had reminded Ray about it only recently, but both had heard it before from their father. Eldon Porter — the most famous Legion who ever lived — had secretly believed that fiends didn't exist in a preexisting form behind the veil.

He believed that when the rift opened, the fiends became something else.

Decided to become something else, Adrian thought now.

The hellbringer. The mutants. What if those were decisions?

The idea of "deciding what to become," on the few occasions primordial form was considered and not laughed out of the room, was always meant figuratively. Adrian always assumed his father meant "decide" in the same way water "decided" to go one way or another at a fork in a river.

But was it possible he'd meant it literally?

"I thought I saw him the day at the quarry," Adrian said. "Dad. Going into the rift."

"I know."

"I don't think it was actually Dad."

"Obviously."

"But it was someone."

"You said you saw a Legion. Legions don't enter rifts."

Adrian's head bobbed almost subconsciously.

His logic was on autopilot, connections now making themselves. They came one after another: a string of unconnected knowings that were apparently all part of the same thing.

Nothing was random. Everything was connected.

With meaning, just like Mom always said.

Like his father's death had meaning. Specifically, Eldon Porter's dying had caused ... *all of this.*

"Matt told me once that Dad entered a rift. As a Legion. That's why I thought he was going to Hell."

"Hell doesn't exist," Ray said.

"It does if we say it does."

Adrian's daze must have finally tugged Ray's attention. He glanced at the screen, where the SWAT team was approaching the porch again.

Then he looked at his spaced out brother. "You okay, Ade?"

But he wasn't. Everything had connected. The coincidental appearance of the hellbringer that killed his father had started what was happening today.

And what was happening at Devil's Castle was about to finish it.

With a whimper instead of a bang.

"It's not luck." His head whipped toward Ray. "Jesus Christ, Ray — get Kaur on the phone."

"*What?* Why?"

"Listen to me." He focused on making Ray understand, and as fast as possible. "Matt can't open a rift that big without a ton of Zen. After it perforates, he'll have all he wants, but he can't open it in the first place without a hell of a lot more than he can possibly have right now. I knew something was missing. Call the captain, Ray! *Call him now!*"

"Ade, I ..."

"*The Element! In the weapons! In the Stitchers' packs!* The entire Brigade's on-site, dammit! The whole goddamn First and half a dozen others who heard the squawk and came running! Don't you see? The only way to get enough Zen Element in one place to open the last rift was to paint them all a target!"

Ray's jaw dropped. "It's a trap."

The SWAT team's ram struck the door.

There was a flash, and then the feed died.

Then a rumble underfoot. The shockwave of sundering worlds, heading for the station at the speed of sound.

25

HELL ON EARTH

ayhem descended in the station house like a pall.
First, there was the television. It flashed as the signal out at the Devil's Castle overloaded and the broadcast stopped. Adrian found himself gaping; there had been no sound after the strike of the battering ram but still his mind served him up a banquet of noises that he hadn't actually heard.

A phantom boom to go with the flash of light, maybe the screams of whatever had gone wrong. His mind made it an atomic bomb, with a frenzy of post-explosion.

Second, there was a single bleat from every computer. Inside Adrian's pocket, his phone made a series of sounds he'd never heard before. When he pulled it from his pocket, the thing's face was glowing bright blue.

Adrian ran for his bag, looking for something. Meanwhile Ray was fiddling with the TV.

"It's out," Ray said.

"I know it's out. Where's—?"

"I don't mean the live feed from the site," Ray clarified. "I mean everything. All the channels." He kept flipping. "But that's not all. The phones are out, too. Cells. Landlines. Internet. Everything."

Adrian was on a different mission. "Where's that EM meter I said Laurel gave me?"

"What kills all communications?" Ray was saying. "Not just over the air, but—"

"RAY. The meter."

"What's it look like?"

Adrian didn't answer. He'd shown Ray some of the equipment Erika had brought to the apartment at Laurel's request — stuff from her lab at GEN, recovered and smuggled out, another lame cover story offered to Erika in explanation.

Laurel had had a hunch what a "fully perforated collapse" might look like, what it might require, and what they all needed to watch for as the drama unfolded. But when she had handed the electromagnetic meter to Adrian, they'd still thought Ray was the saboteur. Ray had probably barely heard Adrian when he showed them off in the car ride over. There had been too much going on.

The car. Adrian ran outside, returning within seconds. The meter had been in the console compartment.

"Find what you needed?" Ray asked.

"Look outside."

"W ... *What?*"

"Just do it."

Ray went to the window. He turned back into the room looking like Adrian felt. Both men saw things daily that would have challenged their Catholic upbringing, but those atrocities had always appeared inside a rift's border.

Now, the very sky had been stitched with a crimson spiderweb of light. The sun was buried behind a battalion of clouds, the horizon somehow lit from below all the way around.

"Was that it?" Ray asked. "Did Matt open the rift?"

"I don't know."

"Does it look worse in the direction of Devil's Castle? Do you think everyone's dead?"

"*Ray.* I don't know."

He was trying to focus on the EM meter. Trying to remember the settings as Laurel had explained them. "I don't know if I'm reading this right, but it's like there's a massive electromagnetic disturbance causing—"

Alarms brayed from the gear room. Adrian pocketed the meter and both men scrambled to address them. There were four Stitching rigs left in the room — Adrian's, Matt Baker's (because technically speaking, he was on vacation), and two spares. The rigs themselves were ringing with alerts.

"What's going on?" Ray had little familiarity with Stitching rigs. He was a Legion. A battler, not a thinker.

Adrian was still bent over his own rig. "That was the Zen Element leakage alarm. It's toxic."

"But the Legions have been collecting Element for—"

"It's not nearly as toxic in its raw form. Stitching rig filler rods are something like 99.3 percent pure. *That* stuff will melt your face off." Adrian was turning each rig over, already wishing he'd fetched protective gloves. "One of the rigs must be leaking."

"Are we in danger?" Ray asked.

"Not necessarily. The detection threshold is really low. It wouldn't do much good as a warning if it didn't go off until levels were fatal." He shoved the last of the rigs back with frustration. "They're all fine. All seals intact."

"Maybe the alarm is faulty."

Adrian shook his head, already trying to figure it out. "All four alarms went off. All four aren't faulty. It's like there was a spill or something." He looked at his brother. "Now would be the time to level with me, if you were refining your raw Element on site."

"Of course not! Who the fuck even knows how to do that?"

Right. Adrian had been down this explanatory road before. Raw Zen was useful only for low-grade (and mostly safe) applications. Turning raw Zen into refined Zen weaponized the element and added to its potency, amplifying its energetic potential by a thousandfold or more, but the process was well-guarded and inefficient at small scales.

Of course the Legions weren't doing it, nor was anyone with the small amount of raw Zen the Legions sold off. This was something else.

He wanted to call Brennan. He knew all about Zen refining. His group had perfected the refinement protocol used by the rendering team today. But how could he reach Brennan with communications busted? Adrian needed to understand this. Right now he didn't even know how much exposure they were getting. It might be nothing. Or it might be deadly.

He grabbed two emergency breathers and Stitcher coats, then handed one of each to Ray.

Ray dragged the coat on. "We have to do something. We're the only ones left."

"There are other Brigades. Other Legions. Other Stitchers."

"Yeah, but they don't know there's a saboteur. Or that it's Baker. Nobody else is seeing past convenient to *way too* convenient. Anyone else who tries to approach whatever just happened out there won't know they're walking into the same trap."

"They might be dead, Ray."

"And they might not!" His breathing was shallow, his face turning red with impotent action. Ray's solution was always to charge in — to *do something*. He must feel trapped right now, having to stop and measure. "Goddammit, Adrian ... we can't just sit here!"

"Laurel," Adrian said, realizing.

"What? What about her?"

"I need to know why the Zen alarms are going off. We're going to need Stitching rigs. We won't be much use to anyone if some Element spill somewhere kills us. Normally I'd call Brennan's lab. Doesn't even need to be Brennan. That Erika woman would come over and explain it, no questions asked. But I'm pretty sure they all went out to the site. Laurel, though ..."

Other than those who studied its use in forensic fashion, she might be the person around who most understood Zen Element. And Laurel was, Adrian suspected, just down the street.

They ran outside, headed for one of the unmarked and fully-equipped vans, when he heard the squealing of tires. Not a surprise; less than five minutes had passed since the sky turned murderous and citizens were starting to panic.

Cars sped down the streets. Shouts echoed around every corner, along with the sounds of destruction: crunching, smashing, the tinkle of breaking glass. Society was a whisper-thin veneer over anarchy. Something Ray said when he was drunk was all around them now.

But this tire-squeal was closer. A small gray Toyota cut hard into the station parking lot, annihilating a spray of plastic trash cans.

The car jerked to a halt. Laurel popped out.

"Breathers," she said, ironically out of breath herself. "We need to be wearing rebreathers!"

Although Adrian had set out specifically to find Laurel and

ask the question she seemed to be answering, he found himself paralyzed.

She ran all the way to them before he snapped out of it.

Laurel was holding up something the size of a small tablet. It seemed to be a different kind of meter. She waved it like an accusation. "There's Element in the air. The pure kind."

"It's *in the air?*"

"Where are your rebreathers?" Then she saw they were wearing them, hung low instead of over their faces. "PUT THEM ON!"

Adrian did, but at the same time he dragged Laurel back into the station. He pulled a spare breather and gave it to her. Once it was over her mouth and nose, she settled down a little.

She consulted her meter, tapped on its surface for a while, then pulled the mask down to talk.

"It's okay," she said with an audible exhale. "My alarm went off." She indicated the meter. "I rushed over. I didn't want to take any chances, so I didn't think; I just ran. Do you know how toxic refined Element is?"

Adrian nodded.

"But there's not that much." She held the meter up, but it meant nothing to Adrian. "We should wear them when we're not talking or eating or drinking, but we'll be okay unless it gets worse."

"Why would it get worse?"

"Depends what's causing it."

"I thought it was the Stitching rigs leaking. Our alarms went off, too."

She shook her head. They sat at the break room table. "It's not your rigs. It's coming from somewhere else. If I had to guess, it's coming from whatever just happened to the sky."

"The Brigade rushed out to Devil's Castle to get Matt at his cabin. I think it was a trap. Did the rift open?"

"I think *a* rift opened. There was one more rift needed to complete the circle of perforations, so that's probably what happened. Fortune is now perforated in a nice, neat circle if you look at it from their plane; I think that's what this is."

"But it hasn't ... like ... ripped along the perforations?" Adrian asked.

That's what they were afraid of. The last rift was bound to be bad, but the entire collapse the completed perforations made possible would be much worse.

"We'd know if that happened," Laurel replied.

"How?"

"We'd probably be dead. The notion of planar collapse is highly, *highly* theoretical — much more Brennan's field than mine — but I get the feeling we'd end up looking around and basically seeing Hell on Earth. Probably couldn't breathe, the way you can't breathe inside a rift. And it'd be hotter than a furnace."

Again she held up the meter. "But this would do us in first."

"We've seen thousands of rifts," Ray said. "It's never put refined Element into the air that I know of."

Laurel nodded. "I'm trying to understand it. I want to find Erika; she'd know. But the phones are out."

"We saw that, too."

"Normal rifts exhale a small amount of raw Zen Element. *Raw.* That's what's in fiend blood as well: *raw* Element. But the refinement process ..."

Laurel stalled, cogitating, probably trying to find a simple way to explain this to non-scientists. "We subject raw Zen Element to very specific atmospheric conditions to separate it out. It's similar to gas chromatography, but for production, not analysis. I don't know for sure. It's not really my field. I can only guess that something about this 'Perforation Effect' recreates those conditions. If the bottom falls out and we get the whole 'Hell on Earth' thing, refined Element might come down like rain. I'll give this to Baker: If he's doing this because he wants a lot of Element, I believe he's about to hit the motherlode. He won't even have to refine the stuff. The only real downside is that he'll be dead. We all will."

"Are the breathers enough protection?"

Laurel thought. Then she nodded. "I think so. For now. Breathe mostly through the breathers and that'll probably be plenty. Both refined and raw Element are mutagens, but at these concentrations I don't think it'll hurt to get much on your skin. Just don't go splashing around in it. This right now is probably no worse than risking a mild sunburn."

Ray nodded, curtly and only once. He stood with an air of decision, soon enough retrieving his Legion gear from the back room.

"You're going," Laurel said.

"We're the only ones who have some clue what happened. They might all be dead out there, but they're not all that's at stake. If what you said is true, the perforations are done but the floor hasn't dropped out yet. Until Fortune rips away along the circle or rifts, we might be able to do something."

"Or you might not." Laurel smiled with an untimely joke. "Is this a good time to ask you again when we can leave the city?"

Adrian smiled. He reached for Laurel, then slipped a hand through her dreadlocked hair, around to the back of her head.

"Don't do that man thing," she said as he pulled her closer.

"What man thing?"

"The thing where you run toward danger and tell me to stay behind for my own safety."

"I'd never tell you what to do."

"You need me. That asshole's trying to turn all of Fortune

into one giant Zen refinery, and there aren't many people who know Zen chemistry as well as me."

"I said I'd never tell you what to do."

She moved closer. "I'm not going to thank you for that."

"Okay."

"Because then it's like I thought I needed your permission."

"You think too much."

They moved even closer. And kissed.

"The world is fucked," she said. "No matter what happens here, the world is a shitty, chaotic, unstable and unreliable place. You know that, don't you?"

"There are places in the world, still, that aren't like Fortune."

"And when this is over, we'll leave this shithole and live in one of them."

"If we're not dead," Adrian agreed.

Chest to chest, heads on each other's shoulders, Laurel said, "What if the next place is just as bad? Just as weird? Just as fucked-up and randomly terrible?"

The answer was something they said all the time, usually in bed, during the afterglow. Adrian was obsessive and always in his head, but Laurel alone could make him relax: smell the flowers, feel the NOW of now. Laurel was a pessimist. Adrian, with his firm belief in plans and meaning and order, had always been her ray of hope. They were each a control rod for the other. She made his world make sense, and he made hers.

"Then we'll move to Detroit," he said. "It's terrible anyway."

26

HIGHER GROUND

It was much worse at the source. Matt Baker's cabin was on a picturesque rise with a view of a valley and a river (or at least, the rise had *once* been picturesque): the perfect place to get away from it all if you didn't mind palpable bad vibes and finding the occasional black-clad depressive dead on your lawn.

But now the sky directly overhead was the diseased black and red of burned flesh shot through with blood poisoning. The red spiderweb over all of Fortune and the surrounding areas had its center there, the air beneath smeared gray as if waiting for rain that never came.

For the longest time, nobody in the Brigade van could see the rift itself. It only gave evidence: an auroral glow that undulated in large, shimmering sheets not unlike the true aurora at the Earth's poles. Only once they rose to higher elevations could they see the land, and what had been done to it.

The usual approach to the old park came from the lower lands, from the south. Those roads, they saw as Ray drove them closer, were blockaded. Not by police, or even by humans.

In some cruel callback for the Porters, the roadway's primary guardians were a pair of massive-horned hellbringers. Smaller fiends representing many different classes crawled back and forth: halfheads, bloodhounds, spiderlings, Fat Joes. Credit Ray for his foresight: If they'd rounded the last bend in the road instead of stopping short to survey the scene, the things would have seen them. Come after them. As things stood, they'd been able to crouch among the Teardrop trees — the only plants that seemed to thrive near the Point other than thistle — and observe the scene with binoculars.

The fiends were protecting the site. They seemed measured. Patient. It almost looked like they had a plan ... but even insects could protect their hives.

Despite this, Adrian for one was beginning to feel like he'd been snowed. For fifty years now, humans had known how to handle fiends. The rules of riftfare almost made it easy, though dangerous. Everyone knew that only one class of fiends came from a rift, and everyone knew rifts opened one at a time. Nobody believed in primordial form; fiends did not adapt or ever change their stripes.

Fiends did not strategize. They did not make plans. They were like animals; they didn't *think*.

They certainly didn't lay traps — something Adrian supposed Matt had technically done rather than the fiends ... but looking at the guards he couldn't shake a weird feeling that this was too organized; the fiends almost seemed to be in on it.

Communications had never gone out before. For the longest time, only one rift had ever appeared in any one place at a time, and even then always inside the Gore Point. So why had everything changed over the past few weeks? Why had so much more changed *today*?

Adrian felt like a sucker hustled by sharks at a billiard table. Maybe humanity had never *really* understood the fiends. Maybe they were smarter than anyone gave them credit for. Maybe they'd only shown mankind what they wanted mankind to see.

It felt like a long con. As if the fiends had been sandbagging all along, just waiting for their chance.

It's lucky for them that Dad's rift happened to stay open just a tiny bit too long, Ray had said. *Everything since happened because of it. It's only possible because* one little thing *went wrong twenty years ago.*

Had that thing really *gone wrong?* Or was it part of the same long con?

The hellbringer wasn't supposed to be in Eldon's rift. It had only shown up when that most important of rifts needed to be kept open just a little bit longer. It was a little too coincidental for coincidence.

They got back into the van. They drove as high as they could, moving lateral to a line of guarding fiends that looked to completely encircle the cabin at a radius of about a mile, maybe less or maybe more. From a tall peak, they were able to use their binoculars to look down on the cabin.

But then they finally saw the breadth of the rift. It wasn't hanging in the sky like most rifts, but had instead cracked the rock below like the fissure that had drained the black lake. The auroral glow was coming from beneath, inviting like a pond made of magic. Only if they were able to look directly down into it would they see the Hell that waited.

"Look," Laurel said, pointing. "In the paddock."

There were trees in the way. Her eyes were sharper than both men's and the sky shimmered with heat haze, so at first Adrian saw nothing. Then he realized that what he'd taken as livestock were actually human beings. Judging by the presence of multiple Brigade, SWAT, and police vehicles but a total lack of dead bodies, they had to be the Stitchers, Legions, cops, and others who'd so recently been about to break down the door and end this. They were completely naked. The fiends had taken their gear, Adrian guessed, but didn't know or didn't care to stop stripping when they reached clothes.

"At least they're alive," Adrian said.

"But I think we can give up on them helping out," Ray countered. "Look. There's a pile of scrap just past the gate. I'll bet it's what's left of all their riftfare gear. Matt must have removed the Zen, then trashed the rest."

"I don't think Matt did it alone," Laurel said. "I think the fiends helped him."

They sat with that. Until Ray asked his questions. "Now what? How do we close this thing?"

Adrian almost laughed. They had four Stitching rigs but only one person who knew how to use them. They could see hundreds if not thousands of milling fiends that weren't swarming like idiots but instead seemed to be waiting for someone to show up and test them. The crowd of demons included many classes. Ray couldn't fight all of even one class, let alone several.

The ground shook with the heavy feet of several of those classes' bosses, each of which had likely widened the original rift as they crawled up the earthquake-size fissure to emerge from it.

The idea of *"closing this thing"* was beyond absurd. Same for the yet-unspoken nobility of "rescuing their friends."

They were three people. Limited training. No way to call for help.

This wasn't *movie*-impossible. It was the real kind of impossible.

Laurel said, "Maybe we should set our sights on something more achievable, like keeping it from getting worse."

"Honey, this is about as 'worse' as it gets," Ray replied.

"It's not. If Matt's map is accurate, this last rift completes the perforated circle. The area inside the perforation is weak now. I'll bet all the old sealed rifts have reopened all over town. But *Fortune is still here.* It's hanging by a thread, but here. Let's focus on keeping it that way."

"How the hell are we supposed to do that?" Ray asked.

"Someone probably has to set it off. One final rift has to open, somewhere in the middle of the circle. Look. The wall on this side is mostly windows. Do you see Matt inside?"

Adrian looked. "No, but that doesn't say anything."

"If Matt opened the rift, why isn't he here?"

"Now hang on a second," Ray said. "We're miles away. I can barely tell who's got long hair from this far away. He could be in a corner we can't see. He could be in the bathroom. Or maybe they stripped him naked and threw him into the paddock with everyone else."

Adrian was shaking his head. "No. Look at how they're behaving. Look how organized it is. We were wrong about them, Ray. We've been wrong the whole time. This almost looks like a stakeout. It might as well be FBI down there instead of fiends."

As he said this, an upright halfhead walked past the wall of windows, the jaw on its lower half chattering and what passed for its brain exposed.

Adrian finished. "If they've fooled us for this long, they wouldn't betray Matt now. They need him."

"For what?"

"To open the last rift, like Laurel said. They must not be able to do it themselves." Adrian pointed near the paddock, at the pile of scrap. "I'll bet every ounce of Element's been stripped from the gear. Somehow they must have sucked some of it out to open the rift in the ground, but stripping that gear happened *after* the rift was open. Taking it apart took manual work. It took hands. The fiends did it. That means they're still sitting on a stockpile of Element. Because they still need it. They need it to punch the perforated bottom out of Fortune. And that means Matt's still with them. Still on their side. So Laurel's right: Where is he?"

"In the bathroom," Ray repeated. "In a corner we can't see."

"He's in the middle of the circle," Laurel countered. "That's the only place he can be."

27

ANOTHER

There was just one problem with Laurel's theory.

Yes, it made sense that until the bottom fell out of Fortune and Hell rose to fill it, Matt would still be useful to the fiends. And *yes*, that meant he'd have to step inside the circle of rifts and presumably open one more. But where had he gone?

Rifts only formed a circle on the fiends' plane, not on the ordinary one. From the normal side of things, the "perforated circle" looked scattered and random. That meant its middle could be anywhere.

They'd managed to creep closer to the cabin without being seen. Managed to get a straighter sightline into the cabin, where Matt still hadn't been spied.

"You don't know he's not dead," Ray said. "Not for sure."

"I know that it won't matter if he's dead!" Laurel snapped back. This was one reason they'd broken up. Even in simple conversation, they managed to irritate each other. "If I'm wrong, we waste time. The end comes anyway and we die anyway, and everyone else probably dies, and then who knows what happens next. But if I'm right — if Baker's *not* dead, but instead headed off to open the last rift — our next move might actually make a difference."

"Okay, genius," Ray said. "Then what's that? He could be anywhere."

"Not *anywhere*." Adrian had been working this out, and unsurprisingly he agreed with his smart girlfriend instead of his break-things-first-and-ask-questions-later brother. "He didn't drive because his car is still out front. He probably can't drive. But you already knew that, right?"

Ray didn't answer. Communications had failed all over town, but this close to the rift, other kinds of electronics seemed equally busted. Riftfare equipment was quadruple-shielded specifically because rift energy was known to be disruptive, so fortunately their rigs still worked ... but the van had suddenly died when they inched too closely. Power stopped flowing from the battery. The alternator stopped charging it. The starter solenoid wouldn't engage. Ray had needed to wrench it to a stop, without the aid of power steering, to keep from plowing into a tree.

"So he's on foot," Adrian concluded. "But even then, we've been watching for a while and we haven't seen anyone leave."

"Maybe he left before we got here," Laurel said.

"Or he's still there, and hasn't left at all," added Ray.

"Either could be true." Adrian wanted to pull up his photo of Baker's map, but without his phone he had to work from memory. "But I think this area around here is all part of the same 'chunk' of land relative to their plane. I don't know that he has to get to the exact center of the circle to do what he's got to do, so he could probably be anywhere inside it ..."

"Great," Ray said. "That's only ... *how* much area to search? Two hundred square miles, if the distances stay the same?"

Adrian lifted an eyebrow and kept speaking. "But I'll bet farther in is better. Meaning, not walking distance."

"You're guessing," Ray said.

"It's a good guess," Laurel agreed, and Ray made a face that suggested displeasure at being ganged up on again. "So we're left with two options. The first is that he's out there in the woods somewhere, maybe with a fiend escort and maybe not, carrying ... what — sixty, seventy pounds of refined Zen? Even if it's somehow shielded well enough not to kill him, that's a lot to ask. He'd have to cross at least three or four miles to have a chance at being on a plot of land that ends up near the center when viewed from their side."

"That's a lot to ask," Ray said.

"Right. Which is why I think the second option is probably true. And it's that he took a shortcut."

Ray looked around. "What shortcut?"

"You're thinking like a human," Adrian said.

Then Ray thought, and understood.

Laurel nodded. "My money says Matt walked right into one rift, and came out of another."

28

THE CHASM

So they descended the slope, sticking to ravines and low places. Vegetation was sparse and strange in the area, but unlike in the heart of the dead zone there at least was some. The three of them crawled beneath fallen branches that made overhangs covered in dead undergrowth. Dirtied their bellies with black soil that wasn't much like normal soil.

As they came closer, Adrian would swear the air itself seemed to thicken, with something other than humidity. Breathing took more effort. His thoughts grew discordant. And looking at Ray and Laurel, he wasn't the only one.

The feeling made him understand Suicide Flats, which wasn't far away. Dying would be easy here. It might feel like a relief ... respite from all the hopelessness ahead.

Laurel pinched him. "Hey."

He looked back.

"It's all the Zen in the air. It's kind of like being smothered by carbon dioxide. Before it becomes lethal, it just kind of ... puts you to sleep. You don't get to sleep right now, Adrian. You owe me dinner. At the Cheesecake Factory. Which is two miles from our new home ... which, when this is over, will be far, far away from here."

He tried to smile, then marched on.

The ground had sundered in a place nature had already weakened: the floor of a shallow valley. As they stayed low, still a good distance from the cabin, freshly opened ground at their feet gave way to clay, then rocks, then to a bile-color imitation of groundwater.

Soon it was a cut, then a wide slash, and eventually pixie shimmers sparkled around them and Adrian knew the edge of the true rift — situated in this ripped-open part of the earth — was not far ahead.

Ray was more cautious than the others. The rift's most extreme corner breathed a steady draft of warm air. It wasn't loud or as boiling hot this far from the thing's center.

Adrian and Laurel stood to approach it, but Ray stayed back.

"Where are the fiends?" Ray asked. "They were guarding it."

"The epicenter's still a half hour ahead," Laurel told him. "You said it yourself. 'People don't enter rifts.' Only Stitchers — but only a few feet over the event horizon, and only for as long as it takes to pinch shut the inside."

"So basically, they don't think we're this stupid," Adrian said.

Ray mumbled something about that being just great, just wonderful. Then he emerged, walked to the edge of the thing, and leaned over it enough that its exhale blew his hair back. "This is a bad idea."

"We can scour Fortune instead if you want," Laurel said with an edge in her voice. "Remember, though, that what looks like the center from their side could be anywhere on our side. So we have to search the entire town. Everything inside the

Rampart. Maybe we can call for air support that won't come. Or maybe we can try to spot Baker with a drone that won't fly because this fucking thing fried everything's circuits."

Ray looked like he might protest. Then he said, "Now I remember why we broke up."

And Laurel replied, "Yeah. This is why."

Ray began taking readings. Like the suits, armaments, and Adrian's Stitching rig, the meters still worked. They were made for riftfare; everything else was not. Laurel had been keeping an eye on the ambient levels of refined Zen Element the entire time, making sure it didn't kill them. Despite expectations to the contrary, levels near the rift were no higher than those at the station. Things seemed to have reached stasis.

But that probably wasn't good news. Baker was gone, and the fiends were out of their comfort zone on the human side of the rift. If levels were no longer rising, everyone on the other side of this fight would want to break the town open. Rip off the Band-Aid and get it over with.

Temporarily alone, Adrian and Laurel stood face to face and exchanged unspoken words.

"It'll be okay," Laurel told him. "Matt did this. He crossed through their dimension by going into one rift and out another."

"You think," Adrian said.

"GEN's findings suggest their plane can be survived for short amounts of time."

"*Short* amounts."

"You've gone in before. Think of it like a sprint."

Adrian looked at the massive, red slash beneath the surface of the Earth. "I can't see anything. I'd have to get over the middle and look down. What if there *are* no other rifts? We have to jump in. We might just keep falling. Might not be able to get out, if there are no other holes nearby to run through. Heat protection and rebreathers only help for so long."

Laurel tugged his jacket shut. "Hey, I've got a joke for you. What do you call it when you've gone through your entire life believing there's a reason and a pattern and a purpose to everything, but then something comes where you have to take action without any idea if you were right? What if your mother always told you that everything had meaning, but suddenly you can't see what that meaning might be, and you have to soldier on anyway?"

"This is a terrible joke," Adrian said.

"What do you call it?"

"Dumb?"

"Faith. You call it faith."

It made Adrian think of priests and churches. Of Heaven and Hell. All the stuff that Ray never believed in, but that Adrian, though he'd tried to remain rational and stoic, had never entirely shaken.

"You're not going," he said.

"I don't have a heat suit. Besides, someone has to monitor things out here where the equipment still works. I'll see your signature when you come out. I'll keep an eye out. If the cavalry comes, I'll tell them where to find you."

"If we live," Adrian said.

She took the folds of his coat, pulled him toward her, and kissed him. "Come back to me."

29
SHORTCUT

They were alone when they entered.

Laurel said her goodbyes, heading the other way back to the van. She needed to retrieve some equipment she could possibly hotwire. She was an engineer, after all. And a biologist. Maybe it was the call of death that made him watch her go, considering her brilliance.

Ray stopped Laurel before she left, then handed her a collapsible Rollard he'd grabbed when they'd taken the rest of their gear from the van the first time. Adrian turned away, not wanting to see his brother presenting the weapon like an engagement ring: sweet more than practical.

"Swipe with this end, stab with this one," he demonstrated.

Laurel nodded her gratitude, oddly touched.

The rift's exhale, a hundred or so yards closer to the center, was the low drone of a vacuum cleaner. At the epicenter, it would probably be like the exhaust from a jet.

Adrian looked down. He could still see nothing. They were used to point rifts. The only other elongated, slash-style rift they had dealt with was the one on High, and that had nearly taken their faces off.

For all they knew, they could barely see the other plane (a blur of red and the smell of sulfur) because this wasn't truly the rift itself. They might jump in, then go nowhere. They'd simply keep falling until their lungs gave out.

Ray looked up, put on the Stitcher's hood he'd taken from the station gear room, then jumped in with both feet.

Adrian took a long second to clear his head, then did the same.

ADRIAN LANDED UPRIGHT, surprised he hadn't fallen over.

There didn't seem to be any sound in this place. At first Adrian thought he was deaf, but then he caught a steady drip-drip-drip that began and ended without rhythm — a sound whose source he could not see.

He and Ray had both secured the loose ends of their asbestos coats and the seldom-used heat-resistant pants that went with them, sealing the works against the hoods to create the thing Laurel had said she didn't have: a full-fledged heat suit.

While on the job, Adrian almost never bothered to go full suit. Stitchers hopped in; Stitchers hopped out. Thanks to the steady outward movement of air from the fiends' plane to the normal plane, no oxygen made its way in through a rift.

That was the bigger problem: a Stitcher's inability to breathe. Incursion and excursion was typically so fast and so shallow that heat was barely an issue. Now it was.

Adrian reached down and clicked on the miniature air handler clipped to his belt. It *might* keep him from scalding. For a little while. But the handler wasn't much — not like a home's air conditioning, which even GEN hadn't been able to make travel-sized — and mostly served to prevent sizzling.

Hot was to be expected — soon to be lethal hot, if they didn't find a way out. Ray — who looked more astronaut now than Legion — pointed at the sky.

Adrian looked up. The rift's opening was only about ten feet above them, showing gray skies and the red-web pattern. But it had no edge. Nothing to reach up and grab, assuming Adrian could even jump that high.

The tiny radio that went with the full heat suit crackled in his ear.

"This little decal," said Ray's voice, and at the same time the Ray-astronaut pointed to one side of his face. "The decal I can see in the corner of my eye, inside the hood. The colored thing. Is that a thermometer?"

"Yes."

"I don't think it's working. It says it's only sixty degrees inside my suit."

"It's in Celsius. So almost one-fifty."

"Okay." Ray nodded. "It feels like one-fifty in here."

"Outside temperature is right around three hundred."

"That's not too bad."

"Also Celsius. Nearly six hundred degrees to you and me. And rising. Rifts act like wounds. The longer you're inside, the hotter the air around you becomes."

"What are the suits rated at?"

"Seven hundred."

"Celsius."

"You don't understand Celsius. That one's in Fahrenheit."

"Jesus." The Ray-creature spun around clumsily, but the air around them was milky and unclear, with no visible features. No other rifts. "I thought you guys entered rifts a lot hotter than this one."

"It's sort of a limit case, Ray. We're in and out with a full Brigade right outside. We don't usually plan to hang out for long."

The thought made him look up, at the enormous tearing rift they couldn't reach to exit.

He wished he hadn't.

They scouted. The ground was soon hot even through their boots, the jackets and pants no longer providing more than a skein of protection from the smolder. Adrian picked the fabric away from his neck, feeling like he was laying on top of a stove-top. It was easy to get lost — not just from their starting point, but also from each other.

The air was like soup. Like fog with ill intentions.

"Ade. Don't move."

Adrian froze. A foil sheet connecting his hood to his jacket pressed against one cheek, burning him. He rolled his eyes toward Ray, then down where his brother was looking.

His legs had disappeared beneath the long, undulating body of a Bimmer-class sense serpent. He had no memory of how Bimmer-class fiends were fought. Or how they attacked, or what they did if they got you. Adrian had made it his business to never be this close to the fiends, and even Legions didn't like to touch them.

Could they dissolve protective gear? Did they bite, and from where — head, tail, or everywhere along their length? It was usually better to be finished off by a fiend if one managed to attack you. They reveled in human pain.

"Don't worry. They're blind."

Adrian wasn't comforted. Clearly the thing knew he was here; it'd entwined itself around him. Did it think he was a fiend? A rock? A tree?

Very slowly, Ray removed his multi-function weapon — the one he'd been given for when the two of them were on a mission alone. Force wasn't what would make the difference on this most unusual of repellances, so it seemed smarter to have a small ability to fight any class of fiend than to burden himself with bigger weapons able to fight a few classes very well. Even the best weapons wouldn't do them any good if they were attacked while alone. Ray had a pea-shooter, but at least it was something.

"Wait!" Adrian said. "You're going to shoot it? Use your Rollard!"

"Sense serpents coil up when they're injured. It'll squeeze into you with poison spines if I cut it."

The serpent had started to move more quickly around his legs. Sentient spaghetti, issuing a hissing, rattling sound. From the body itself, because Adrian had no idea where its head was.

"Ray? Why's it doing that?"

"Because they're blind. Not deaf."

It knew he was here. It knew what he was.

Ray took aim.

"Ray? Ray, wait!"

Ray fired, spitting three glowing punchball rounds. Two of the three struck the serpent's body, causing it to hiss, retract, and recoil.

"Run," Ray said.

"But what if it—?"

"Forget the serpent, asshole! I'm more worried about *them!*"

Adrian looked out, following Ray's pointing arm. The serpent had been holding so much of his attention that he'd missed the line of fiends now racing toward them. They were all shapes, all sizes, and the herd would be upon them in thirty seconds.

Everywhere else around them, the air stayed scalding, suffocating red mist.

"THIS WAY!" Ray yelled.

He ran. Adrian, deciding to trust his brother, ran with him.

Fifty sprinting feet on, Adrian was jerked sideways when a hand from nowhere dragged him in a new direction.

"Here! Through here!"

Adrian felt himself slowing — probably the reason he hadn't kept up. The torpor had come on him slowly — just like Laurel had said outside, just like lulling to sleep.

He looked down and realized his left leg wasn't working. It must be the serpent, the final one-third of which he could now see slithering ahead of the fast-approaching wall of enemies.

Something hit him from behind. He fell forward and it was like jumping into an ice bath. Into a sunny day from abject darkness.

Ray was over him, ripping his hood violently away, staring into his face with intensity, slapping his cheeks even though right now all Adrian wanted was bedtime.

"Weld," he said.

"What?"

"SPOT WELD THAT MOTHERFUCKER OR I'LL KILL YOU MYSELF!"

The shout woke Adrian in an instant.

And the situation's reality slapped him in the face: Ray had just pushed him through a rift and they were back in the sane world ... but that same rift was still open behind them, and for damn sure it wouldn't let loose with only one convenient class of fiends for Ray to fight.

He blinked. His head cleared. Stitching was elegant; spot-welding was more for the rare emergency shit-show. His practiced hands found the right toggles on the rig's nozzle, though, and just in time he managed to blast three fat blobs of Zen resin at top, bottom, and middle of the eye-shaped rift.

Then it looked like a shirt-front pressed open by a too-fat belly, straining at the welds as if they were buttons.

The fiends hit the rift. They reached and swiped through like prisoners trying to come through bars.

Adrian watched for a while. But then he saw the serpent climbing above the bottom weld, preparing to slither through the gap.

He focused and Stitched, until the rift was gone.

30

SAINTS AND SINNERS

drian blinked again.

He came awake, not remembering when he fell asleep.

Ray was above him, kicking him in the face instead of lightly slapping him until Adrian finally sat up.

"Did I pass out?"

"Sort of."

"For how long?"

"Five, ten seconds. Technically speaking, you weren't asleep. Actually, you just died."

Adrian sat up the rest of the way and nodded at an empty doser can on the concrete floor. "Adrenalix. You feel paranoid?"

That was an understatement. Adrian's world had jumped up to ten, everything hyperactive and heart-slamming.

Ray nodded. "For the serpent. It spined you. It would have spread and killed you for sure. So I had to kill you instead."

Adrian looked again at the can. He'd never used Adrenalix before, but it was part of every standard emergency kit and they'd of course learned all about it. The stuff wasn't adrenaline, but instead a chemical analogue that GEN had somehow calibrated to work like a double-defibrillator. In the space of half a second (two seconds or so after administration), it stopped the heart and then attempted to re-start it.

Attempted was the operative word, though the trainer had assured Adrian's crew that it "usually worked."

Among the Legions, Adrenalix was often called Soul Balm, because after it was used on you, you were essentially living your second life. Priests hated it, but they hated a lot of things.

"I feel like I could climb walls," Adrian said.

"In about two minutes you'll feel like warmed-over shit. The come-down is supposedly hard. And you're welcome."

Adrian looked where the rift had been. He'd managed to Stitch it before … dying. "We're safe?"

"I haven't exactly had time for the tour, but I think so. This has to be where Matt came through. It's the only hole I found."

There could have been dozens of other open rifts around them. But the answer felt right, through all this amped-up haze. Nearby rifts could be felt from this side, and it turned out he'd mostly felt the one they'd come through from the fiends' side as well. He'd missed the sensation at the time, probably because of the serpent's poison.

Adrian stood, his high already fading. They had entered an expansive open space — not just a hangar, the place was big enough to park a blimp.

"So what do you think, Baby Brother? Are we still in Kansas?"

Adrian almost recognized the place. He wasn't sure how or from when, but it had a familiar vibe. Maybe he'd come here with Laurel. Before she'd hooked up with Ray, just after she'd made the absurd decision to move *into* Fortune while all the sane people were running away from it. Nobody came to this place. Residents were usually born there, and knew no better.

Laurel said she'd come for the science. Adrian was crushing on her at the time, and found her answer bold and sexy.

They'd come alone. Adrian had mistaken it as her being interested in him, but in truth he'd been a famous Stitcher and she'd been hungry for a tour. Laurel wasn't working at GEN just yet, but Adrian had pulled some strings to impress her. He knew forensics, and Brennan — not yet head of forensics, but well-respected — knew GEN.

The hangar had been in use for Gore Point recon aircraft at the time. That's why he'd been slow to recognize it. The planes had been moved to a Point-adjacent airport years ago. The building had been officially decommissioned for nearly a decade.

They heard a sound like the final gasp of a drowning man. A vicious sucking of air, followed by a cough. Noises echoed around the cavernous space like a stirring of bones.

Adrian and Ray startled.

Their heads darted toward the sound, realizing it'd come from the secondary hangar bay, invisible around a corner. Ray stripped his protective gloves and put a finger to his lips. They hadn't been keeping their voices down as much as they should, but whoever was over there sounded like he'd just come awake with the heaving inhale of untreated apnea.

They drew conventional pistols.

Then they approached and peeked to see Matt Baker on the floor, stirring feebly.

"Stay where you are," Ray said, moving in with his M9 up.

Adrian followed, kicking wide in case he tried to flee.

Matt looked momentarily confused. But then his face cleared into something serious.

"Don't get up, Matt," Ray said. "Get on your knees. Cross your legs behind you. Hands where I can see them."

Matt complied. Mostly. Except that he held something

almost like a grenade in his second hand. "You should have been a cop, Ray."

"Throw that away," Ray told him over the sights of his weapon. "I'm not screwing around."

Matt half-laughed. "Oh. You don't want me to do *that*, Ray."

Adrian inched closer to his brother. "Look at his leg."

Ray did. Adrian couldn't be sure, but it looked like a small Adrenalix container had been strapped to Matt's ankle, visible now below his pulled-up heat suit. There was some sort of gadget build around it.

Adrian, coming back to normal now, thought he understood. Matt was wearing some sort of an auto-injection rig — something GEN had been toying with. The device had been built specifically for human incursions into the other plane, but got shot down by congress because humans entering that other place was crazy.

If a person was attacked without a team of Brigade-mates around them, nobody would be present to give them First Aid. Auto-injectors supposedly watched the wearer's vital signs, then triggered an Adrenalix injection automatically if it thought there was a need.

That would explain the gasping. Matt might have been wounded while crossing the rifts but still managed to stumble through. He'd made it across the floor, then collapsed. That's when the rig had shot him full of adrenaline analogue and woken him with a start.

Understanding rippled through Ray. Auto-injectors were a human thing. A GEN thing. A thing Matt couldn't access on his own because production had stopped and even Kaur couldn't have found one if he'd even known they existed.

So Matt had an accomplice.

A *human* accomplice, with access to the very best goodies.

Goodies, Adrian was willing to bet, like the device in his hand.

With a flick of fingers, Matt allowed something to pop free from the device and clatter to the floor.

"Who else is here?" Ray demanded.

"Nobody. I can do this on my own. I am the flaming sword."

"Matt? What's that in your hand?"

"A key."

"To what?"

"To the Kingdom of Heaven."

Ray was slowly approaching, arcing inward. His pistol hadn't wavered.

"This isn't about Heaven. You know that, Matt."

He almost laughed. "It is for me. Maybe not for you. All I have to do is open the door."

"And you think God will save you?"

"God *has.*"

Ray inched in farther, but then Matt brandished his device with a warning. "Ah-ah."

"This is over."

"It's far from over." Then Matt rolled to his knees and finally to his feet, daring Ray to shoot him. He had a limp, though, and his leg was bleeding. "I've already seen what happens here. Seen it when I pray. You can't kill me. I'm immortal now."

Ray cocked his weapon. He'd always had a flair for the dramatic. "Let's find out."

But Matt was unconcerned. "You never liked me, Ray. You thought I was weird. Even when we were kids, and our dads worked together, you thought I was strange. I even did you a favor. I told you what would happen to your father. He sinned.

And then they took him, the way guardians always take the sinners."

Adrian looked at his watch. One of the things Laurel was planning to observe from the van was the clarity of the airwaves. Rifts opened like nuclear blasts sometimes, and just like nukes they sometimes had short-term effects to precede the long-term ones. Laurel was hoping the comm blackout was like an electromagnetic pulse and would fade in time. Then she could call the cavalry. And just as Adrian had worked out where they were (GEN's mostly-abandoned legacy campus), Laurel's instruments would know it too, by now.

Maybe they could stall. It would be better to face whatever came next with Legions and Stitchers behind them.

"What was his sin, Matt?"

"He opened the gate. He courted the demons and asked them in."

"Oh, go fuck yourse—"

"He was on the job, Matt." Adrian raised a palm to stop his brother. "Same as your old man."

"'*Precious Eldon Porter,*'" Matt mocked, childlike. "Always first in the press. Always got the raises. The fame. The bonuses. The *credit*. I told you back then that rifts could be entered. I told you he'd done it. But did you believe me? Of course not. Not me, or my father. Why did we matter? We were just doing the Lord's work!"

"So now you're going to make everyone else pay? You're willing to kill everyone just so you can earn a few million dollars of filthy—"

"THIS ISN'T ABOUT MONEY! I'M NOT TAKING ANY MONEY!"

Then, as if surprised by his outburst, Matt used his free hand to smooth out his jacket. He lowered the grenade thing and eyed it like a mystery.

"You can't win. Don't you see? It's activated." He shook the thing in his hand. "Now all I have to do, to open the gate, is to let go. You can't dive at it and throw it away and think you'll stop it. You can't get to it and hold it closed. You can't even throw your body over it to protect the rest."

"Why are you doing this, if not for the money?"

Matt sneered, still pacing as two guns tracked him. "Look around you. Look at what this city has become. The Lord said, 'Do good work and I will reward you. Do evil and I will punish you.' But man is flawed. Man was tempted. Man turned his nose up at the Lord and said, 'You do not command me.' Then he finally opened Hell at our feet. *We stare into Satan's kingdom every day.* We fight his minions. And yet still people say, 'It's somewhere else.' 'It's another plane of reality.' They say, 'We don't know what this is, that we fight.' But the demons that come here are abominations. They have horns and sharp teeth like animals. Every day we fight Hell, and yet still we disbelieve the Lord's warnings." Matt shook the device. "But they won't disbelieve when the sky descends, and Hell takes over."

"So this is some sort of a fucking *quest?*" Ray demanded. "Some sort of religious bullshit?"

"Ask your brother. Ask him what your mother said, after your father died."

Ray looked at Adrian, but Adrian said nothing.

"You came to *me* the next day, didn't you, Adrian?" Matt's voice was mocking. "Not to your brother, but to me. Because when vengeance came to your father, finally you believed me. Of course you rationalized it all away. But why don't you tell Ray the rest? Have you gone to confession? Have you told anyone else about your mother's dreams, of Eldon burning in sulfur?"

Adrian snapped, advancing three quick steps. He centered his pistol on Matt's forehead.

"Do it," Matt said.

Adrian cocked his pistol. So much for Ray being the only dramatic one.

"DO IT!"

Adrian felt himself shaking with the rage of betrayal. He'd been weak. His crises of faith were few and far between, and strictly speaking he was a nonbeliever. But his upbringing was a habit; he couldn't shake the feeling of brimstone at his back when times got tough.

After Mom told Adrian all about her dreams, he had been alone, Laurel still with Ray. He'd needed to get it out. He couldn't talk to his brother because Ray didn't believe anything. He couldn't talk to his mother because Mom believed too much. Twice he'd found himself accepting Matt's comfort as the only port in the storm. In truth Adrian didn't know what he believed.

"*I said do it! Do it!*" Matt rushed forward, slamming his forehead into the muzzle of Adrian's pistol. "*Do it! Kill me!* I'm dead either way. So go ahead! Make me a martyr! What will it tell you tomorrow about Satan, if you kill a man in cold blood today?"

Matt stepped away and smiled. "The hard way, then."

He casually tossed the device over his shoulder, and—

31

BATTLE ROYALE

Adrian ran after Matt's hurtled device.

It didn't matter that he told them that it couldn't be stopped once activated.

Ray, displaying the coolness in extreme circumstances that the public loved him for on TV, stayed put. His weapon tracked Matt as he turned to run. Ray saw it coming, and shot him once in the leg.

Then he walked to where Matt was bleeding, took Matt's pistol, then kicked him hard in the stomach.

"For my father." He turned back and kicked him again. "And my mother."

Then he joined Adrian with the device. It was less grenade-like up close — more like a dead-man's switch for some larger implement. A trio of sealed Zen filler rods were secured to its side like miniature dynamite. Adrian assumed the big rip was like an avalanche in waiting. It would only take a bit of Element to blow Fortune open now. The process needed a nudge to get the snowball rolling. Presumably that's what the filler rods were for.

The top of the thing was flashing, and speeding up. Like some sort of a countdown.

"Can you disarm it?" Ray asked.

Adrian shook his head. "It probably *can't* be disarmed. I wish Laurel was here."

"Because you want her to die?"

It was an inappropriate joke, but Adrian shook his head, taking the question as serious. "She works with stuff like this all the time. Look. This is a GEN device."

Ray looked. Adrian was right: the device had been made with GEN parts. His silence spoke volumes.

"We're in trouble, Ray. That thing on Matt's leg looks like GEN, too. This is a GEN warehouse. Matt can't be in this alone. Someone a hell of a lot smarter is pulling the strings. They sent him into that rift. Sent him here, and gave him this." Adrian held up the device, now blinking faster and faster. "I think we're about to wish you'd let the serpent get me."

"Brennan," said Ray.

Adrian nodded. "I should have seen it coming. He held us behind when the call came. He fed us all the clues at the right time. His lab does this kind of work."

"Are you saying Brennan *wanted* us to solve it? *Wanted* us to find Matt?"

"Makes sense, right? Brennan's nowhere near the epicenter of what's about to happen, but *this* needed to be." Again he indicated the device. "Enter Matt. This way, Brennan can save himself. Probably on his way out of town by now, maybe driving a car that'll act like a giant Zen collector. Just scoop it out of the air when the boundary shatters. He led us to Matt, and we told *everyone else* about Matt. Sent them into the trap with the fuel needed to open the cabin rift. If there's a world left when this is all over, people will want answers. Luckily, the famous Porter

Brothers already told everyone: It was crazy Matt Baker, acting alone."

"But *we* know. *We* know he was only using Matt."

"Yeah," said Adrian. "There's just one problem with the idea of us exposing Brennan to the world. I don't want to rain on your parade, but—"

"I get it." Ray tossed his chin toward the end of the warehouse. "Run. Toss it out."

"Won't make a difference. It's not a bomb. I don't think it matters where it goes off now, unless you can open a rift to Antarctica or something."

"Goddammit, Adrian, we can't just sit here and let it—!"

The frenetic blinking suddenly stopped and started glowing a solid yellow-green instead. There was a flash of light from all around, but none of the filler rods attached to the thing detonated, broke, or began leaking.

Instead, it began flashing again ... slowly this time.

"It didn't work," Ray said, exhaling, turning to laugh maniacally at Matt as he bled on the floor. "Shitbag set off his doomsday weapon, but *it didn't—!*"

Then the entire building shook — just once, as if a giant had kicked it.

The concrete floor spiderwebbed from end to end with cracks like a smashed windshield. An enormous, horrible roar started slowly, then built steadily. The sound came from everywhere at once.

At the hangar's end, a very different kind of rift formed. Neither Adrian nor Ray had ever seen one like it before. Instead of being slitlike, it was perfectly round. Instead of acting as window to the familiar, red-tinged fiend plane, its core was solid black. It had a multicolored aurora like most rifts, but this one was making slow circles around the center like water orbiting a whirlpool.

"Shit."

"Shit."

They backed up. There was no point in glory now; now was time to flee.

But then the fiends came, and so much faster than ever before.

There was no dramatic pause between opening and exodus. Fiends slipped from the obsidian portal as if emerging from ink. Whatever black substance comprised the new rift clung to each fiend briefly as they came, then snapped back and made ripples.

Adrian and Ray both turned, but a new kind of flying fiend — like massive hummingbirds with the dead-eyed heads of old dolls — zipped instantly past them to guard the exits. The things pressed the brothers forward, and when Adrian and Ray turned back toward the portal, they saw halfskulls and stilt-walkers and slithereens coming at them in a sprint.

Since the dawn of riftfare, fiends had only ever shambled. Speed was another area where the other plane seemed to have been holding back: sandbagging, showing the humans lesser abilities so they could surprise them later with all they could actually do.

They formed a circle around the humans, not yet attacking.

Ray looked at Adrian. Adrian looked at Ray. Everything in the past thirty seconds had been a surprise: all improved fiends but still no engagement. Not far away, they heard — but could not see — Matt Baker beginning to scream.

It took longer than it should for him to stop whimpering. They'd made it last. As much as Adrian hated Baker right now, hearing those sounds made him hope the other man's faith was true. Hopefully he'd gone to Heaven. *Nobody* deserved what those screams implied.

"Take this," Ray said, shoving his multifunction weapon at Adrian. "I've got all I need."

Adrian was taking in the thousands of creatures around them. The portal kept emptying like a clown car. It was standing room only, sporting members of every fiend class Adrian knew plus several he doubted *anyone* knew.

He eyed the black rift. It was different. His gut called the difference *deeper*.

This was a *deeper* portal that Matt's GEN device (Brennan's device) had opened. Milton said in *Paradise Lost* that Hell had levels. This felt like proof.

Layers and layers. All the way down some dimensionless void.

And Adrian realized: *We've only ever seen the tip of their iceberg. We've only ever seen what they showed us, and we were arrogant enough to believe we would know if there was more.*

"Ray, we can't possibly—"

"TAKE IT!"

Adrian realized something else: Ray didn't think they could win this. He only wanted to go out fighting.

They stared at the fiends. All teeth and claws, waiting outside a naked circle — as if for the opening bell — dripping with saliva and rattling breaths.

"I wish I could think of something cool to say." Ray didn't sound afraid, but that was his defense. Of course he was terrified.

Adrian hugged the multi-function tighter. He'd set it to battle the Soluze class, because Soluze were fought with blunt force and conventional weapons. A full-size Soluze weapon would throw bullets and shrapnel, but this little one was more like a shotgun that never ran out of ammo. It would act like a second Rollard ... and Rollards were what Legions used on every first wave, because nothing was immune to getting cut in half.

It was like a kung-fu movie; they only came at Adrian and Ray one or two at a time. Adrian thought he'd forgotten the Legion-skills training every member of the Brigade took in bootcamp, but it came back to him with the comfort of an old pair of sneakers. He had to pivot and fire, but every fiend was differently exposed. Some, he hit what passed for legs. Others, the head.

Ray slashed like he always did. When he easily mastered the few that came on at once, they charged even faster. Adrian assumed he'd be in trouble soon; unlike Ray, he needed room around him to blast because his weapon wouldn't slash and cut like Ray's was doing.

But the trouble never came. They never pressed tight to him. They never squeezed the huge mob tight on Ray. Instead they slashed and shot, shot and stabbed. Bodies fell and formed a wall, which new fiends climbed, crawled, or flew over. When the dead mound pressed too tightly, Ray backed up and began to climb out of them.

Adrian followed, eyes wide and uncomprehending. The fiends' open area moved with them.

They weren't being overcome. Or truly being surrounded.

"What the fuck's going on here?" Ray said as he swung his weapon. "Talk to me, Ade."

He was too out of breath — from working the weapon, from exertion, but most of all from the adrenaline fugue of battle — to answer.

Not that Adrian even had one. Unless this was Hell for the boys who spent their entire lives battling demons, and the answer was an eternity continuing the war without reprieve.

This is our punishment. It won't end. We will just fight. And fight. And fight. Never losing, or making progress. Forever, and ever, and ever.

Activity came by the odd black rift.

The rift itself swelled, dilating like a camera's iris, becoming twice and then three times its previous size. The top of the circle touched the hangar roof far above, aurora sluicing along the corrugated metal.

Something emerged. More massive and muscular than Adrian had ever seen. It made the hellbringers from earlier look like action figures. Its skin was bright red. It had horns the size of school buses, pointed forward like a bull. The fiend had to be more than a hundred feet tall to fill the hangar so completely.

"Uh, Ade?"

"I see it."

The thing seemed to sit instead of advancing. Even sitting, it more than dominated the space.

The fiends came and came. In an endless procession, never an insurmountable wave. The huge red thing watched. Waiting.

The frenzy increased. Pressed closer. Ray bloodied the floor, bloodied himself, bloodied Adrian.

Adrian turned and fired, turned and fired. Most of the time he merely wounded rather than killed the fiends.

When they thought they might finally be pressed-in-on and their nightmare might finally conclude, a booming sound (almost like a voice) echoed through the hangar.

The fiends stopped as if frozen.

Adrian looked up, realizing that he'd just heard the behemoth thinking. He didn't need to understand their language. The beast had said, *ENOUGH.*

The fiends backed away, retreating to huddle near their leader.

"What's happening?"

"I don't know, Ray. I haven't got a goddamn clue."

"They could have killed us. But they didn't." He looked at the monster. "What the fuck's it there for, Ade? What is this — some sort of a game?"

"Not a game," replied a very human voice. "A test."

They looked. Someone from Denny Brennan's GEN-adjacent forensics unit was approaching, but it wasn't Denny Brennan.

It was Erika Dale.

But not as they knew her.

32

THE LONG CON

She walked on two legs, but those legs seemed oversized beneath Erika's loose-fitting slacks. They appeared bent backward, and where they emerged from the cuff, Adrian saw hooves instead of feet. Her fingers looked too long. Although it was hard to be sure from where they were, her eyes seemed to be different as well: no white around the iris, but instead yellow, maybe orange, or red. Her pupils no longer appeared round. More like rectangles laid on their sides.

"A test," she repeated, "for the legacies of Eldon Porter."

"*You,*" Adrian said.

They had gone to Erika for advice several times. She'd helped them. She worked at GEN. She told them exactly the clue that had led Adrian to discover Matt and his map, and told them all the ways the world needed to worry about perforation.

Erika was the mastermind, not Brennan. How had he missed it? She was the one who knew how to open rifts. She was the one who thought she could control them.

"Me," she said, not sounding quirky at all. "Me, but better."

"What happened to you?"

"Improvements." Then she looked at the big demon. "Family."

"You think they're your family?"

"I think I don't have any on our plane." Her voice found an edge. "Mom dead from cancer. Dad dead two years later. No siblings. No friends. Not for Erika Dale: She's too weird, too freaky. It *had* to be Matt Baker."

She looked toward the corpse, visible now that the ground had been cleared of fiends. It didn't look human. Maybe it was skin. Definitely it was red-soaked clothes. But where were the bones?

"Some friend," said Ray.

"He was," Erika replied without irony, walking over on her new hooves, clacking like a horse and buggy. "He did what had to be done. Soldiers of the first phase always come out hungry. We couldn't let them have you, but this still requires an offering. A sacrifice. And obviously it couldn't be me."

Ray was eyeing the grenade-thing Matt had brought here. Its top was still flashing. Erika saw him looking at the device, then walked over and kicked it beneath the waiting fiends' feet.

Then she looked at Adrian and Ray. "Maybe you should sit down. I don't want you running. It'd be a shame to kill you after all this work."

Ray stared defiantly.

Adrian did nothing, standing beside his brother by default.

But then the massive fiend at the back started to stand, eyeing both of them and grumbling in its language. Ray and Adrian took a seat. Everything was strange and jumbled. Instead of worrying about the obvious, Adrian fretted some uncomfortable thing in his back pocket. Pea-sized and hard, pressing into his ass.

"You're experimenting with Zen Element," Adrian said.

Erika nodded. "It's a mutagen. I suspected for a long time that it was what made primordial form possible."

"So it's true. Primordial form."

"Of course it's true. They don't have a preferred form in their plane. They become what they are right before they enter our side, or when they see one of us on theirs. They can sense us, you know. Our feelings. Our thoughts. They become what we think 'demons' are."

"This isn't Hell. They're not fucking *demons,*" Ray said.

"If you wish. But they come from a deep place. A hot place. They take the form of nightmares." Erika looked down at herself. "And what they do, so can we."

The big thing made sounds at her. It wasn't projecting, but the base level voice filled the room like icy fire. Erika made sounds back at it.

"You understand their language," Adrian said.

"It's not really a language. It's a feeling. Every living creature is a little empathic. Live with them for a while and you'll get the gist. If you're open to the emotions that come. Speaking to them is really just projecting what you're feeling."

"Bullshit," said Ray.

Erika grunted toward the behemoth. It slammed its fist on the ground, shaking the hangar.

"The perforation hasn't burst yet," Erika said. "I assume you noticed."

"But it will," Adrian replied, thinking of the device she'd kicked into the throng.

It must be a two-stage thing: The first counting-down opened the black portal and the second, presumably, would shatter the worlds. He hadn't known there would be an intermediate phase.

But there was obviously plenty that Adrian had been in the dark about.

"It will." Erika nodded. "The sundering will release enormous amounts of Zen Element. It's the only way to create all that we need."

"To sell? To be rich?"

"To change the world. You think I'm the bad guy. You think I've done wrong. Betrayed you. Betrayed everyone."

"Sure betrayed your buddy." Ray glanced again at Baker's not-really-a-body-anymore.

"Matt was a believer. He will go wherever his soul wants to go. And does it really matter if he's gone forever? Matt went willingly. Believing to the very end. That's all any of us ever have: our experience, our belief, our personal world constructed as true but really as subjective as everything else. Matt got the purpose he needed. A way to right what he felt was wrong. A measure of redemption, I suppose. His goal wasn't to survive. It was to end this life believing that another place might be better."

She half-smiled. "My own plans are grander. The sundering will kill this city. If you think that pleases me, you're wrong. But it's a fair trade. A sensible sacrifice. So far we've been limited in what we can do with Zen because of its short supply and government interference. There will be anger and loss and grief when Fortune falls. Followed by hope. Zen Element healed your own injuries in days instead of months, Adrian. Or have you forgotten?"

He shook his head. They needed a way out of this — but how?

"When it's on this plane, refined Zen is anti-entropic. It *creates* energy instead of losing it. All the world's problems stem from deficiencies and shortfalls, but after this there won't *be* any deficiencies or shortfalls anymore. We'll be able to make food available to everyone, disregarding costs of transportation and growing. Healthcare will change forever, and cost next to nothing. Zen could have cured my mother's cancer. It can *still* cure yours."

"You're insane. A purge that big won't only take Fortune. Fiends will spill everywhere. They'll take down the Rampart."

"You're thinking like a human. We always put ourselves at the center, don't we? The creatures you call 'fiends' aren't that different from us. They didn't ask to come here. They didn't ask for us to rip through into their world."

"We *didn't* rip into their world! Not until you came along?"

Erika smirked a little, as if she'd been waiting for someone to say that. "Are you sure about that?"

Ray and Adrian traded a glance.

"Your father was the first Legion, but ask yourself if he was anything like the Legions you know today. He fought, yes. But he studied, too. Half of what GEN knew when he died came from Eldon himself. You must have heard his theories growing up."

They said nothing.

"I'll take that as a yes," Erika continued. "I don't suppose you ever wondered why. While everyone else was treating them like a scourge to eliminate, why was your father opening books, working with early GEN, cooperating with the government, trying to understand?"

"He was a curious person," Adrian said, knowing the answer was lame.

"He was *informed*," Erika corrected. "The first fiend to enter our world through the very first thin spot was part of an exploration team. They wanted to see what was here. But then someone figured out that thin spots created Zen. Someone else realized that at scale, they could purify it and end up with a substance of immense value. So they asked their lead man to look inside. To open a hole and make contact." She laughed. "The 'fiends' believed our intentions. As soon as he figured out how to speak to them, they told him how to do it."

"You're lying."

Erika again made sounds at the big beast. Its response was more mumbles, but this time Adrian thought he heard the words *"Eldon Porter."*

"I don't really care if you believe me or not. But it was their idea to test you, not mine. It doesn't matter to me if you fail."

"Test us how?" Ray asked.

"When the perforation is blown open, Fortune will become uninhabitable. The refined Element made by now by the perforations and in much greater quantity by the sundering kills us. The heat kills us. Their atmosphere will suffocate us. All of us are going to die. The only solution is to no longer be 'us.'"

"Jesus," Ray said. "That's what's happening to you. You're becoming one of them."

"Cured my asthma. Healed the bad leg I had since I broke it as a kid. No more headaches. The heat doesn't even bother me. I can hear them better, and they can hear me. I no longer strike them as human. Under their instructions, I've turned Element from poison into a panacea. When Fortune perishes, I shall thrive."

She nodded at the big demon. "It's a collaboration. Me and them. They're not evil. Their motives are simply incompatible with ours. They tell me there will be balance when it's over. Once their world was ripped-into by your father, more rifts came naturally. I told you that rifts beget rifts. The damage can't be undone: not by us or them. All they ask is to have an oasis in our world. That's why I believe them when they promise they won't cross the Rampart. They don't want to conquer the planet. Nature is fragile and they know it. They're offering equilibrium, not conquest."

"Offering," Adrian repeated.

Erika nodded. "For you too, if you want it."

Adrian was starting to understand. The fiends had never come at them to kill in that last battle. They had instead been testing the mettle of offspring from the first collaborator they had known — because even Eldon, who had started all of this, was only curious, not malicious. The world had suffered for his best.

"Go fuck yourself," Ray said.

"Are you sure? The sundering should happen in under five minutes. I was given a grace period as gratitude for my assistance. You see, it's hard to be in the middle, where I am right now. I'm not quite human. Not quite fiend. It takes a middle ground to change over safely. I'll complete the process before the sundering, and you can too. But choose quickly. Nature is delicate and this is your cushion. This is your only chance. There won't be another."

Adrian remembered Erika saying something like this before: *Nature is like a perfectly balanced spinning wheel. Change one tiny thing just a little bit and it throws off the balance.*

The big demon made a sound. Maybe it was Adrian's imagination, but he swore he understood more this time — not the words; this was more holistic than language.

"It wants me to tell you—" Erika began.

"—that they didn't want to kill him," Adrian finished.

That surprised her.

Then she smiled a little, nodding slowly. "So you do have something of your father in you. Yes. That's exactly what it wants you to know. After the damage was done, and rifts began to multiply and threaten their plane and ours, we developed riftfare. We developed the Brigades and Legions and eventually Stitchers. The damage was confined to the Gore Point as long as it happened naturally, so we — humans — more or less adapted. But it wasn't as easy for them. Ecosystems are fragile. So much energy was leaving their world that they started to suffer their own sort of energy crisis. Because there's no such thing as *anti*-entropy — not in an absolute sense. We talk as if Zen violates the laws of thermodynamics, but that's not true. It only violates the laws on our side of the rifts. But all the energy provided by the Element has to come from somewhere."

"It comes from their plane," Adrian said. "Doesn't it?"

"Yes. And it's bleeding them dry. They can't provide for their own population. Food no longer grows. It's like what happened to the dinosaurs, when that meteorite dust cloud blocked out the sun."

That was a strange thought: thinking about fiends as a people in their own right. If Erika was correct, they were starving. He didn't want to consider the specifics of what she had said: *food no longer grows.*

"They had to get to *this.*" Erika spread her arms wide, meaning all the tumult that had happened over the past weeks, culminating today. "It was the only way they could survive. They didn't know Zen could be refined and made more powerful. It doesn't work in their world; they literally can't understand its physics. But when they saw that perforated rifts had the potential to tear larger holes — holes that somehow *generated* refined Element — they knew that was their way out. Refining Zen let them get more out of what they had. It stabilized the system."

"So this was all one long con," Adrian said. "Years and years of making us think we were in control."

He flinched as he shifted position, rolling over the hard, pea-sized thing in his rear pocket. Subtly, he reached back and removed it. Looking down at the thing, he felt himself transported to half a day ago in Ray's apartment — a time that now felt eons in the past.

He almost pitched it, but some instinct told him not to. Then he began to remember why: This was *Erika* in front of him. Erika with the dead mother. Erika, who'd revealed other things about herself, too.

"Exactly," she went on. "When rifts appeared on their side, they always waited until a Brigade was ready to fight on our side before letting it rip the rest of the way through. They only became a single class upon emerging from a rift, knowing they'd overrun Brigades easily if they came as they pleased."

Adrian found himself thinking of the mutants: partially transformed fiends caught unaware so far from the Gore Point, unable to take definitive form fast enough.

"They let us kill them. They aren't like us in that way; the death of individuals isn't much different for their group consciousness than shedding skin cells or cutting fingernails. They let us win. They played soft, like an adult allowing their kid to win at a board game. But they realized a bit too late that we'd developed a newer, better Stitching technology with the potential to stop the bleeding on our side. And stop new rifts from appearing, if we could get ahead of it. But what was good for us wouldn't help their side at all."

The big demon made a new sound, and Adrian needed no translation. Its thoughts and emotion clearly said, *It was the only way.*

"They had to keep your father's Brigade from getting ahead of the damage. If they'd closed the rift on that first try, when the Stitchers first prepared to move in, it would have all been over for our plane — 'over' in a good way. But a small delay would change that. They needed a way to stall, and there was no other way than to send a fiend the Brigade couldn't handle quickly. None of the Legions were equipped for a hellbringer.

Eldon was front of the line. Pulling its punches would have blown their cover."

The demon's sounds now told Adrian directly: *Your father was worthy. He was strong. You are like him, in that way.*

"You should be flattered," Erika said. "They are picky about character. If you had any flaws that bothered them, they would not be inviting you to join us."

Become like her, the big demon said. *Take the serum. Transform, and become us.*

A small halfhead stood from the crowd. It was holding the GEN device, now flashing very fast.

It chattered like castanets. The big demon nodded. *Time ends. Join us now.*

Erika took a small pneumatic injector from her pocket, bared the skin of her arm, and pulled its trigger.

Whatever was inside acted quickly, causing her arm to boil and twist as if from within. Her mouth changed shape. Her hair began to fall out. Her stomach protruded and her eyes bugged. It looked painful: nature's carefully-balanced wheel doing its best not to tip and shatter.

Change one tiny thing just a little bit and it throws off the balance, Erika had told him and Laurel days earlier. *The system starts to collapse.*

Adrian felt the hard thing in his right hand, remembering how it got there. It was from his fight with Ray. Ray had wanted to eat after their tussle, but he'd broken his teeth. He'd thrown the open bottle at Adrian instead.

Adrian pressed into it with his thumb, turning it to crumbles and dust.

Erika extended the injector for either brother to take. Her voice had already changed — become more like gravel, more like a smoker's.

"I'm particularly surprised they want you, Ray. You're so

proud. So driven by ego. They don't like cocky people. They don't appreciate arrogant asshole showboats like you, claiming all the glory for themselves."

Ray looked at the injector. "Go fuck yourself."

She laughed a little, not at all displeased. She didn't want the Porters. Erika would rather the apocalypse kill them.

"As you wish," she told him. "Stay. Be human. Wait for the end ... or let the army I command kill you."

Now Adrian was the one to laugh. The building was shaking, presumably as the timer reached zero. It was an absurd, terrifying time to be jolly.

He looked at the demon instead of Erika. It was staring right at him.

So he felt into his feelings, finding it less difficult than he imagined. And to the demon, he tried to repeat Erika's words, *So proud. So driven by ego. Asshole showboats, with all the glory for themselves.*

The demon didn't flinch, perhaps understanding that the same applied to Erika herself: *also* proud, *also* ego-driven, *also* scratching for glory. In the fiend's eyes, Adrian thought he saw permission for what he was about to do.

"Wait. I'll do it," Adrian told Erika.

Surprised, she turned toward him with the injector halfway extended.

But Adrian didn't take the injector. Instead he raised his hand, and blew the crushed peanut in his palm directly into her face.

Her transformation didn't protect her from her old deadly allergy. Almost immediately her hands shot to her throat, anaphylaxis taking hold. She fell to the ground, choking.

"Someone once told me that nature was delicate," Adrian said as her throat closed. "Make one little change at a crucial time and the whole thing collapses."

The fiends did not react, watching it happen instead. The shock of Erika's reaction was vastly magnified by her transformation. She choked and gagged. Her skin roiled and her joints snapped. Hair grew; hair retracted. The bones of her hands ripped through her skin, claw like and long. Her head swelled. Contracted.

She clenched and her abdomen exploded, spraying the floor with brown fluid.

Like what spills out of a bug when it's stepped on.

33

DEALMAKER

The big fiend was still watching Adrian when it was over.

All the others stood around motionless as the timer flashed faster: thousands of eyes and eyeless forms, waiting as if for a speech to commence.

Adrian stood. Ray stood beside him.

"Adrian?" Ray asked, eyeing the fiends. "Now what?"

Adrian ignored his brother. He tried to tap his feelings — his gestalt *impression* of what he meant to say rather than the words themselves. He wasn't sure he had the trick, but he still had to try.

It seemed to *want* him to try.

You can end this. You can stop the sundering.

And the demon's sounds conveyed: *We can.*

I will work with you. I will find allies. Let me try. We can find another way. I am not like Erika. I do not care for glory.

You are noble. But you are only two men.

The thing flashed faster. How long could he possibly have before this part of the world became a dead limb of history?

His thoughts raced, but too many of them went to Laurel. Horribly, only now was he realizing how much he loved her. How much he *needed* her. She deserved a better life than he'd given her. She was a smart woman. She could have left him any time to strike out on her own. Tragically, it was her unswerving faith in Adrian — her hopeless love for him, though he did little to deserve it — that stayed her hand. He was the reason she was about to die. She'd leave this world trying to help him any way she could, murdered just the same when Hell came to Fortune.

Only Laurel mattered right now.

I will go with you, Adrian told the demon, safe knowing that Ray did not understand their conversation. *I will do whatever you need.* He eyed the injector still in Erika's hand. *I will become like you, and I will help you make the refined Element you need.*

The sundering will make far more Element than you ever could.

Adrian shook his head, summoning humility, knowing that to boast through this way of communicating would sink him.

No. You do not understand my species. The Rampart is small compared to the rest of our world. They will not let you be. They will not consider Fortune lost, but a fair trade and allow things to remain as you want them. They will come for you. With bombs and disease, they will come for you. If they fail, they will come again. And again. We are not a peaceful species. We kill. We conquer. It's what we do.

The big demon was shaking its head. *We do not want that.*

Then let us try to help you, Adrian said. *Don't break the worlds. Keep it whole. Keep your secrets. The world is used to rifts. You will be left alone if you stop this. So let us try. Let us try to work together.*

You cannot. You do not know how to manufacture what we need.

Adrian looked down at Erika's dead body, wondering if

he'd acted rashly. Erika knew all about refining Zen. If she hadn't been so homicidal, *she* could have helped them. She'd wanted to go with them anyway.

Although, she would never have settled for taking orders, or doing as she was told.

He needed to give them someone else. To save the city — to save his people — one person would have to spend eternity in Hell.

The device flashed faster. And faster. Who knew what needed to be known? Who was expendable?

He thought of J. Dixon. Dixon was a snake; Dixon could go and nobody would care. But Dixon knew nothing about Zen Element.

Brennan, Adrian blurted. He had to say it quickly. He had to pretend he still thought Brennan was the bad guy, not Erika. Although really, were they sure he wasn't? Brennan ran the lab. Brennan must know what Erika did with her time. In the space of seconds, Adrian convinced himself.

Brennan is bad. Or at least suspect, because he knew Erika. It's okay if they take him. It's okay if he worse-than-dies.

Adrian imagined himself tomorrow, looking in the mirror. Trying to forget this terrible dilemma and its ugly solution.

Take Denny Brennan, he thought all of a sudden. *Take the scientist. The one in the lab.*

Adrian focused hard, trying to bring Brennan's face to mind so the fiends would know who he was ... *somehow*. But he was brand new to this. What emotion conveyed *Denny Brennan*? What sequence of sounds?

He might be doing it correctly, but his emotions were jumbled. Everything was inside him right now: hate, love, legacy, death.

Adrian only knew urgency.

So he sent it out: *Brennan. Let Brennan show you how to refine Zen Element.*

He focused on Brennan's internal image, batting away the images of all the other people who would die if he failed — everyone he loved.

His mother, his brother, his friends, and most of all Laurel.

He pushed them to blackness and forced himself to see only Brennan. Brennan in his lab coat. Brennan sitting in his office. Brennan's voice, his clothing, the car he drove.

Adrian focused without shame, knowing shame would come tomorrow.

Brennan. Brennan. Brennan is the one you want.

The demon rose to its full height. It tweezed the device the other fiend was holding between its massive fingers, turned to the portal behind it, then reached through to someplace unknown where it could do no damage.

The air changed. Somehow Adrian understood that it was over, that even the rifts around the perforation were closing.

The smaller fiends turned, filing through the black portal first. The big demon then stood alone, even more massive now that the room had cleared. It looked at Adrian and Ray and gave what sounded like a warning:

The deal you wished is made. You will keep your word. This plane will be yours for as long as the scientist is ours.

Will you take the scientist now? Adrian asked.

The demon grunted one last time. *It is done. We have her already.*

It stepped through the portal, which closed behind it without a trace.

And then in that second, without needing to verify — without needing to call, because he was quite sure communications had resumed — Adrian shivered as he realized something terrible.

We have her already, the fiend had said.

Her.

During his moment of decision, Adrian had been thinking of everything at once. Every*one* at once. Everyone who mattered in the moment. He didn't truly know their language. He'd simply tapped his feelings, and now he understood: *the wrong feelings had come out.*

"What the fuck was *that* all about?" Ray asked.

Adrian's legs gave out. He fell hard to his knees.

"Adrian?" Ray asked, looking down with concern.

Adrian fished the phone from his pocket. It was working. He needed to call Laurel. Laurel.

Laurel.

He wanted to call Brennan to make sure he was gone. To make sure the fiends had taken him instead of anyone else. But he already knew that Brennan was just fine — on Earth where he'd always been.

So Adrian called Laurel instead. Her phone rang. And rang. And rang.

When it clicked to voicemail, his imagination wrote a clever new outgoing message for her, which it played for him while her actual message spooled off:

Hi! You've reached Laurel Gantry. I can't come to the phone right now. I can't come to the phone ever again. If you'd like to leave me a message, I'll call you back the second Hell freezes over.

Adrian dropped the phone. He sagged as if all the bones had left him, gaping at where the portal had been. Where the fiends had gone. Where he knew, without question, that his confused mind had bargained Laurel away forever.

There was meaning and order and a plan for the world after all, just like Mom always said ... and that plan was Hell itself.

"Adrian?" Ray said.

He started shaking and couldn't stop. Ray's voice became the echo at the end of an impossibly long, impossibly dark hallway.

"Adrian? Are you okay?"

GORE POINT WILL CONTINUE

Hell has only begun for the walled-in town of Fortune, for Ray, for Adrian ... and especially for Laurel, abducted by demons into their unearthly plane.

Preorder the next book in the series (City of Fire) here (it comes out December 10, 2024).

*(... or, if you want to get it **four months earlier** (in eBook, paperback, or a SIGNED SPECIAL EDITION HARDBACK), you can get it here on Kickstarter in July.)*

THANKS TO MY SUPPORTERS!

112 amazing readers helped bring *Gore Point* to life in truly swanky form via a 2024 Kickstarter campaign. **My extra-special thanks go to the following top-tier supporters:**

Jef Michiels
Anthony Erdmann
Jason Kelly
Bradley Cronn

Thank you from the bottom of my heart for supporting my work. You're the best!

ENTER THE TRUANTVERSE

When it comes to stories and the worlds they live in, books are only the beginning.

Visit JohnnyBTruant.com/join to get my best books sooner and cheaper than the other stores.

My list doesn't suck like so many author email lists. Seriously. It has unicorns.

Also by Johnny B. Truant

Winter Break

Pattern Black

Pretty Killer

Cursed

The Bialy Pimps

Namaste

The Target

La Fleur de Blanc

Axis of Aaron

Devil May Care

Screenplay

The Island

Burnout

Sick and Wired

UNICORN WESTERN:

Unicorn Western

The Wanderers

A Fistful of Magic

Shimmer to Yuma

The Man Who Shot Alan Whitney

The Spectacular Seven

Open Meadows

The Unforgotten

The Magic Bunch

Unicorn Genesis

FAT VAMPIRE:

Fat Vampire

Fat Vampire 2: Tastes Like Chicken

Fat Vampire 3: All You Can Eat

Fat Vampire 4: Harder Better Fatter Stronger

Fat Vampire 5: Fatpocalypse

Fat Vampire 6: Survival of the Fattest

The Vampire Maurice

Anarchy and Blood

Vampires in the White City

Fangs and Fame

Game of Fangs

INVASION:

Invasion

Contact

Colonization

Annihilation

Judgment

Extinction

Resurrection

Save the City

Save the Girl

Save the World

Longshot

THE INEVITABLE:

Robot Proletariat

The Infinite Loop

The Hard Reset

Cascade Failure

Reboot

En3my

DEAD CITY:

Dead City

Dead Nation

Dead Planet

Dead Zero

Empty Nest

THE DREAM ENGINE:

The Dream Engine

The Nightmare Factory

The Ruby Room

The Pandora Core

www.ingramcontent.com/pod-product-compliance
Lightning Source LLC
Chambersburg PA
CBHW032021310726
48972CB00002B/493